SEDUCTION
Of A Butterfly

WHAT READERS SAY

Seduction of a Butterfly-The Art of Forgiveness, grips your heart and ministers to your spirit. It follows the journey of an accomplished woman whose life shifts in an instant-from the height of joy to the depths of brokenness. This is more than a story, it's an experience you won't be able to put down and one that will leave your soul stirred long after the final page. "Weeping many endure for a night, but joy comes in the morning." – Psalm 30:5

Gail Goodwin-Webb , *Gospel Artist*

After the first few paragraphs of *Seduction of a Butterfly-The Art of Forgiveness,* I felt like crying. An educated woman is found clutching a note in her hand, saying, *unfit to live fit to die* –lying in squalor. By the time I reached the end of the first chapter, I was just plain "mad." But then I remembered the heart of the title... "Forgiveness." The story reminds us of God's grace, his presence in pain and hope that refuses to die. It's a must have.

Charlesetta Copper, *Minister of God*

SEDUCTION
of A Butterfly

The Art of Forgiveness

A Novel

Patricia J. Monserrate

Broken No More
Arlington, Tx

Published 2025 by Broken No More
Arlington, TX

ISBN
Paperback: 979-8-9993677-0-9
eBook: 979-8-9993677-1-6

Library of Congress Control Number: 2025914386

Edited and Proofread by Write Books Right

Book cover & interior layout design
By Eddie Egesi, Apricot Press (an imprint of Apricot Branding)

This book is dedicated to my two best high school friends, Charlesetta Cooper and Renee Foster. Each of you has touched my heart in an everlasting way. I learned how to love myself, no matter how other people viewed my outer appearance. My prayers are you will long remember the impact you had on the life of a petite, shy girl with a speech impediment. May you continue to allow God to use you.

"Unfit to Live. Fit to Die"

Penville, North Carolina 1980

TABLE OF CONTENTS

CHAPTER 1
Lost & Found

May 17, 1980
New York, NY

A young woman's body lays unconscious in a pool of blood, her hand clutching a moist, tiny paper. On the paper is an ominous statement: *Unfit to live, but fit to die!*

The night, voided of its twinkling lights, felt heavy and oppressive, almost supernatural in its darkness. Twenty-six-year-old Grace Forrester, a recent graduate with a master's degree in art conservation, had fallen into a bottomless pit.

Tattered newspapers surrounded her smelly body as feces lined her cardboard bed. Broken remnants of exquisite dishes and glasses were strewn across the floor, their dangerous sharp edges waiting to cut someone. A shredded wedding gown, smeared with red stains, was strewn in a far corner of the room.

Grace couldn't hear the loud banging on her door or a woman's voice on the other side shouting, *"Go, get help!"*

Moments later, men in uniforms burst the door open. The smell of death assailed their nostrils, and without thought, they stormed inside the hell of the unknown.

The automatic sliding doors swished open as the ambulance attendants rushed the unconscious Grace inside the emergency room. The fluorescent lights buzzed overhead, casting a stark, clinical glow. The waiting area was full of patients, moaning and crying, with bloody noses, cuts, and broken bones. A nurse on duty rushed past patients, her face etched with worry, muttering to the attendants.

"What do you have?" the nurse asked.

"Suicide attempt; she's unconscious."

The nurse turned to the older woman standing behind the stretcher, her lips trembling. "Are you a family member?"

"No, I'm her neighbor, my name is Mrs. Martha Henderson."

"Please have a seat, Mrs. Henderson. We will be out shortly," the nurse instructed.

Lying flat on the stretcher, Grace was barely breathing as attendants attached a face mask that delivered oxygen and quickly wheeled her through the closed metal doors.

Martha, sitting on one of the beat-up chairs in the waiting room, clutched her purse to her chest. A strong scent of booze from the man sitting next to her assailed her nostrils, causing Martha to turn sideways. With her gentle smile and crinkled eyes, she knew the moment she had a fleeting glimpse of the new tenant across the hall that she had a sad story to tell. She immediately felt a link to her and monitored the sounds coming from her next-door apartment, and when these sounds ceased, she intervened. The petite woman, now teasing death, seemed to Martha like an adorable child.

A symphony of coughing and hacking greeted Harold Henderson in the ER waiting room as he searched for his mother, Martha, through a maze of people. He felt uneasy about his mom being alone in the emergency room. Harold finally saw his mother sitting on the edge of her chair while a scruffy man tried to lay his head on her shoulders.

The moment Martha saw her son, she called out, "Harold, over here," as she waved her hands.

Harold loves his mom's qualities of nurturing; however, he is afraid that one day, her irrepressible goodwill will explode in her face. "Mom, you shouldn't have ridden in the ambulance."

"Ms. Forrester was close to death, and she needed someone praying for her and helping her."

"Mom, when are you going to stop this madness of interfering in other people's lives?"

"Until God stops me."

"But why must you always get involved with total strangers? Dad always said you would give our last piece of meat to a stray cat."

"Son, on your job, I know you must meticulously track and analyze reports, but this is a human being's life, not numbers."

"Look, everyone has their own path to chart; why should we interfere?"

"What does the Parable of the Good Samaritan teach us?"

"To treat everyone as our neighbor with compassion and kindness regardless of who they are or where they come from."

"Correct, son, and Ms. Forrester is our neighbor; let's just pray she hasn't finished what the devil wanted her to do."

Moments later, a man in a white doctor's coat, wearing a stethoscope around his neck, called for Mrs. Henderson. Martha cautiously raised her hand and, with Harold at her side, went to stand in front of the doctor.

"Madam, you're not a relative, just a neighbor, correct."

"Yes."

"Do you have any information on the young lady who was brought in?"

"Only her name, it's Grace Forrester," Martha said. "But I can get more information from the landlord."

"Good, but I fear that she may try taking her life again. Therefore, we are going to keep Ms. Forrester for now."

"Can we see her now?"

"Not now, but you can return when it's daylight; she will have a room by then."

Martha nods, her face grim. For a few moments, mother and son were quiet. After expressing their appreciation, they turn and leave the hospital for home.

In the early morning hours, Grace sluggishly woke to the smell of antiseptic and the sounds of screams and yelling. She wiggled to get loose, but something was holding her arms down. Moving her eyes from side to side, Grace saw nothing but padded walls. Peering above her head, she squinted at the bright light overhead. Then, something cool was rubbed on the back of her hand, but the slickness quickly turned to a jab of pain. She flinched and turned her head to see a nurse securing an IV to her hand with tape. Her thoughts were foggy, and she screamed, *"Let me die, oh please, let me die."*

A hush fell over the normally bustling psychiatric ward, with every hospital worker speaking in quiet tones. The nursing staff was baffled by such a heinous act performed by a stunning, petite woman. "Does she realize how close she came to snuffing out her young life forever," one nursing attendant asked another.

"You're a lucky young woman," the nurse begins. "Honestly, you should be grateful to be alive..." the nurse let the last four words lag.

"Take a good look!" Grace snickered. "I'm worthless, so why bother with me? Nothing's going to change." Grace saw hesitation in the nurse's eyes. "Run, you frightened rabbit... everyone else has."

The nurse's limbs tingled from fatigue, but she grieved for the young, troubled soul.

"Try and rest; your neighbor promised to visit later today," the nurse said as she left Grace and went on to her next patient.

Grace wondered what neighbor? She solemnly stared at the padded walls. What would happen now? She had deliberately disobeyed God's word, Exodus 20:13, *"Thou shalt not kill."* In essence, she tried to murder herself. What would her parents say? What has happened to her passion for preserving and protecting cultural heritage? Was such passion only for art and not human life? She desperately craved to erase the past ten days. Her romantic notions about finding true love were a farce.

～

Born and raised in Penville, North Carolina, Grace had a smile that came from deep inside her. With her long, thick, pitch-black curly hair, she enthralled anyone who entered her space. During her formative years, due to her speech impediment, she endured daily bullying, especially from the cool kids. However, one day, three brave girls came to her rescue, and a friendship was developed that lasted for two decades.

For long moments, Grace lay prone on her smelly, bleached sheets. Images of her lost hopes and dreams of May 7, 1980, remain etched in her mind. That wonderful feeling of elation as she received her master's in art conservation and the anticipation of marriage to the most exciting man, she had ever met suddenly evaporated.

Her lips vibrating, Grace whispered, *how can I describe the pain I'm feeling, Father? It's beyond my wildest dreams to see what I've waited for so long, marred by the devastation of deception.* Her life-long definition of happiness has vanished. Closing her eyes, Grace relives the previous ten days.

⁓

It is Wednesday, May 7, 1980; Grace's face is beaming. She smooths her graduation gown once more as she eagerly waits for her name to be called. There's nothing quite like the feeling of finally achieving a long-term goal.

Soon after the graduation celebration, Grace dashes into her dormitory. A white satin gown greets her. With her mother's help, Grace carefully slips into her white wedding gown. The delicate lace cascaded over her skin as her mother's skilled hands gently adjusted the intricate beading on the bodice, creating a shimmering effect that caught the light. Grace's eyes sparkle with tears as the delicate veil is placed on her rolling curls.

With a mix of anticipation and love, she prepares to meet her father, who's waiting patiently outside her dormitory. Stone's heart leaps for joy at the sight of his daughter's timeless vision of elegance. Gently holding her hands, both parents walk with her to the campus chapel.

Arriving at the chapel fifteen minutes before the 3:00 p.m. ceremony, Grace's father, Stone, holds open the door so she can enter the side entry to the pastor's study. The door creaks open, revealing a dazzling light filtering through the stained-glass window. Not wanting to wrinkle her lovely wedding gown, Grace holds herself ramrod straight, her gloved hands holding her bouquet of lilies, her face hidden by the shadows from the sunlight.

As the minutes ticked by at rapid speed, her loving mother, twin brothers and three devoted friends periodically peek inside the room at the anxious bride. A nagging sense of doubt that she couldn't dismiss lingers in the back of her mind. Gazing up at the towering etched image of Jesus on the cross in the window pane, Grace silently prays.

The constant sounds of the chapel's front wooden doors opening and closing disrupted the stillness within the pastor's study. With the set time approaching, she became mindful of the time and started hearing every tick-tock from the clock. Grace nervously waited for the sound of the wedding march.

Grace sighs and thinks about how restless Reese has been during the last four months. Perhaps it's the stress of planning the wedding, she rationalizes. But she couldn't erase wondering about his nervousness or the absence of his parents for their rehearsal dinner.

Soon, questions begin bombarding her thoughts. Where is Reese? Our families and friends are waiting. Where could Reese be? He must have had an emergency. Yes, that's it. She visualizes Reese's adoring face, apologizing profusely at her from a gurney. Her breathing quickens, but the clock in the pastor's study continues to tick loudly.

Her thoughts alternate between worrying about Reese and thinking about the next step in her professional life. Grace recalls the day she received news of her internship with a prestigious museum in Paris. She decided to treat herself to lunch and met the most gorgeous specimen of a man, Reese Butler. Drawn to his frightening charisma as a moth to the flame, he took her heart hostage. Though many beliefs in their lives were vastly different, within months of dating, they were engaged and planning a wedding.

Agitated by Reese's lateness, Grace continues to grip her bouquet, murmuring tightly, *Reese, where are you?* Stone joins her by the window to soothe her nervousness.

When the study's door next opens slightly, Grace is startled, her eyes searching; she calls out, "Reese?"

"No, my wee one," Stone sadly stated. "It's your mother."

As Grace slumps in a pew, her mother comes into view, followed by her brothers and girlfriends. Their expressions of concern ripped through Grace's heart. Grace eyed them closely as they gathered around her.

"Just tell me he's okay," Grace's eyes encompass the group.

"My sweet daughter, we had our doubts about Reese…but we trusted your decisions about him and were happy for you both." Her mother, Labella's features soften. "This note… is from Reese's roommate… he's gone." She lays the note in Grace's lap.

From the time she was a little girl, Grace hated confrontation or any unhappiness. She observes her father kneeling nearby. Finally, she stares at the folded piece of paper entrenched in the folds of her gown and looks at it as if it were a burning ember, frightening to open.

"Grace?" a voice spoke from behind her, drawing her attention from the note.

"Yes, Zory, what is it?"

"Aren't you going to read the note?" Zory asked animatedly, without thought. Her green eyes ignited with curiosity, her short bob haircut swinging from side to side.

"Zory! Have a little respect for Grace's privacy," Nora, another bridesmaid, tactfully said, though her hazel eyes aimed fiery arrows at Zory's impulsive behavior.

"We all feel this ordeal is nerve-racking," the third bridesmaid, Penelope, interjected while fingering her long brunette hair, her dark brown eyes begging for peace.

With a growing tightness in her chest, Labella pushed the lovely bouquet of white and purple lilies aside and sat next to Grace. Her mother helps her open the folded note. As she does that, Grace makes a squeaky noise as she recognizes Reese's flawless handwriting. She exchanges shocked glances with the small group attending her while they hold their breath. Her mouth quivers while making no sounds. Beholding her daughter's anguish, Labella fights back her rising anger.

"My pet, I'll read it," Labella softly commands, gently removing the note from Grace's hand. The small group listens intently.

Grace…this is one of the hardest things I've ever had to say, but I finally dare to tell you. Our time together has been wonderful, and I will always remember the day we met. But… I've found out that my old girlfriend has never stopped loving me. As I tried to reason that I wasn't in love with her, I failed miserably. You deserve someone who truly loves you and your God. I hope one day you can forgive me. I'm sorry, Reese.

Labella methodically folded the note, placing it on the table near Grace. Every word ripped apart a piece of Grace's heart. Clutching the note, Grace stares at it as though its poisonous words could further hurt her, but at the same time, she does not quite believe what she has read.

"You must be wrong," Grace rants at her mother. "He'd never do that!" Color bleeds from Grace's face.

Labella leans forward. "Tranquila, Grace." Labella reaches for her hand, but Grace snatches her hand away, shaking her head.

"No, Mamí, this can't be true."

"I just don't understand why Reese would do this to Grace," Stone's voice bellowed.

"Why would he do this to us all?" Labella snapped.

"Mami, Papi...I know it's not what you expected," she said with tears streaming down her face. "I wasn't aware that Reese thought it wasn't right."

Grace's mind raced to those wonderful eighteen months they had been together. She recalled those quiet moments of watching movies and enjoying impromptu picnics and nights of stargazing. Her thoughts jumped from memory to memory, like cooking meals together at his off-campus apartment and volunteering at the local community center for wayward teens. Their entire relationship played out in her mind.

"What do you mean you had no idea?" Stone asked in a distraught way. "You must have suspected something."

"Maybe I felt something was off a little," Grace whispered.

"The planning all these months, we've all been counting on this day," Labella said.

"After what we've done for the two of you, Reese just walks away," Stone said resentfully. "We warned you not to marry out of our faith!"

"I know, Papi," she said softly. "I loved him. Perhaps I tried to make him fit into a mold that didn't suit him."

"And this…this wedding?" Stone said emphatically. "He didn't dare to tell you beforehand."

Grace nods, her face etched in pain. Avoiding everyone's gaze, she leaped to her feet, holding the note in her hand. She yelled out, "No, it can't be. He promised never to leave me."

Grace violently ripped her veil off as the note fluttered through the air to the floor. Abandoning her pride, she bolted out of the room toward the sanctuary doors. Breathing heavily, she paused, and minutes later, she seized the doors. Grace stealthily approached the sanctuary unnoticed. She saw family and friends who had filled the pews. They seemed excited and were chatting, anxiously waiting to see the enchanted bride.

Freshly cut lilies fiercely assailed Grace's senses. She slowly gravitated to the pews adorned with sheer white swags decorated with small bouquets of colorful shades of purple lilies. Through brooding eyes, she could see the covered arch of white and lavender lilies spanning the altar. The officiant was patiently waiting standing behind a lush bench in the center, smiling, awaiting the bride's appearance.

Breathing rapidly, she fiercely walks down the aisle, her fingers sweeping over the pews. Her gown scrapes against the whimsical lantern candle holders. The moment Grace appears, the officiant signals the organist to play, and music begins to fill the chapel.

Disillusion in full bloom, Grace softly begins to hum, "Here Comes the Bride." Stunned at her appearance, the jabbering of the guests turns into gasps. In a ghostly way, Grace proceeds down the aisle.

The eyes of family members, friends and guests widen, a mixture of curiosity and apprehension on their faces. A collective murmur ripples through the audience; People start to look at each other in confusion.

Grace reaches the two steps to the altar; the officiant's smile fades as Grace stands before the gateway to a glorious life, now dead. Falling to her knees, she moans and groans. The audience uneasily shifts in their seats when Grace yells at the top of her lungs: *"Your words... spoken ... were pointless... your promises were bogus... all our time together wasted... I curse the day I met you... Reese.* With each word, Grace's heart becomes colder.

The audience gasps, and the music abruptly stops as Stone, a man of dauntless bravery, along with his two sons, rushes from the back of the chapel to the altar to rescue Grace as she continues to scream. Stone silently ceremonially ushers Grace back down the aisle to the solitude of the pastor's study.

The officiant clears his throat. "It seems that Reese is not here today," he said in a somber tone. "I understand this is a difficult moment for all, but we must take a moment to collect ourselves."

After a moment of silence, everyone looks on sadly as Grace's brother, Wyatt, remains in the chapel while Edmond goes to the small reception hall to have a word with the caterers.

"We are sorry, but there will be no wedding today," Wyatt announces. Please proceed to the reception hall, where my brother, Edmond, will help you retrieve your gift. All other gifts sent directly to my sister will be forward at a later day. You may also take a slice of cake with you, but all the other food will be donated to the campus cafeteria."

While the officiant was escorting the guests to the reception hall, everyone was expressing support and under-standing.

"This is a tough situation," said Stone's father. "But she's of good Scottish's stock."

"She's a wonderful person," Labella's mother stated. "She will find someone who loves her."

Grace involuntarily shivered as she returned to the eerily quiet private room. The queasy feeling in the pit of her stomach didn't help. *Was this really happening?* Looking around the room, she saw stunned faces filled with gaping mouths as reality was coming in for a fast landing.

"What type of rogue dumps my daughter?" Stone yelled as he wrestled with his rage.

"He's a selfish brute," Zory howled... "and a coward," Nora and Penelope ranted in unison.

"Listen, everyone," Labella said, kindly working to express her thoughts clearly. "Our expectations that a marriage was going to take place is very unsettling for us all. But we must put our frustration and anger aside for the sake of Grace."

Stone nodded to the group. He understood the pain his daughter was feeling. At the moment, his thoughts took him back to the day an unusual tackle on the football field caused him to lose all his possessions and almost his life. The question he put to his daughter was full of meaning.

"Grace, what will you do about your internship?" Stone asked as he studied the color draining out of her face.

Grace didn't answer, and she repetitively twisted the engagement ring on her finger.

"Don't let that coward win," Zory interjected. "You earned that internship."

Grace looked completely unhinged.

"I can't go," Grace whispered. "I let Reese hold the tickets."

At that moment, Wyatt and Edmond returned to the room, eager to inform their sister that Reese's parents weren't a part of the bewildered guests. However, the heated conversations caused them to remain silent.

"What!" Stone's rages. "He kept the tickets we gave to both of you as a wedding gift."

Labella stared at her daughter's dejected expression.

"My sweet loveable bear, please settle down," Labella blurted. "You obviously are not aware that your sneers are scaring everyone."

Labella warmly hugged her husband and was able to get a small chuckle from him. He honestly didn't realize what his actions were doing. Stone fashioned a quieter demeanor.

"Please forgive me; I am sorry for my behavior," he reached for Grace's hand and kissed it. "What are your plans concerning the internship?"

Grace slowly turned to her father. "I can't think about taking the internship now," she said, her voice dripping in pain. "I think I should stay in New York."

"Don't allow Reese the satisfaction that he won," Zory interjected. "Go to Paris!"

Stone's brows knitted, keeping his tone carefully neutral. "Grace, I don't see any reason why you should miss out on this wonderful opportunity."

"I agree with your father," Labella interjected. "Why are you so comfortable about your decision?"

This inquiry gave Grace pause. "Because until just now, I haven't thought I would be living in Paris without Reese. What do you think, Papí?"

"We think it's a great honor, but we wouldn't force you to leave. I can't promise going to Paris or staying here you won't be miserable. But I do trust the Lord you'll make a wise choice."

CHAPTER 1

"Do you agree, Mami´?"

"Yes, Grace, I do, but please understand that you'll lose your dorm apartment in four days. I have doubts about you finding an apartment."

"I'm aware that things aren't looking great at the moment, but I need some time for myself."

"I don't believe you truly understand the gravity of your situation." Stone spoke again.

"I do… Papi´, please don't be against my choice. My mind won't change." She glares at her parents. "I'm sorry."

Stone tries again. "Where are you going to find an apartment in such a short time… especially in New York?"

Wiping her face with the back of her hand, she insists: "I will find one."

"Getting an apartment without a prospect of a job is almost impossible," Labella explained.

Grace tilted her head, her jaws set in a frown, her gaze fixed. Stone chuckled a little, seeing himself in her.

"I've got an idea," Stone commented. "If you find an apartment, your mother and I will pay your rent until you're employed. But if you don't find an apartment or job, you'll come home."

"We'll stay and help her, sir," Zory joyously jumps in, assuring them.

Nora and Penelope's hearts sank. Nora only requested two days off from the hospital, and Penelope didn't want to leave her little boy with her mother-in-law for too long.

17

"That idea is awful, Zory," Grace pleaded. "My dorm is a studio with one bed."

"No worries," Zory was careful to keep her biased emotions from her voice. "We're wasting time talking; we can do this."

Had Grace known from the beginning, Reese would abandon her, she would be celebrating her accomplishment, not sitting on a hard wooden pew, devastated. Would she ever move past his deception?

"Oh, Reese," she whispered, "will I ever not miss you?"

So much has happened in four days. Grace found an apartment with the help of her girlfriends, and now alone in her brownstone apartment, she's once more haunted by Reese leaving her at the altar. Lost in the emptiness of her heart, Grace moans and repeats over and over, *"I'm defective; I will never find happiness."* Distraught, she resorted to using old newspapers as a makeshift bed on the cold floor in her living room. As Grace smooths a portion of the newspaper, a lump forms in her throat, and she has trouble catching her breath.

She glances at one of the newspapers lying on her makeshift bed and sees,

"Mr. and Mrs. Farrell of Chicago are proud to announce, after a brief separation, that their daughter, Laura, and her longtime boyfriend, Mr. Reese Butler of New York City, married on May 7, 1980. Both will join the family's law firm after their long honeymoon in Paris."

Grace swayed back and forth, bawling, *"No... no...Reese. How could you? What a fool I've been! You...lied to me...you never loved me. You took our tickets for your honeymoon with that woman!!!"* Reality flew and disappeared under the trampling of Reese's rescinded love.

While screams ripped through her, her face became distorted with agony, her features contorted in a terrifying grimace. Grace slowly moved across the floor to the wedding gift she kept from her parents. She gouges the wrapping paper open, exposing the exquisite bone China set. Grace grapples with the bubble wrapping for a moment. Then, she quickly flung each enchanting dish against the kitchen wall. Grace hollered at each dish with an interval of swearing affirmation. *"I believed and trusted you. How could you betray me?"* She squeals as she hurls each exquisite piece of China, toward the wall, *"I loved you. Why didn't you tell me about Laura when we first met?"*

Completely depleted, Grace slouches in the middle of total obliteration while hope drifts away.

In the following days, Grace lived a homeless life within her apartment, metamorphosing into an altered person. She was unrecognizable due to the induced starvation and absence of showers. Her apartment was filthy, and her body was a mere skeleton. Her once silken curls were coarse and matted. A still, small voice tormented her daily, whispering, *"You have no reason to live; your only option is death."* It left her sinking into a state of desolation.

CHAPTER 2
Whispers In The Dark

Penville, North Carolina

"Stone?" Labella's voice was low as he sat down at the breakfast table.

"What is it, Bella?"

"Did we do the right thing leaving Grace so quickly after her wedding fiasco?"

"Yes," he chuckled, a familiar response to Labella's doubts and fears about their children. "God's loving hands will protect her."

"I don't think she was ready to be left alone," Labella said softly, remembering Grace's strained voice when they left New York.

Labella watches her calm husband sip his hot coffee. For a moment, she thought about how whenever Grace encountered obstacles, she rarely asked for help.

"Grace was placid when we left," Labella crooned.

Stone nodded. He was troubled by Grace's exhibition at the wedding chapel. Every memory of that day gave him a slight pang. He was still combating his anger at how Reese treated his daughter. He was halfway through his pondering before Labella commented.

"Why the blank look," Labella said, recognizing doubts.

Stone put on the most persuasive face he could muster. "It's nothing, Bella."

"Spill it, Stonewall!"

"I've already talked with Wyatt and Edmond, to manage the clinic for a few days. We're leaving Thursday."

Labella reached across the table, squeezing his hand.

"I love you, Stone Forrester," she said softly.

Stone wanted to continue the warmth of her hand, but he had an early session with an injured pro athlete. He rose from the table, kissed Labella, and left.

Labella continued to finish her breakfast, worried that she hadn't heard from Grace and concerned after the conversation she had with Grace's girlfriends the previous day, expressing their concern for their friend. *"Mrs. Forrester, we knew Grace was hurting, but for the first time, she didn't share her emotions with us. We didn't know how to respond to her silence or the discarded minuscule fragments of pictures littering her living room and kitchen. Her wedding gown was slashed into shreds. The whole scene made our farewell awkward and sad."*

Labella wondered what would greet them when they arrived at Grace's in a few days.

The loud doorbell jolted Stone Forrester from a deep slumber. Disoriented, he glared at the bedside clock, his mind racing at full speed; who was calling at four on a Sunday morning? Before he could reach for his robe, Labella stirred.

"Stone?"

"Go back to sleep," said Stone, putting his robe on. "Someone's at the door."

Labella caught sight of the time, and before Stone could say another word, she was grabbing her robe. Leaning against Stone's back, they headed to the front door. In the semi-darkened entryway, their eyes adjusted to a uniformed man standing under the porch light with a yellow envelope.

Stone and Labella slowly read the telegram over twice before looking at each other. With labored breathing, Labella tries to comprehend the contents. *Grace tried to kill herself. She's in -New York Memorial Hospital. Please come quickly. Her neighbor, Martha Henderson.* After collecting their thoughts, they made plans to leave immediately.

New York Memorial Hospital

"Mom, why the rush?" Harold asked Martha, who was standing outside the church after Sunday morning services.

Harold Henderson has been driving his mother to church every Sunday since she moved in with him several years ago. Since the passing of his father, he wanted to make her life easier, and loving her made it easy to do.

"I need to go to the hospital to check on our new neighbor."

"Mother, we've done more than our neighborly duties last evening. Why do you want to stick our noses in deeper?"

"She's a child of God who has lost her way, and she needs our help."

Harold knew his mother's statement wasn't a stretch. Not an overly emotional man, he was appalled at the conditions he witnessed at how his neighbor had been living. However, he watched in amazement at how his mother took control of the situation, making sure the neighbor had a fighting chance at life.

"But… why us mother?"

"Why not us, Harold? We are put on this earth to be an effective instrument for God," she whispered.

"Yes, but when you called the paramedics several nights ago, she spurned our help. And it's rumored in the building that she spat at the landlord when he walked into her apartment with the telephone man."

"First of all, I don't pay much attention to rumors, and you shouldn't either. Secondly, the landlord had no right to walk unannounced," Martha emphasized.

With flowers in hand, Martha walked into the hospital room an hour later, only to find Grace seemingly taking a nap. She was on the verge of leaving when Grace opened her eyes.

"Good afternoon, Grace," she began, putting the vase of flowers on a table nearby. "I'm Mrs. Martha Henderson, your neighbor across the hall."

The next several moments, Grace listened suspiciously to Martha who informed her that arrangements had been made to clean her apartment, and her parents had been notified.

"I'm so thankful that God brought you back from the brink of death."

Grace, who had no real desire to speak to this woman, remained mute. She regarded the soft, weathered features of the stout, mature woman standing by her bed. How and why did she invade her universe?

Martha's heart ached at seeing the dark circles and sunken face of the young girl in the bed. This young woman was literally starving herself. Cautiously, Martha reaches for Grace's bound hand, holding it as a mother would do for her wounded child.

"Don't you worry, my child, you're not alone," Martha smiled.

Frowning, Grace wanted nothing to do with this nosey neighbor. She just wanted to be left alone.

"Go away," Grace snapped. "I don't need or want your help..." she muttered, turning her head to face the padded grey wall.

Harold chose that moment to enter. Quietly, he stood by his mother and tried to read her expression but was distracted. His eyes strayed to the frail woman whose face was staring at the wall. He wasn't certain, but it appeared she had rejected his mother's kindness.

Harold touched his mother's shoulders in an embrace. "Are you ready to go?"

Ignoring his question, Martha spoke directly to Grace. "Grace, this is my son, Harold," Harold nodded, but Grace refused to face her visitors.

Only by the greatest force of will did Harold hold his tongue. At the very least, he wanted to tell his neighbor how rude and ungrateful she was acting. Working to remember his mother's teaching to love those who don't want to be loved, he readied himself to follow his mother's lead.

"Grace, we'll be back later this evening before visiting hours are over," Martha whispered. Laying her weathered hand on Grace's shoulder, Martha viewed Grace's closed eyes and saw her silently moving her lips. Mother and son departed.

Catching a glimpse of Martha and Henry's backs, Grace screeched at them. "Skedaddle…and don't come back. Oh, yeah, keep your nose out of my business."

Despite the beaming sun, Labella shivered with cold-ness, scurrying inside. Riding alongside Stone in a taxi from LaGuardia Airport, she held her hands tightly clasped on her lap. She was hurting for her daughter, wondering what pitched her over the edge to cause Grace to take such extreme measures. Labella swallowed hard, trying to summon the courage to speak what she was thinking.

"Stone?" she solicits. "It's hard to gauge what torment Grace went through alone."

"Maybe she imagined a bleak future, no reason to live; only death was appealing."

"That's impossible!" Labella proclaims. "She has a loving family who cares."

The ride from the airport to the brownstone was draining for Stone and Labella. They were disconcerted to find Mrs. Henderson wasn't home. Thankful they had a key, they slowly entered Grace's apartment. Instantly, they faltered at the haunting smell of filth, human waste, and dried blood on the floor. Labella leaned against the wall by the door, her arms wrapped around her stomach, and wept uncontrollably.

Stone shudders, his teeth clenched. He surveys what could've been his daughter's eternal tomb. With a slight lurch, he crouches down beside the makeshift cardboard bed, scarcely keeping his snack down.

Several moments later, a middle-aged man with an empty expression greeted them; his dark, tangled hair reminded them of a swamp.

"Who are you people?" The landlord crackled. Ignoring Labella, he cuts over to Stone. "How'd you sneak in? Beat it!" The landlord yells. "See here, the clean freaks need to clean after the dead broad."

In a few quick movements, Stone stood to his full height, looking down at the stocky man, his eyes narrowing. "My daughter is not a broad, and she isn't dead!" Stone boomed.

"We're not leaving, so if I were you, I wouldn't linger. Send in your cleaning crew."

The landlord stared up at Stone, taking a moment to respond.

"Okay...sir," he snorted and turned, leaving the bewildered parents behind.

The apartment was in shambles, and it told a story of brokenness. Labella collected the ripped gown before the crew could pitch it in a huge bin. They saw the dried blood on it. They shook their heads, looking around. Their love for their daughter mixed with the agitation they felt that their daughter had lost sight of God's love.

New York Memorial Hospital

Stone, Labella, Martha and Harold had established a good rapport during the last four days. Working together to maintain a solidity around Grace, gradually, they saw a little bit of light entering Grace's eyes.

Grace sat quietly in the back seat of Harold's car, inhaling the fresh morning air. It was a treat to be outside instead of inside the antiseptic room, where she had revealed her intimate thoughts and emotions to a reserved doctor. The tension at her first session with her parents was too much at times.

Harold and Stone maintained a light conversation, giving Grace space. As the car maneuvered through the streets, Grace became restless and started checking out her surroundings.

Looking out the car windows, she saw tall brick buildings with fire escapes, specialty stores, and an older woman dragging a trolly full of groceries.

Miraculously, Harold found parking in front of the brownstone on the Upper East Side. Unsure of what she would find behind her apartment door, Grace climbed the steps, filled with panic and fear. Reaching her apartment, she turned the doorknob with trembling hands. With an appreciative sigh of relief, Grace gazed at a refreshed, furnished, cozy apartment.

"I hope you don't mind. We've prepared supper for everyone," Labella smiled, hugging Grace.

"Martha and Harold," Stone begins. "We're thankful for all you have done for us."

"Let's eat," Martha chimed in, putting dishes of food on the new dinette table.

With bowed heads, Stone led the group in the blessing of the food. *"We give thanks for this wonderful meal and for allowing our Grace to see a new day."* Watching her father pray, Grace found it comforting to have such a loving and God-fearing family and neighbors.

Early Saturday morning, on her knees in the living room, Labella prayed for Grace's restoration and guidance. She had reluctantly bid farewell to Stone earlier and felt a little slighted by his leaving. However, she knew that if he felt it was essential to stay, he would have done so.

On all prior occasions, Grace had always fared well on her own, but not this time. Today, Labella hopes Grace will share what's in her heart. Hearing footsteps, she ended her prayer.

"Is that you, Grace?" Labella asked, arising from her kneeling position.

"Yes, I've napped sufficiently." Grace sat down on a bar stool in the kitchen. For a moment, they were silent.

"Dear, how are you?" Labella asked, taking the other bar stool next to Grace.

"I'm taking one day at a time, Mother."

"Should I be concerned about you? It's been an immensely rough two weeks."

"Don't fret; in time, I will smile again," Grace said, reaching for a carrot stick from the platter on the counter.

"Estoy contenta."

They sat quietly for a moment longer before Labella rose to add milk to the cooked mashed potatoes. Detecting uncertainty in Grace's mannerisms, she asked: "¿qué pasa?"

"I've let you both down," said Grace in a hushed tone.

"No, Grace," Labella said, forgetting the potatoes. "God has a divine purpose for your life. I'm trusting him to guide you through this moment of pain unto victory."

"I'm having trouble believing that."

"We are never prepared for a painful life, but the lessons we learn are always positive."

"Mother, I was so gullible," Grace blurted out.

"At times, we all feel that way. Being left at the altar will damage anyone's self-worth and create doubts."

Grace nodded, doing her best not to let her thoughts roam wild. Before she could resolve their conversation, Labella resumed preparing dinner. Labella's smile gives Grace just enough confidence to believe.

"Grace," Harold begins as they sit down to eat, but Martha interrupts, "He has found a job for you." Both mother and son erupted in laughter.

Shocked, Grace gently lowered herself in her chair and studied Harold. His announcement, unbeknownst to him, had infiltrated her thoughts. Continually receiving financial support from her parents had been most distressing for Grace.

"What does it involve?" Grace questioned Harold, finding his probing eyes on her.

"Working the information desk in a museum," Harold said, remembering hearing about her missed internship in Paris.

"When do I start?"

"Monday," Harold explained. "I know it's crazy, but your father said you could do it."

"Oh, mercy!" exclaimed Grace. Unable to speak further, she lowers her head.

Unable to join in the conversation around the table, Grace fights within herself. Should she accept the job? It's a far cry from restoring precious artifacts. In addition, she's happy one minute and depressed and angry the next. Can she truly reenter society?

❧

"What time does the clock read?" Grace asked Martha over lunch.

"One o'clock," Martha flashed her a brilliant smile. "Are you nervous?"

"Outrageously," Grace admitted, feeling a bit sick.

It has now been exactly two weeks since she began working at the museum, Monday through Thursday. She did enjoy interacting with the customers and using her knowledge of art history. Although Reese was constantly in her thoughts, Grace went through the motions of living, even agreeing to attend an event with Harold.

"You've plenty of time to dress before tonight's event."

"Why am I going?"

Martha explained. "Harold's boss gave him two tickets, and he roped you into going with him," she said, clearing the table. "Besides, you haven't seen the Guggenheim Museum."

"But I have nothing…" Grace halts in the middle of her sentence when Martha holds up her hand.

"Not to worry, you've got a black dress, that will do fine. Think of Harold as your adoptive brother," Martha laughed.

Even Grace smiled a little over this and then noticed the time again.

"I won't need to mingle, will I?" Grace asked.

"Actually, Harold's nervous, too."

Grace nodded. "Thank you for everything you've done for me, Martha."

"What have I done?"

"Only saved my life and encouraged me daily with words of wisdom, kindness, and tenderness."

It was too much for the neighbor. Tears rushed to her eyes, and Grace moved swiftly to her side, kissing Martha's warm cheeks.

"I must go; thanks for lunch," Grace said, rushing out the door.

With a wave from Grace, she was gone, and Martha sat alone in her kitchen. The afternoon sun grew warm, and right now, Martha didn't want to move from her spot. While enjoying the sunray's warmth from the open window, Martha's mind was on the painful longing behind Grace's dark brown eyes that she couldn't dismiss. She shook her head a little at how often Grace avoided looking directly at people and attending social functions until now.

For a moment, Martha found a strange and exciting feeling spiraling through her. Eager to have some quiet time in prayer, Martha didn't stay long in the kitchen. She knelt at her prayer chair with a heart filled with wonders and hopeful expectations.

Harold moved his hand beneath Grace's arm as they walked from the underground garage directly onto the street. A flickering tapestry of stars woven across the canvas sky greeted them. The moment Grace gazed at the unique design of the bowl-shaped masterpiece of concrete before her, her mouth opened, and her gloved hand embraced her neck. The spiraling structure that seemed to reach out to the night sky left her speechless.

"Well, Grace," Harold said as he turned his attention to her. "How does it feel to participate in society again?"

"It's somewhat scary," she admitted, shifting her eyes from the unforgettable sight.

Harold smiled, steering her inside the museum toward the winding ramp, highlighting the open rotunda. They heard music from an electric guitar. On impulse, Grace ran her hand across the smooth, dimpled walls.

"I'd missed an opportunity to visit this museum with my classmates," Grace surprisingly explained softly. "Instead, I went on a picnic with Reese."

Seeing her distant look, Harold tightened his grip on Grace's arm. Entering the private area, the instant laughter and clinking of stem wine glasses unsettled Grace's small moment of pleasure. She saw scores of people mingling around a water fountain, drinking, eating, and discussing art. Grace thought maybe she committed too willingly.

"This was a mistake," Grace whispered to Harold.

He looked at her without a change of expression. "Now, I know it can't be easy for you being here, and I'm clueless as to what you're feeling. But I know that you can't break the cycle of chaos inside of you if you run."

Grace watched Harold's face carefully. He was so much like his mother, transparent. They didn't talk further until Harold introduced her to Mr. Mike Brennan, his employer, and his wife. Hearing Harold giving high praises about her knowledge of art conservation, Grace's cheeks flamed with embarrassment.

"Ms. Forrester," Mr. Brennan announced. "I believe you would be interested in meeting an associate of mine," he said, motioning to an elderly gentleman on the opposite side of the room.

Grace watched an impeccably dressed European man approach the small group; his smile was wide. At that moment, she wanted to bolt.

"Bonsoir," the gentleman nodded to everyone but suddenly turned probing eyes on Grace. "I would like to introduce myself; I'm André Dupré, director and owner of Dupré Museum," he said politely.

Grace barely lifted her eyes. "Nice to meet you. I'm Grace Forrester, originally from Penville, North Carolina," she explained in a subdued voice.

"A pleasure to meet a fellow Carolinian," he exclaimed. André watched her eyes soften at his words, though she bit her lower lip.

Interrupted by the faint chimes announcing the auction, André moved behind the pocket-sized woman with sad, brooding eyes. When the door was opened, she vanished inside with her companion without a backward glance.

André had deliberately asked Harold to clear the way for him to speak privately with Grace. After the auction, he found Grace sitting alone in an alcove, immersed in a modern art piece on the wall. He stood quietly alongside her for five minutes before he spoke.

"It was brought to my attention," André said, avoiding making eye contact, "That you've missed an opportunity to intern in Paris."

Suddenly, Grace looked up with a face like thunder. "How...how do you know that?" she asked, clutching her purse.

He turned and spoke directly to her. "My friends, Mr. Brennan and Mr. Henderson." "Why?" Grace snapped.

"They're certain you can learn a great deal as my mentee," said André.

Though she turned her gaze from him, André was sure he had her full attention, therefore, he continued. "I don't know the reason you didn't take the internship, but I sense you're intelligent with a passion for art and its history."

"I'm sure you're capable of finding someone more quali-fied," Grace stated, her eyes fixed on the painting.

"Ms. Forrester...my interest is somewhat selfish." He cleared his throat. "I'm in dire need of an art conservator."

Grace looked at him, confused. "Mr. Dupre´, I thank you for your kind offer, but I'm not interested in any internship or job," Grace explained, turning her gaze again to the art piece.

Hoping she would look at him again, he pleaded. "Ms. Forrester, my museum is in Penville, and I must hire someone before I return."

36

"Penville?" she questioned, avoiding his eyes.

"Oui," André´ exclaimed.

Receiving only silence, he took out his business card from his wallet and laid it near Grace.

"Ms. Forrester, please think about my offer. I will wait for your call," André silently walked away.

⁓

"How are you, Grace?" André asked. He couldn't help but notice Grace's tenseness as she stood alongside him.

"I'm well, Mr. Dupré," Grace whispered.

It was early Monday morning, and they were at the Metropolitan Museum of Art, reviewing ancient Eastern art pieces. Thinking back three weeks ago, Grace couldn't imagine her life could almost be normal. She felt confused and was still fighting a war against self-doubts and insecurity; normalcy seemed impossible at times.

Grace discovered André was born in Switzerland in 1914. His family had fled to France due to war. They left their life of luxuries to stay alive. In 1945, the Dupré's returned to France and rebuilt the House of Dupré, a horse breeding farm. André's journey of losses and rebuilding instilled in him the goal of *never fearing failure but fearing not trying.* At the same time, he had become a well-educated and wealthy man.

"Don't you think it's time you call me André?" he asked. He watched Grace's head immediately lower.

It wasn't difficult for Grace to enjoy the beauty and history of ancient Eastern art pieces. She shadowed him, examining an intriguing 1825 secretary-bookcase... striking the 1194 BC Head of King Seti II wearing the Blue Crown... and the 1379 Mandala of the Sun God Surya. With all her heart, she couldn't believe, in a short time, the knowledge she had received.

"Are your parents excited you are returning home?"

"Yes."

Less than a week later, Grace stood in the middle of her empty apartment of seven weeks. Her crusty landlord was more than overjoyed to break her lease. Looking out her window for the last time, Grace saw that summer was in full swing. Not only were giggling kids on skateboards zipping between parked cars, but animal owners in shorts, their chosen attire, walked their jubilant dogs.

"Are you ready?"

At the sound of Andre's soft voice, Grace spun around from her place at the window to find Martha and Harold next to him.

"If you were musing over the past, Grace, please don't," Martha said.

"You've no reason to be unhappy about leaving; the time has come for you to move on," Harold blurted.

"Don't forget your adopted family in New York," Martha murmured.

Picking up Grace's luggage, Andre´ nodded to the silent young woman and went to wait for her in the hallway. Grace, with a wad of tissues in her hand, solemnly bid her adoptive family goodbye, then turned and walked out the door.

CHAPTER 3
The Ripple Effect

Penville, North Carolina

Some of Grace's pleasures since she returned home were working with André and introducing him to her parents during their family's annual Fourth of July party. Approaching the back door of the Dupré museum, she recognized how time was fleeting and knew she must cherish each moment. The large, handsome stone building stood alone on a rural street against the backdrop of high mountains with white caps.

The morning had moved so swiftly, the end of the day was fast approaching. Grace had all she could do to concentrate on the paperwork in her hand. She was concerned about the direction of her thoughts. It's true all these weeks, she'd been hiding from her girlfriends, but she had been unprepared for the incident at Sunday services the previous day.

Seeing longtime friends and meeting new ones was somewhat overpowering. However, Zory, Penelope, and Nora without speaking with her, blocks Grace's exit from the pew. Without any fanfare, Nora pushes in front of the others.

"Grace," she whispered, "We haven't seen or spoken with you since you've returned home; why?"

"I...I..."

"We were really looking forward to having a girl's night out."

Zory briskly pushed Nora aside.

"If I didn't know better," Zory bubbled over, "I'd think you've been hiding from us."

"Not exactly," Grace said, her voice shaky. I needed time to find a place to stay and get acquainted with my new co-workers at the museum."

Zory grunted at her timid remarks.

Penelope, the married friend with a child and husband, rejected Zory's rash statement and tried to appeal to Grace's conscience.

"We have no reasons to be harsh with Grace," Penelope explained.

Zory flipped her hand in an upward movement, rolling her eyes and pushing Penelope and Nora to the side as she huffed and puffed, walking to the edge of the pew.

Grace realized the motivation behind their intervention was to show her they felt snubbed. Getting back into the groove of living in Penville was going to take some time. She knew forgiveness was in order, but when and how, she wasn't sure.

The following weekend, large canvas tents had erupted in an open field across from her home. Grace posed a question to herself. "How about a walk along the trail?" All alone, she headed down the nearby trail toward the waterfall while sunrays glittered through the gaps in the trees. Enjoying the gorgeous shaded walk through the woods, Grace spotted an astonishing variety of beautiful mushrooms—and even caught sight of a mother deer and fawns running across the trail. Smiling, she continued her walk.

A couple hours later, reaching the town's bakery, Grace selected freshly baked blueberry muffins and sweet lemon tea. Catching her breath, she sat on a bench near the water fountain in the town's square and shared her muffin with the few pigeons circling the area. Basking in the heat, Grace closes her eyes and starts her ritual of relaxing. First, she concentrated on her fingers, willing them to go limp. One by one, R-E-L-A-X, Grace properly told her hands and arms. Slowly, they started to obey her, and after several minutes, she was in her quiet place.

Grace's eyes flew open at the sound of a soft cough. "Hi, Andre'," babbled Grace. "How long have you been standing there?"

"Not long. Just thinking about our first date," Andre' chuckled with his eyes twinkling in mischief.

"What brings you into town on this glorious afternoon?"

"I was looking for you," he said, his voice and eyes teasing.

"One would think you might be having second thoughts," she teased him, unnecessarily brushing imaginary dirt off her jogging shorts, her eyes down to keep from laughing. "One might suspect that your new conservator is a fake."

"I shall leave this instant without telling you my good news."

He said this so swiftly and funnily that Grace laughed.

"Have a seat, and let's have a chat."

When André sat next to her, he introduced the news. "We've started negotiating to acquire a fascinating exhibit."

"What does it have to do with me?"

André stared straight into her eyes. "Everything!"

"Why?" she gulped. "I haven't completed my probation period."

"You've proven to the board of directors and me that you're a talented art conservator."

She nodded, pondering his answer.

"Grace, please understand, you're the daughter, Bridget, and I didn't have. She died so young…" he paused. "I'm like a proud father, seeing his daughter succeed."

"Every day, I'm grateful for you," she beams. "During the lowest point in my life, you saw the real me."

"Readiness is the word of the day," said André. He stood and bowed, disappearing in the crowd of tourists mingling around the town's square.

Dupré Museum

Mrs. Stella Hastings, André's trusted secretary, recalls the first day she encountered Grace. Without prompting, she enlisted herself to look after the pint-size bundle of suppressed joy. Older than Grace, yet young enough to be an older sister, she allowed Grace to call her by her first name.

"Grace!" she gushed. "Mr. Dupré wants you in his office."

"What if I say no way," Grace teases her.

"How many times have I said you can't hide in your chambers endlessly," she responded, laughing. "Get cracking, little one."

Grace made a funny face, putting her tools down.

Stella whimsically stated, "Who can resist those jewel-like brown eyes and sweeping eyelashes?" giving Grace's back a little push.

Minutes later, they find Mr. Dupre´ standing in front of a large painted mural opposite his desk. Stella nodded to Grace to enter. On the far-right corner of his desk was a silver and glass column clock engraved with André's motto: "A man who doesn't fear failure will succeed, but a man who fears trying would be a failure." He turned to greet his guest.

"Well, Grace, the time has come to show your talent to the world."

For a long minute, they stood muted, admiring the art on the wall. André linked his arm with hers, leading them to an area with chairs for conversation.

"You have the Worthington exhibit!"

Grace's mouth flew open, but no words were uttered. With a deep, satisfied chuckle, André lounged back in his chairs, underscoring his smirk.

"The trustees all agreed you're the best person for this assignment."

Grace fidgeted, wondering why she was chosen.

"Apart from me, I can name several more qualified art conservators."

His voice dropped to a near whisper. "Stop second-guessing

yourself. You're our qualified art conservator for this project.

Standing abruptly, frowning. "You don't understand, Andre'," Grace dashes away from the chairs, staring at the ceiling. "I just can't," she states.

"Come here, Grace," he implores her. "I truly understand your feelings," he said as his features softened.

Grace reluctantly walked back to her seat, choking with emotions. "This is so hard."

André takes her hands and helps her to sit down. "I know, but I also know you'll succeed. Believe in your self-worth... now let's get to work."

They spent the next two hours talking about the Worthington exhibit. Arrangements were being organized for her to meet with the Board's Director, Mrs. Caroline Worthington, in two weeks at the New York Historical Museum.

⁓

Twenty minutes away from Penville, in a rural community, cars pulled smoothly into the circular driveway, one behind each other. To calm their curiosity, Grace's guests mingled for a few minutes outside, greeting one another. Hearing the commotion outside, Grace opened the door and was apprehensive to see all her guests had arrived simultaneously.

"Wow," exclaimed Zory, stepping inside the front door.

The guests could view fine woodwork even from the entryway. A tapestry in rich sea colors displaying a small Italian village hung in the living room. Beautiful furniture in coordinating colors of the tapestry was scattered throughout, with an ornate grandfather clock near the front door.

"Everyone, come in," Grace said as she greeted friends and family.

"Little sister, it's nice of you to invite us to dinner," Wyatt remarked, laughing as he followed everyone inside.

"Yes, it is," Grace smiled.

"It seems we're underdressed," Labella commented, her eyes resting on Grace's soft pink evening gown. As she scooted by her guests, her gown billowed behind her.

"What's with that look on your face?" Grace stated.

"Can you shed light on why we're in jeans and you're not," Zory challenged her.

A small laugh escaped Grace. It was so like Zory to be sarcastic. Nevertheless, all eyes were still on her, clearly waiting for a reply.

"Let's eat, dinner is already on the table."

Grace's guests did as they were told, awed when they saw the table decorated with simplicity and sophistication. Grace smiled when all her seven guests were seated around the table, and they recited a prayer of thanks. Over homemade lasagna and Caesar salad, the conversation focused on the growth of the Forrester's Athletic Clinic and news from town.

Stone, seated near his daughter, leaned close and spoke what was on the tip of everyone's tongue. "How long are you going to make us wait?" Stone beamed. "This wasn't a casual invitation."

All eyes turn to an excited Grace. "We're waiting," Labella chuckles.

Grace's breathless account of her new assignment left the group in total silence, except for one person.

"You don't mean the well-known Worthington Steel family?" Zory asked in excitement as she leaped from her chair, tipping it over.

Grace nodded.

As was expected, everyone was shocked and speechless and started speaking at once, and all Grace could do was stare at their faces.

"One at a time, please," she said at last as her family and friends laughed.

"Do you think you will enjoy this assignment?" Labella asked.

"I confess, I have doubts, Mother, but it sounds delightful."

Nora and Edmond offered to serve the dessert during the conversation.

"When do you leave for New York?" Penelope's voice was rather soft, taking a spoonful of ice cream and pound cake.

Just before Grace answered, she wondered if she would have another breakdown. Could she handle being in New York so soon after she nearly took her own life? Her breath was stuck in her throat; she couldn't allow those memories to hinder her assignment.

"I'm leaving in two weeks."

With little ceremony, the group moved to the living room, taking remnants of their dessert plates. Talking all at once again,

46

enlightening Grace on what she needed to pack or purchase. She was overjoyed with every suggestion. The last statement from the group was, "Don't forget family, friends, and your humble beginnings."

From inside the safety of her quiet bedroom, returning to New York could be a challenge; picking up her bible, she read about Abraham's willingness to leave what was familiar to him. Trusting and believing in God for strength, Abraham began a new journey. Grace couldn't help but wonder what awaited her on her new journey.

Worthington Estate – Long Island

Lance Worthington arrived at the Worthington estate on a cool, crisp evening with a gentle breeze, perfect for a stroll through the gardens. However, death prowled around Sterling Worthington, Sr. Lying in a huge four-poster bed, Sterling Worthington, Sr., breathed with labored breath; his flesh clammy and his complexion pale beneath his bushy mustache. His eyes were open and fixed upon the venomous disposition of his grandson.

The older man was addressing his grandson near his bed. "Do you understand?" he repeated hoarsely with great effort.

"Do you understand why it was done that way?"

Lance Worthington, the forgotten grandson, stood by the bed. His sharp, bluish-green eyes scrutinized his grandfather's drawn brows and his wrinkled hands clutching the sheets.

Standing erectly with his imposing stature and broad shoulders, he spat out, "I don't understand. Too much time has passed," he said as he turned away from his grandfather's face, his heart throbbing with anger and sadness.

Lance's grandfather, Sterling, could see the anger and hatred in Lance, and he desperately wanted to atone for his sins against his daughter-in-law and only grandson.

"You…and your mother…will be… comfortable," Sterling gasped, his breathing even more labored. "You won't have to worry about anything."

"Thank… you." Lance mouthed.

"I must do what's right," Sterling muttered. "I can't rest in peace… with the Worthington's name stained. "You'll be restored …as the rightful heir," he spoke through parched lips while his chest rose and fell heavily.

"I did love you…Grandson…" his words slowly dying, his eyes closing.

Caroline Worthington, completely obscured from everyone else in the room, foregoes her lace handkerchief, letting tears run down her cheeks. She regarded her beloved husband with a smile as he spoke to their grandson for the first time in over thirty-two years. Going pale, she whispered, *I love you, dear husband, and I will honor your wish.*

Sterling, Sr. died an hour later. Carefully and quietly, the Worthington clan gathered to lay to rest the founder of the Great Sterling Steel Company, Mr. Sterling Worthington, Sr.

Worthington's Steel's business offices and factories were suspended for ten days following the funeral of the founder and CEO, Mr. Sterling Worthington, Sr. His wife, Caroline, confident in her abilities, maintained a timeless and classic style, now embedded in her DNA, in carrying out the details surrounding his death.

Caroline, in a tailored black dress, sat at her writing table, finishing the last of the condolence correspondence. Her thick grey braided hair was swept up in a bun. Much as Caroline wanted to believe the day wouldn't be as bumpy as the last ten days, her heart beat a little fast as she left the library to speak with the family. She covered the distance rather swiftly, only to be disappointed because the family had already departed to other parts of the estates. She dialed for her personal maid.

"Kindly alert the family to assemble in the drawing room in one hour."

"Yes, madam."

Caroline stood at the fireplace, studying her wedding photo. *This life is what I was born to do*; she quipped to the photo. Can thirty-two years of rejection truly be forgiven and forgotten? The family wasn't aware of the recent change to Sterling's will, now, as the sole executor of the Worthington's fortune, Caroline is certain she will receive a barrage of criticisms. She was determined to demonstrate a single-minded focus to carry out her husband's dying wishes.

Next Day, Sterling Worthington, Jr., with his prim, combed chestnut hair, was always surrounded by a scowl. His long, lanky body, impeccably dressed, was heightened by his tendency to make everyone seem beneath his social standards, wealth, and wasn't worth his time or respect.

However, he was no match for his domineering father, who demanded perfection in every area of his life and those around him. Yet Junior sought his approval, becoming his father's puppet. When his son, Lance, was born with clubbed feet, his father advised him to leave his wife and deformed baby boy, and he obliged. Strolling inside the library with grandiose flare, Junior perched on the settee, forgetting his wife, who was lagging behind him.

"Mother, what's so important?" Junior asked with a self-satisfied smirk and pompous attitude.

"Don't be so melodramatic," Ava Worthington's voice dripped with mockery from the door. "What's your hurry? Have you lost sight of your wife?" Ava chuckled, her crinkly voice cutting like a knife.

Ava, the only child of the Redding Hastings, the oldest wealthiest family in New York, was forced on her twenty-first birthday to marry Sterling, Jr. After barely two years, he discarded his family after she gave birth to Lance.

Forsaken by the Worthington's, she strove to maintain proper appearances, manners, and adherence to social norms. Dressed in a black ruffled collared dress, coordinated with black and silver chunky accessories, Ava was a formidable opponent to her ex-husband; she flashed her devious witchy eyes his way.

"What's with your spiky white hair," Sterling laughed. "You look like an old punk rocker. I'm astonished Mother included you in this charade of family unity."

"You're so inept," Ava hollered, sashaying to the chair farthest from the sofa and settee. "How dare you try and belittle me when your mousy wife needs an overhaul."

"Both of you cease immediately," Caroline hissed.

The hatred between her husband and his first wife wasn't lost on Betty, Sterling's current wife. She seamlessly sat down beside her husband and laid a hand on his shoulder, but he brushed it off. Considering her position within the Worthington family, Betty kept her eyes downcast, looking at the carpet.

Betty Starks was raised by wealthy parents who constantly critiqued her sense of fashion and social manners, which caused her to be uncertain about her self-worth. Being both witty and educated, she caught Junior's interest. Betty was astounded when a five-year courtship with Junior materialized into a marriage proposal. Her parents were elated that she was able to attach herself to such a financially strong family. Even now, years later, Betty questions why Sterling had chosen her.

"Sorry, I lost track of time," Lance Worthington said congenially, rushing through the door, his fingers running through his neatly combed raven hair. He stopped and surveyed the room. "Hello everyone."

All five heads turned at the sound of a male's breathy voice.

Raised without a father, Lance's mother taught him that following the rules would lead to rewards. On his grandfather's deathbed, Lance met the two most important men in his life—his father and his grandfather, who he had not met previously. His grandfather's dying wish empowered him to remain at Worthington's estate, even after the funeral. However, Lance was looking forward to his obligations being over so he could return to his life in New York.

"Come and sit next to me," Caroline asserted. His curiosity spiked his interest in the impromptu gathering. Taking her outstretched hand, Lance sat next to her on the sofa.

"You may begin, Mr. Devon," Caroline motioned to the gentleman sitting behind the vast ornate desk in the library.

Mr. Mark Devon, having conducted a textbook reading of wills to the families of a deceased one, sat stoically for several minutes. Considering Mrs. Worthington's instructions, he knew that the beneficiaries were unaware of current changes to the will. The puckered mouths, tightened fists, and lifted chins brought a menacing mood to the room. He knew that this meeting could rapidly turn ruthless.

"It's alright, Mr. Devon; please start; time is precious," Caroline stated, perceiving his fear.

Taking her cue, he inhaled deeply. "Good day, everyone," Mr. Devon said in a firm tone. "Let me say I'm very sorry for your loss. Mr. Sterling Worthington, Sr. was a great caring man. At the request of Mrs. Caroline Worthington, I will begin to read the will of Mr. Sterling Worthington, Sr."

I, Sterling Worthington, Sr., of Long Island, New York, on this date, August 5, 1980, am of sound mind, and I am writing this holographic will with the intent of setting forth my wishes for the disposition of my estate after my death.

Projected on the wall, the artist had skillfully captured Sterling Worthington, Sr.'s strong personality in the portrait behind the desk where Mr. Devon was reading the will. Sterling Jr. stared at his father's chiseled jaw as though his father was in the room presiding over the disposition of his inheritance.

A chill shuddered through his body, even though the warm rays of the afternoon sun rested in the library. With great effort, Junior tried to make sense of what was being said. He listened to the familiar symphony of Mr. Devon's voice. The eerie grin plastered on Ava's face caused Junior's breath to quicken. It wouldn't be the first time his father had made him play by his rules.

"That isn't Father's will," Junior exploded, his nostrils flaring. "The date is wrong! I won't be insulted," he yelled, approaching Mr. Devon like a cheetah stalking its prey. Betty gasped at her husband's back, clutching the fabric of her dress, fearful about what he might do.

Caroline, extremely irate, firmly admonished him. "Sterling! sit down!"

The outburst from a composed Caroline was unexpected. Loud gasps pierced the silent room and caused Junior to withdraw, showing his displeasure.

Caroline nodded to Mr. Devon to continue. Regaining his composure, he proceeded.

"I will forgo the preliminaries of the will and read what each of you *is* waiting to hear.

I give all my real estate, stocks, bonds, and the company owned by me at the time of death all rights that I have under any related insurance policies, to my wife, Caroline Worthington, if she survives me. I also give the Chairman of the Board position of the Worthington Steel Company to my wife, Caroline Worthington, if she survives me.

I give the sum of 10 shares of the company's stocks and a seat on the board with a yearly stipend of one million ($1,000,000) to my son, Sterling Worthing, Jr., if he survives me. The stipend will be forfeited if he doesn't participate in the board's activities and/or sells his shares.

And I give my CEO position of the Worthington Steel Company to my grandson, Lance Worthington, who I foolishly rejected if he survives me.

Standing, Sterling snaps angrily, "I can't hear any more of this madness. Father was sick and out of his mind when he rewrote his will."

Caroline flinched, laying her hand against her breastbone, looking defeated. With a flip of her hand, Mr. Devon dutifully put all the documents back inside his briefcase and navigated to the door without a word.

Sensing an incoming struggle, Caroline adopted a quick stance, holding everyone's attention as she sat behind the desk. "Sterling," she angrily said, "Son! Sit down and be calm."

"Why?"

"I need to explain your father's changes."

"I wouldn't be surprised if Ava pressured him," he grunted.

Lance frowned at his father. "You have gone too far…the fact of your greed and misdirected love disgusts me. We don't want your precious money."

"Finally, your father realized you were an unsuitable husband and father," Ava laughed.

"That's enough," Caroline declared.

Sterling gasped. "You mean you agreed with Father's will?" What's the matter with you, Mother?

"Your father was dying…he wanted to remedy a wrong we caused." Caroline took a deep breath.

"The CEO position…that should be mine!"

Caroline carefully focused, controlling her movements and speech. "Your father and I lost three decades of not having our grandson…your son… in our lives. An injustice was committed, and I promised your father we will never be separated again."

"Why must I have to suffer?" Sterling railed. "Ava never wanted anything from us."

"The matter is settled," Caroline commanded, rising from her chair and addressing her family. "I'm going to take a nap, and I expect everyone for dinner," Caroline said, leaving everyone in disarray.

Drunk with happiness, giggles arose in Ava's bosom. Her eyes, sparking with pure joy, met Lance's for a fleeting moment. However, without warning, an angry Sterling stood in the middle of the room, yelling and shaking his fists in the air.

"I'm not staying for dinner."

"But your mother is expecting us," Betty pleaded.

"This has nothing to do with you…other than you'll have less money to sponge off me," he flared. "Are you coming?"

Lance and Ava watched a woman shrinking before them.

"I hope we'll see you tonight," Betty lamented.

Ava nervously drummed her feet on the Persian rug. After Sterling and Betty departed, Ava fixed her eyes on Lance, and joyful tears liberally flowed down her cheeks. Ava twirled around the room. Her gaze stopped at the majestic desk with the black leather chair, a representation of Worthington's power and riches; now, it was available to her son.

"Do you understand what that old man has done?" Ava asked slowly.

"Yes, but why is it important to us…we're doing fine without their money."

"Foolish boy," she sternly scolded him. "You're now responsible to continue the Worthington legacy."

While chirping birds sang noisily in a tree outside the library's window, an invisible barrage of questions surrounded Lance.

"Mother…must I…"

"Stop right now!" She interrupted. "I don't care why that old man's heart turned warm, but you'll not deny your inheritance."

What had seemed like a long-ago memory was finally in front of Lance. Meeting his grandfather was without any ceremony, but Sterling Sr. gave these words to him: *you are now the torchbearer for the Worthington's legacy.*

CHAPTER 4
Fractured Memories

Penville, North Carolina

Grace had a sense of trepidation about what was going to happen when she reached New York. After a fifteen-hour day of packing her clothes and tools and everyone giving their final counsel and well wishes, she was completely frayed as she boarded the train for more than an eleven-hour ride to her destination.

The moon's silver glow across the landscape made the night seem almost as light as day. As she looked out at the dark landscape, Grace saw various sleeping towns dark, except for the scurry of dancing lights from the street's lampposts. The noise of the slow-moving wheels bending around the high white-tip mountains and the sounds of the train's fast-moving wheels on the flat lands both resonated in Grace's sleeper car. After a while, the rhythm of it became hypnotic, lulling her to sleep. The overnight train ride was a welcoming relief since she teetered on the edge of complete exhaustion.

New York, New York

The day was beginning to wake up as the sun was yet to rise, fully carrying its summer heat. The early morning light delivered a soft, muted feel, much like an impressionist painting. Leaning her head against the window, Grace leisurely enjoyed the first hint of dawn painting the sky. Unfortunately, her stomach twisted into knots when the train entered Grand Central Train Station in New York.

Arriving at the Plaza Hotel's front desk, Grace received an engraved envelope from Mrs. Worthington. Inside her room, she read the note from Mrs. Worthington. It explained that an unexpected complication had arisen, and they would meet within a couple of days. Grace called Mr. Dupre´ about the correspondence from their benefactor, and he told her to spend the time in New York enjoying herself until she was called to begin work for the museum. Grace went down to the hotel's restaurant for lunch. Later that evening, she called her former neighbor Martha, informing her that she was in town. Early the next morning, Grace moseyed through the bustling hotel to Harold's awaiting car.

"Hello, Martha, hello, Harold."

"Hello, Grace," Martha and Harold said in unison.

Excited to see each other, the three friends suddenly grew quiet after the greetings. Martha asked, "How was your train ride?"

"Uneventful, but I must confess I'm nervous about being back in New York.

"How did you get this project?" Harold asked.

Grace laughed a little. Grace gave them full details of how the project came about. She explained how she loved working with André and spending time with her family and friends back home in Penville. She felt like a tourist with the Hendersons, touring Central Park, enjoying each other's company and then going out to eat some wonderful food.

On the third day, the front desk rang to inform her that a car was waiting for her downstairs. Grace hastily rushed downstairs, thankful she had eaten breakfast and dressed before seven. Outside, she saw a chauffeur standing near a long black limousine, and after she introduced herself in a timid voice, the chauffeur smiled and offered to assist her.

Meanwhile, at the Worthington Estate, Ava was in the library. Her lips were tightly pressed together, and her features constricted. She was brooding over who the stranger was that Caroline didn't want her to meet. Suddenly, she took action, swiftly marching downstairs to the servant's quarters in search of Caroline's maid, Ivy.

"Tell me the name of Mrs. Caroline's guest," she demanded, shocking Ivy into silence.

Ava took her silence as a defiant move.

"Ivy, give me an answer now!"

"Madam, the mistress instructed us not to disturb her until her guest leaves," Ivy gawked at Ava.

"I'm not a servant," Ava bristled. "You will tell me where they are."

With Mrs. Ava's new status, Ivy was afraid of losing her job. Not sure what to do, Ava took Ivy's delay as an insult, placed her hand on her hip, turned her nose up and stormed from the area, determined to search every inch of the house. The maid looked on bewildered.

When the limousine pulled up, the driver buzzed, and an opulent huge iron gate with a massive W emblem opened. While Grace was riding through the gate, the bright sunlight reflected off the massive, well-manicured grounds before her. In the distance, she saw a lavish estate of stone surrounded by rows of blooming cherry blossom trees and roses.

The limousine driver helped Grace out of the car. A flaw-lessly dressed man in a black suit and shoes opened a vast decorative wooden door.

Inside the entryway, she looks about her, taking in the antique Persian rugs covering the marble flooring and the elegant beamed ceiling inlaid with rich, dark wood beams, adding a touch of sophistication to the foyer. Peering down the hall, she saw a glittering array of glass, crystals and a white-glazed Steinway grand piano. With some apprehension, she follows the butler.

Mrs. Caroline's faithful servant announced that her guest had arrived as he held open the ornate door for Grace. She gazed at the door.

Caroline, peering out, saw next to her servant a smartly dressed, dainty young woman in a black and white two-piece tweed suit. Caroline instantaneously doubted if this adorable, unobtrusive woman could rise to the challenge.

Discerning that her guest was taking deep breaths to control her fear, Caroline swiftly moved toward Grace. She entwined her arm with Grace's shaking arm and led her to the sofa. Caroline watched her guest for a moment, hoping the young woman would relax.

"Welcome, Ms. Forrester. I appreciate your willingness to come to my home."

Grace nodded. "Thank you for allowing the Dupre' Museum the wonderful opportunity to honor your family's history."

Due to Grace's perfect speech and demeanor, Caroline acknowledged that Ms. Forrester was a highly intelligent young woman. "The Dupre' Museum was our board's first choice. We have heard many great reviews of your fine exhibits."

Grace looked pleased, expounding on how Mr. Andre' Dupre' had used a generous amount of time and effort to ensure the museum was capable of bringing art to life. Delighted for the diversion of small talk, Grace was grateful that she had started to relax and hoped Mrs. Worthington, would enlighten her about why the meeting wasn't held at the museum.

"Mrs. Worthington, may I be so bold as to ask why we're meeting at your home?"

Caroline looked at her guest, her mind still trying to find an approachable way to discuss the subject.

"We have an enormous problem with the exhibit."

Grace was shocked at this news. Her assignment was to determine the exhibit narrative and review all objects and other components related to the exhibit.

Seeing the look on Grace's face, Caroline asked "Having doubts?"

"No, but you might," Grace said.

Caroline shook her head in disbelief; Ms. Forrester was not only intelligent but observant.

"A large painting for the exhibits has been damaged, and it can't be moved."

Flabbergasted, Grace couldn't speak.

Seeing Grace's concerns, Caroline pragmatically posed a question to her. "You're an art conservator?"

"Yes," Grace answered in a barely audible tone.

"My solution," Caroline begins, "is that you remain at the estate to repair the painting."

Grace's mind conjured many problems. She only planned for a week's stay in New York; her tools were at the hotel, and she wasn't sure about living in such splendor.

"I confessed your solution is daunting, but I need my tools to complete your request."

Caroline lifted her eyebrows, quite fascinated by the fact that Grace was candid with her.

"I appreciate your concerns, but there's no need. My driver will drive you back to your hotel and pick you up tomorrow morning at ten o'clock. I will notify your museum of the situation."

So, Grace assented to the assignment, but she was worried about what would await her. She also thought about the impact of staying in New York for an extended period.

❦

Ava somehow learned the location of the visitor and stood outside the door where Caroline was meeting with Grace. Ava silently peeled the closed door from its clasp. Nonetheless, Caroline caught the click of the opened door and whirled around to see Ava. Caroline furious but nods with dignity. Ava enters the room and closely scrutinizes the stunning young woman.

"Mother Caroline?" Ava's eyes only on Grace. "I'm sorry; I assumed your guest had left," she said, her voice dripping with molasses.

"Ms. Forrester, excuse my daughter-in-law's intrusion. May I introduce Mrs. Ava Worthington?" Caroline mimicked Ava's honeyed voice.

Leering, Ava extended her hand. "It's a pleasure to meet you."

Spontaneously, Grace leaned back, unable to fathom the disdain from this woman.

"Nice to meet you, Mrs. Worthington," Grace muttered, her throat closing. Instantly, she turned her attention back to Mrs. Caroline, refusing to believe all aristocrats were rude.

⁓

Lance reluctantly remains at the mansion, tied up in his new reality that has totally upended his prior life. He couldn't believe that three weeks ago, he was enjoying a bachelor's life in New York.

Yet, here he was, feverishly wishing to leave his grandparents' drab mausoleum. Twisting his watch, he couldn't help but think about this new mantle placed on him. Had it totally erased his old life? It was beginning to feel more like an anchor around his neck.

Determined to return to his more familiar life, he sought out his grandmother's faithful driver when a silky voice triggered him to stop. He nearly bumped into the senior housemaid, Rose. While he apologizes to Rose, the chauffeur Charles rushes past him. Lance immediately thanks Rose and follows Charles.

Hearing a man's tantalizing voice, Grace turned toward the door, missing part of Ms. Caroline's instructions. Noticing Grace's unusual distraction, Caroline questioned her while Ava gauged her odd behavior.

"Are you alright, Ms. Forrester?"

Even being preoccupied, she replied, "Yes, I will strive to fulfill your wishes."

"Perfect!" Caroline nodded, weaving her way through doubts. "My driver will be here shortly to take you back to New York."

On the heels of Caroline's statement, Charles rushes into the room, with Lance quietly following him. Lance leaned against the table in the shadows and couldn't escape the vision of an exquisite woman with dark and thick curls around her face and shoulders. Her dark brown eyes and lashes beckoned him, while her creamy bronzed skin would lure any man to her, he thought. Lance, forgetting his surroundings, inches to get a closer view, almost toppling a glass vase but barely catching it.

Grace glances over her shoulder at the sound. Her breath caught in her throat, causing her to cough lightly. Lance shrugged and winked at Grace, who returned a smile. Ava's body stiffened, seeing the interaction between the two.

"Lance!" Ava squealed, giving him a probing look. "How long have you been standing there? Don't dawdle come in."

Lance carefully set the vase down on the table, and with light steps, he covered the distance. After kissing his mother and grandmother, his eyes returned to the tantalizing woman sitting opposite his grandmother. He deliberately fixed his gaze on the woman before him. Grace tried to resist those alluring glistening eyes but couldn't.

"Lance," Caroline exclaimed. "This is Ms. Forrester; she will be staying with us."

"Nice to meet you, Ms. Forrester," said Lance, embracing Grace's hand and letting his fingers dance lightly across the back of her hand, sending a shiver of pleasure through her. Shyly, she glanced up at a raven-haired Adonis.

Ava's mouth was twitching as she began to speak.

"What are you doing here?"

"Actually, I was searching for Charles when he rushed by me. I need him to drive me back to New York."

"Well, Charles is here to take Ms. Forrester back to New York," Caroline stated "but she's returning to us soon."

Grace got to her feet, licking her lips nervously; she sighed and tried to find the right words. She learned in a short length of time that the grandson was dangerous. His towering good looks and his bluish-green eyes were full of fire and seduction. When all the pleasantries were completed, Grace departed quickly.

Alone with his thoughts, Lance concluded the charming Ms. Forrester demanded further research, and perhaps being at the Worthington estate wasn't all bad. She wasn't his usual preference, tall, thin and blonde; on the contrary, Ms. Forrester was petite and curvy. Yet her voice was that of a sultry woman who he could listen to for hours. Delighting both his mother and grandmother, he decided to cancel returning to New York. Lance decided to wait with great anticipation for Ms. Forrester's return.

The following day, Grace anxiously arrived at the Worthington's estate mid-morning. This time, she learned from Charles, the chauffeur, that the sprawling grounds hosted an eight-car garage with living quarters above it for the chauffeur and his wife. On the property, away from the mansion, were several stone quarters for the gardeners, horse handlers, the security gatekeeper and their families. Separate quarters on the lower level of the mansion were for the maids, the butler, and the cook. The estate housed stables filled with award-winning horses, both indoor and outdoor tennis courts, swimming pools, and several other rooms that seemed to hold some mysteries.

Ivy, Mrs. Caroline's maid, led Grace into the library, advising Grace that Ms. Caroline would be in shortly. When the doors closed, Grace's hands moved to her mouth as she inspected the floor-to-ceiling books arranged in the built-in bookcases. Looking out the window, she saw the magnificent rose gardens, which were a testament to the opulence of the Worthington Estate.

Several moments later, Mrs. Caroline entered the library. and Grace's heart thudded with dread when Mrs. Caroline didn't greet her but simply nodded. Bewildered, she solemnly walked beside Ivy, a few feet behind Ms. Caroline. At the end of the long hallway and down two steps, Ms. Caroline steps aside to allow Ivy to open the huge sculpted door.

Standing a short distance inside the semi-darkened room, Grace regarded Mrs. Caroline's cool, cordial manner. A dark current surges through Mrs. Caroline, as she leered at something in the far corner of the room, her eyes filling with sorrow and regret. Gathering her wits, Caroline collected her handkerchief from under her sleeve and dabbed her eyes.

Seeing that Ms. Caroline was troubled by haunting memories of the room, Grace knew a fierce battle had been fought here, where hope and peace were lost, and brokenness won. Deep sadness and melancholy hung over the room,

"Your assignment is in that corner," Caroline pointed to a sizeable covered item. Grace considered the item for several minutes.

"May I inquire what I am restoring?"

"It's a painting," Caroline gave a low moan of despair.

"After my examination, I will have an idea about the restoration process," Grace advised, stroking her hand along the hem of her immaculately ironed and starched blouse.

Mrs. Caroline studied her, trailing her handkerchief down her temple, her cheek, and her chin. "Very well," Caroline said. "I will leave you to your work. Good day, Ms. Forrester."

Staring at the closed door, Grace didn't hear Ivy until she tapped Grace's shoulders.

"Ms. Forrester, if you need anything, use the phone on the desk to inform Rose."

"I will do that," Grace quickly said, refusing to display her concern. Ivy smiled and left the disoriented guest alone in the room.

Grace inhaled profoundly. It was clear Mrs. Caroline was unwilling to discuss the painting with her. Grace walked over to the windows and hastily pulled back the heavy drapes, letting in golden rays from the sun, hitting the wood-paneled room with rich browns and greens.

Leather-bound books filled bookshelves around the walls. Bookshelves hugged the walls, and memorabilia was on display, showing the Worthington family were lovers of sailing. The faded outline over the massive fireplace once flaunted a large painting, which she guessed was the one needing to be restored.

Grace moved the phone to a nearby end table and gaged that the large writing desk would be a useable working space. Never backing away from the challenge of restoring priceless artwork, she unexpectedly perceived the covered painting as an unusual challenge. Grace crossed her arms over herself, delaying her examination.

Minutes later, Grace slowly moved toward the painting and bent over to uncover it. Suddenly, she hears determined footsteps and a howling from inside the room, jolting the quietness. Grace swiftly turned around, observing Lance who was rapidly walking toward her. In contrast to his flirting the day prior, his chest was rising, falling with rapid breaths, and his eyes were a blazing fire. Grace shifted her body to its full, four feet, nine inches tall, and lifted her chin as heat rose on the back of her neck.

"Mr. Worthington—please," she managed to get her words out. "I'm here to restore…a painting. It's time for me to begin my work."

Embarrassed that he had frightened her, Lance turned and became quiet until he spoke.

"Yes," he said contritely. "You're correct; I'm sorry; please proceed."

Grace heaved a sigh of relief and pulled back the sheet covering the painting. It was a portrait painted by Satine Blackstone, regarded as a leading artist. However, a large slash of white paint covered two of the four subjects' faces and a portion of their bodies. The other two subjects were an elderly woman gazing at the seated subject while a young woman appeared longing for an unreachable object.

Mortified by this deliberate act that had disfigured the painting, Grace's fist clenches. She frowned at Lance. "This wasn't an accident," she screamed. "Someone damaged this painting calculatingly."

Lance's nostrils flared. "That's not your concern," he yelled. "You were brought here to repair it, not give your opinion." His brows raised. "We were told you were the best."

Grace steels her emotions and turns back to the painting for an assessment. "Fortunately, the damage isn't too extensive," she assesses. "The portrait was varnished, which protected it. I should be able to dissolve that smear of paint; if not, I'll remove specks at a time."

Lance jammed his hands in his pants pockets. He turns toward her and says, "So, we are clear that your outburst was meaningless, and I can notify my grandmother that you're able to repair it."

Lance displayed his contempt by sneering at her as he turned and swaggered toward the door.

Grace, with her arms folded, screams. "Stop!... This shouldn't have happened. A painting is...something special... an expression of emotions and thoughts. It's personal. I just don't understand how anybody could hurt it this way."

Lance harrumphed, full of unrepressed anger, and he bolted to where Grace stood. "Paintings can't feel," Lance's voice roared. "People are what's important—or don't you believe that, Ms. Forrester!"

Risking her job, Grace stomps her foot; she isn't going to shy away from being bullied.

"Naturally, I believe that," she blurted out. "I'm just trying to figure out what happened. I've never seen this before. A painting burned in a fire and then doused with water, yes. This painting...is different; it was damaged intentionally, and that's what makes me so angry and sad."

Lance's eyes glinted dangerously; he waved at the painting. "You want to know the story about the infamous Worthington family, Ms. Forrester? You want me to tell you the whole ugly truth behind your beautiful painting?"

She shook her head. "I'm so...so...sorry, I didn't me... me...mean to... in...in...interfere." She stopped and took a huge breath. Grace hadn't stammered in her speech in many years. "I just want to understand."

Lance blinked and glanced around the room without seeing anything. "It's not a story for you, Ms. Forrester. People and their emotions intrude on and off the canvas. Just restore the painting." And he left the room without looking back.

CHAPTER 5
She's Poison

Worthington Estate

Grace had been busy in the last several days painfully prepping the portrait. She promptly learned Mrs. Worthington loved order. The Worthington estate had an unfailing schedule for everything. The formalities were new to Grace; dressing formally for dinner was not an everyday occurrence in her life, and she was thankful, she had packed sufficient dinner clothes. However, she did take joy in the harmonious uniformity in the running of the Worthington family.

Since her first day residing at the estate, Mrs. Caroline has been interested in her and her family and Grace willingly allowed her inquisitiveness. However, Ava's constant stares during dinner and breakfast were quickly becoming stressful. In addition, after her heated discussion with Lance, he refused to acknowledge her very existence, completely ignoring her.

Grace was puzzled by Mrs. Caroline's ambiguous silence about Ava and Lance's treatment of her. But she reasoned, she was there to do a job, not become friendly with the family. On her third night at the estate, Grace dreaded having to eat another meal with the family. Immediately after being seated, Mrs. Caroline started the conversation before the first course was served.

"Do you love working at the museum, Ms. Forrester?

"Art is my passion; I see life as a portrait," Grace answered tactfully, having no idea who may have damaged the portrait.

"What an interesting thought," Mrs. Caroline replied.

Quietness fell around the table; Grace eyed Mrs. Caroline. She saw something in the older woman's eyes that she couldn't quite read. Grace found it hard to listen to the rest of the conversations circling the table. She couldn't believe that Mrs. Caroline would make fun of her. During the remainder of dinner, Grace didn't speak. Afterward, she eagerly retreated to the safety of her room.

Early the next morning, swallowed under the smooth silk sheets on her bed, Grace stretched her arms wide above her head. She lifted her face to the warm sun filtering through her drapes. Grace contemplated the different exasperations she'd experienced each day after her arrival. Rising, she dressed for the day's work ahead. Within an hour, she rushed to the smaller dining room for breakfast, not expecting to see anyone. Grace suddenly stopped; Lance was eating his breakfast, a newspaper near his plate.

"You're alive," Lance stated, matter-of-fact. "You're never late; it's nearly 7:30 a.m. Did you work late last night?"

She glanced strangely at Lance, and without acknowledgment of his question, she went directly to the buffet table. After a moment, of being tensed, she walked slowly toward the table, avoiding the scrutiny of his bedroom eyes.

"No ham or skillet potatoes?" Lance said, ignoring Grace's blank face. "You will be hungry within an hour. The kitchen staff will be insulted."

"Toast and eggs are generous," she scoffed lightly. Nonetheless, her heart was ferociously racing.

The corner of his eyes crinkled in a teasing fashion. And even though Grace was blatantly ignoring him, he tenderly put a blueberry muffin on her plate.

"Thank you," Grace whispered.

They dined in quietness for a while. Lance's next words were spoken so softly that Grace had to strain to hear him. "Grace, how about a truce?"

A lump formed in her throat; Grace opened her mouth to agree, but she found her voice wouldn't work. She nodded instead. His quiet smile left Grace in utter shock; she couldn't fully conceal the yearning in her heart for him. While rising from the table, he let his hand touch her exposed arm, which lingered. The skin of his palm burned against her shoulder.

Moved by her discreet nod, Lance left the room, berating himself for his treatment of her. Blinded by his mother's rational words about not mingling with the hired help, didn't stop the powerful attraction he had for Grace. To hold her would be the sweetest thing he could imagine.

After breakfast, Grace departed to the study. Humming under her breath, she used a screwdriver and pliers to pry the nails that held the canvas. With meticulous care, Grace unframed the painting and lightly turned the portrait over, resting it on a clean sheet of glass, causing no harm to it. She focused on the subjects in the portrait. She was certain the elder woman was Mrs. Caroline, and she concluded the defaced men had to be Lance's father and grandfather. The other woman was a mystery because it definitely was not Ava Worthington. It appeared the defacing of the painting was an impetuous act. Who and why would someone do a horrendous act to an innocent painting?

Swept away by tedious and painstaking work, Grace had lost all trace of time till twilight slithered in the room. Grace missed pulling the light switch on the portable lamp near her. She laid her magnifying glass on the desk, wincing as she straightened from the discomfort of bending her back. When she heard the study's door open, Grace was mystified at seeing Lance enter and stand in the center of the semi-darkened room.

Her heart skipped a beat at the sight of him. Oddly, he wasn't properly dressed for dinner. Even in casual dark slacks and a blue turtleneck sweater, he was outrageously commanding. Lance inched closer but stopped near the fireplace. He regarded the damaged canvas, surrounded by strange tools. The lack of progress was too poignant to be amusing.

"It's been four days!" Lance grumbled. "The white paint is still visible."

"An examination had to be made first, then a thorough analysis of the painting's condition, to see if it was structurally sound and it had no crack or rupture," said Grace, fuming.

"You understand, we can't schedule a date for the exhibit until the painting is restored."

"Yes, I am well aware of the situation."

"How much time do you need?"

Grace wet her dry lips, and without speaking, she solemnly gathered all her notes and quietly put them in her black briefcase.

Shame engulfed him, and their conversation had become very tempestuous. Lance needed to subdue the electrifying atmosphere.

"Is there a possibility of a definite date?" He spoke softly.

Stirred by his mood change, she gave a little laugh.

"Honestly, I really don't know at this point. It may take several weeks or a month. It all depends."

"Grace," Lance almost whispered as he crossed over to the desk and stood very still. "I'm leaving in a couple of days."

Grace pressed a hand to her throat. "I'm sure your family will be sad to see you leave."

Moving closer to her. "What about you?"

Recognition dawned on her face, and she gasped.

Lance's mouth curved into a smile. "I want to spend some time with you."

"Um, I really think not…" Her face flushed. "I'm not sure it's appropriate."

"Do you think you can forgive my past indiscretions? Please say yes."

Grace nibbled on her bottom lip. "Yes."

Methodically, Lance took her hands and caressed them. Grace's breaths quickened.

"Please meet me on the terrace for dinner," he said, drawing in a long breath.

Grace turned her face away. Having dinner with Lance Worthington would be intimidating, she admitted. Yet, she couldn't neglect that her heart had been in turmoil from his teasing eyes since their first encounter.

"I should leave," Grace echoed shyly, removing her hands and left the room.

Lance remained, not knowing if Grace had accepted his invitation. Seeking advice, he ended up in his grandmother's private parlor. Other than smiling at her grandson, she patiently waited for him to begin the conversation. After long moments, Lance began to speak.

The servants had done a wonderful job transforming the terrace of the solarium into an intimate dinner for two. The sky was completely dark, dotted with countless twinkling stars like diamonds scattered across a deep velvet canvas. A table for two was covered in a grey brocade tablecloth, garnished with fine dinnerware and cloth napkins. Soft lighting illuminated the silver candelabra, and purple tiger lilies fostered a cozy atmosphere.

Lance had just about given up on Grace joining him. Then, she did arrive, wearing a cream-colored blouse and brown pants, nervously tipping her head to meet Lance's gaze. Clad in black trousers and a greyish-black round-neck sweater, he found himself mesmerized by the curves of her delicate lips.

"My lady, good evening," he said, yearning to hold her in his arms.

Grace nodded. Telling herself not to overact, she moved to the chair, her heart rapidly beating as Lance assisted her with her chair.

"I'm happy you decided to come."

Grace nodded. She wasn't prepared for the intimate setting and its remarkable splendor. Taking deep breaths, she tried unsuccessfully to squish the rising pleasure within her.

"Everything is lovely," she said warmly, her voice softening a bit, simultaneously wondering if his mother or grandmother would be pleased.

Lance, on the other hand, pondered how to romance this incredible woman. Granted, at the moment, all he wanted to do was ravage her lips with endless kisses. In the end, to maintain his composure, he grabbed a piece of bread.

The kitchen staff was very accommodating, and one of the manservants came out to pour chilled sparkling water for the couple.

"A special meal is being prepared for us," Lance stated.

"I can't wait," Grace chuckled softly.

A loveable grin covered Lance's mouth. Each enjoying the sweet fragrance from the surrounding rose gardens, their hearts were quivering with desire.

"Did I hear your grandmother right? Are you a pilot?"

"Yes. It's exciting," Lance laughed. "But I haven't met anyone like you who is passionate about their work like myself."

Surprised at his confession, Grace suppressed a smile.

Shortly thereafter, the servants served a special fine meal, which Grace and Lance wonderfully enjoyed. When dessert was served, Grace nearly moaned.

"I don't know how I can eat another bite," Grace said to Lance.

Lance smiled to himself. "You must taste it; it's crème brulé, a French custard.

Grace lifted her spoon and broke through the caramelized sugar on top. She dipped into the custard, and a delicious mixture of custard and sugar erupted in her mouth. It melted smoothly and richly on her tongue. She savored the flavors for a moment.

"My heavens," Grace cried, enjoying every bite she took. "I love custard, but this takes it to another dimension." Grace glanced toward Lance to see his thrilled expression.

Lance looked at her thoughtfully, and Grace stared back at him because she seemed incapable of doing anything else, and for a space of several seconds, they couldn't look away. She seemed to be at a sudden loss, her hands all aflutter as Lance slowly leaned in.

"Ms. Forrester, I am eager to tangle with the lioness who attacked me for my foolishness about art."

A moment of silence met his remark. "I wouldn't call myself a lioness, only a protector of art and its history."

"You're an incredible woman," Lance spoke in a soft voice. "Let's take a stroll around the gardens," Lance suggested, rising and extending his hand to her.

Grace apprehensively accepted his hand, and Lance linked her arm with his. As if on cue, sounds of music enclosed around them. The path led to several gardens of roses; they stopped to sit on a bench. Lance turned his regretful eyes to Grace.

"Please accept my apologies for my previous rude behavior," Lance went on quietly, his deep voice confidential. "The moment I saw you, I was hopelessly intrigued by you."

Grace could only stare up in stunned surprise. She couldn't move or think, not even when his hand reached up, and gently touched the end of her charming nose.

"I...." Grace began, but her throat felt dry.

Suddenly, Lance felt hysterical joy; her attractive eyes held only warmth and thoughtfulness. Enclosed in a cocoon of peacefulness, neither spoke, only enjoying being with each other. Arriving back at the solarium, Lance didn't want the evening to end, and he needed more time with her.

"I want to see you again tomorrow night," he said as he held her arm tighter.

Grace's eyes closed for a moment, her inner voice howling loud. Don't borrow trouble

Grace, you're only a pleasurable diversion for Mr. Worthington. By Worthington's standards, you have nothing in common. You've been fooled once. Watch yourself.

"Unsure about me and my reasons?"

"Yes, I can't imagine why a man like you wants to see me," she whispered.

Lance chuckled low in his throat, and there was no pomp or ceremony when he began to speak. "No doubt, I'm infatuated with you. This instant, I want to kiss you. Thus, I confess something's preventing me."

Grace bows her head. "Thank you for a lovely evening and your honesty, but it's late."

"Please don't go," he pleaded. "Let me walk you to your room."

Grace watched as defeat clouded his features. It seemed odd; slightly more than sixteen weeks ago, she thought life had dealt her a raw deal. Now, she has caught the attention of an attractive man with a charming smile. What harm could come from it?

"I think that would be fine," Grace replied.

Lance worked very hard to put Grace's pear-shaped face from his mind. He seriously regarded what his mother would do and say if he pursued Ms. Forrester. Tiny as she may be… she was the woman he wanted to know. When he kissed her hand good night, he asked her to meet him at seven for dinner tomorrow night. He said that Grace must meet him because it would be his last night before he returned to New York.

Lance's chest rose with a deep sigh; in his heart, he wasn't certain he could abide by his mother's wishes to stay away from Ms. Forrester. Sounds of soft footsteps outside his door announced someone was lurking nearby. He cast a glance at the door, his ears alert; minutes later, no movement was heard. Therefore, he told himself they had moved on.

From her room, Grace watched as the upper rim of the sun appeared on the horizon, marking the start of a new day. Every thought of the dinner last night left Grace unsteady. Lance Worthington scared her a little, and she knew he wasn't the man for her, but her heart turned over every time she thought of him. A still voice whispered within; *he isn't a believer; remember, Reese wasn't either.* These thoughts abruptly brought her back to earth.

Grace chose not to have breakfast with the family, especially with Lance. She emerged from her bedroom while everyone was still sleeping. Heading to the kitchen, she grabbed an apple, but Ana, the cook, intercepted her, insisting she also take a muffin.

Entering the study, Grace noticed a handwritten note propped up against the phone. The calligraphy on the card was elegant and beautiful. *Grace Forrester, you're booked for a refined evening with Lance Worthington. Meet me in the study at 7:00 p.m.*

It was almost more than Grace could take. She looked for a chair and sat down hard. Her eyes focused on the note. The next hour, she stared at the note, wondering how she would ever get over Lance Worthington. Shaking her head, Grace turned to her work, determined not to think about Mr. Lance Worthington.

Ava ascended from her bed to the sounds of whispering in the hall. Slipping into her plush black slippers, she tip-toed to the door to listen. She hears Caroline's two maids, Rose and Ivy, talking about seeing Lance kissing Grace. *Impossible*, Ava sputters. She thought, I know servants will gossip about their employer occasionally, but she doubted they would lie about a kiss. Ava feared Lance could be interested in Ms. Forrester.

After hearing such unwelcome news, Ava stomps across the floor to her vanity table and slams her body into the chair, planning and strategizing how to wreck any potential romance between Lance and Ms. Forrester. With a dignified tip of her head, she nodded to her reflection in the mirror. *I will terminate this blossoming romance quickly.*

From the moment Ms. Forrester arrived, Ava discerned that she was a threat. Ava considered how she had deprived herself of happiness in life so Lance could have the life he was born into. He had the best schooling, training, and the advantages life offered; without his father's help or his family's money, Lance thrived and became a well-respected man with dignity.

Given the choice, Ava preferred Lance make Rachel Van Fitzgerald, the heiress of the Van Fitzgerald luxury hotels, his wife. Though Ms. Forrester was educated, she didn't compare to Rachel's exquisite beauty or social standards.

Ava heard jubilant voices streaming from the breakfast room. The room became utterly silent when Ava entered, taking in the sight of Caroline and Lance's lowered heads in an intense conversation.

Ava nodded, assuming the conversation was about Lance's new position in the company, so she sat comfortably in her chair. "No need to stop talking on my account; what's so interesting?" Ava smiled at them.

Ignoring Ava's question, Caroline turned her attention to her personal maid.

"Ivy, kindly get a plate of food for my daughter-in-law," Caroline crooned.

Ava glanced at Caroline with reservations, wondering why her question wasn't answered. Pretending she wasn't offended, she spent agonizing minutes nodding at boring conversation until she had enough. Ava pushed her plate to the side with force, and blurted out what was on her mind.

"Lance," Ava stated. "Speculation is circulating around the estate about you and Ms. Forrester."

Caroline immediately dismissed the servants serving breakfast, informing them she would call them if needed.

"Ava, I can't believe you would discuss the family's business in front of the servants," Carolina added.

"Why did you feel I needed to know this information?" Lance dutifully placed his utensils down.

"I apologize, but I found myself in a bit of a quandary," Ava said, squirming uncomfortably in her chair.

"Please tell us what you have heard," Lance's gaze was quite fierce.

"This morning, I heard servants gossiping that you kissed Ms. Forrester last night outside her bedroom."

"That's a lie! I kissed her hand in the hallway," he snarled.

"Why were you with Ms. Forrester?

"If you must know, we had dinner together," he barked.

"Ava," Caroline interrupted. "Lance sought my advice about dinner with Ms. Forrester, and I gave him my blessings."

"How could you do such a thing? Ava spit out the words in fury.

"Why shouldn't I have dinner with Ms. Forrester? Lance exclaimed. "I'm a grown man who can make his own decisions."

"It will be pointless to see her," Ava roared.

"Ava Worthington!" Caroline thundered. "I don't see any harm in Lance seeing Ms. Forrester."

"Allow me to elaborate. Lance shouldn't be thinking about romance, only his new responsibility," she turns to face Lance squarely, looking him in the face. "Have you forgotten Rachel?"

"What about Rachel? We're not engaged. I will make it easy for you. I will see whomever I wish."

Slowly, very slowly, Caroline drew the teapot from its small plate. She pours herself a cup and holds a cup out to Lance, but he declines.

"Lance, tell me about Rachel," Caroline asked.

"I've been seeing Rachel Van Fitzgerald for several years."

"Do you love her?

"No," Lance spoke. "I don't see a future with her."

Ava sat back in surprise. "You what?"

Ava's look became very serious. "You'll marry within your social circle, like Rachel, the heiress to the Van Fitzgerald luxury Hotels chain, not a…"

Caroline cuts Ava off from speaking. "I won't allow you to insult Ms. Forrester, a lady of refinement and elegance who will be a great asset to any man."

"Caroline, I know what's best for Lance," Ava shrieked.

Lance's face flushed with indignation.

"Do you actually believe I would agree to your choice of who I should love or marry?"

"Well," Ava replied matter-of-factly, "Yes, since I agreed to my own father's wishes and married your father, whereas, now, you're an heir."

Lance swiftly came to his feet, standing for a long moment, looking at his mother and grandmother. "When I marry, it'll be for love—not to meet anyone else's standards for pedigree or privilege."

"Lance, please wait," Caroline whispered. "Your position within the family indeed carries a fragile balance, but your happiness belongs solely to you and the woman you choose."

"Ava…" Caroline's voice was clear. "Try to remember we both want the same thing for Lance: to encourage and instill wisdom inside of him. If we don't, Lance will fail."

Lance turns both to his mother and grandmother. "I appreciate both of you, but I must express, Mother, you don't own me, and Grandmother, I'm still angry about the family disowning me. I am attractive to Ms. Forrester, and I will continue a relationship with her," he told them emphatically, barely holding his wrath.

He bent his head, leaving the room. Grace might have been pleased to know that Lance had fought for her.

Grace's work was at a standstill as she let her mind dwell on the night before. Without warning the face of Reese swam before her, and her expression darkened. With an abrupt gesture, she lifted her jeweler's loupe and scalpel, delicately scraping away tiny spattered pieces of white paint. She worked straight through lunch, excited and speculating about what the painting would expose. Thankful for the small tray of sandwiches and cold lemonade Ivy supplied, she had exactly the nourishment and energy she needed to continue working.

Hours later, haunted bluish-green eyes loomed out from beneath the white paint. Squinting to see more of the subject's eyes, Grace dropped her jeweler's loupe at the sound of a timer, signaling her day's work was completed. Putting her tools away, she headed to the sanctity of her room. Though she heard some noises coming from parts of the mansion, she didn't encounter one servant.

Grace sat on the edge of her bed, hiding her face in her hands, weeping in between long sighs of hopelessness. *I don't have any reasons to think he cares for me, she told herself. Grace Forrester, get a grip. Furthermore, what if Ava interferes, and the Worthington family rejects you?* Biting her lower lip, she thought of the way he kissed her hand and the teasing glint in his eyes that seemed to express longing.

Grace knew it was cowardice, but right now, she disregarded God's word in 2 Corinthian 6:14 once more: *Be ye not unequally yoked together with unbelievers: for what fellowship hath righteousness with unrighteousness? And what communion hath light with darkness?*

Grace selected her dress for the evening. It was simple: she had to see him once more; there was no other way. Any feelings she may have for him needed to be eradicated. Walking silently down the hall, Grace was more confused than ever.

Gently, Grace opened the door of the study; she strained to see Lance in the dim room. She paused…in her view, dressed in an elegant black tux, Lance stood at the worktable, staring at the painting. On a few occasions, Grace had watched Lance duck to get through the study's door; now, the room contained his vastness. Her velvety-tapping heels slithered until she was a few feet from him.

"Lance," she said faintly.

He turned, looking down into her face, his expression heartless; minutes later, his eyes pivoted toward the painting again.

"Are you okay?" she asked, finding his gaze disconcerting.

Twisting his hands hard, he spoke with a clogged throat. "Until my grandfather was on his dying bed, I never visited this place," Lance went on softly. "He denied my very existence."

Grace hesitated, a slight pause in her speech, before she finally spoke, revealing her uncertainty about his feelings. "You must have spent a lot of years being angry at him."

"Just so you know," Lance put in, "I am not easily angered, but this painting opens a can of worms."

"Perhaps you should explain why," she whispered.

"No, it's not a grand story to share."

"I will simply listen," she hastily replied.

Even with the celestial white moon, she felt powerless to eliminate the darkness of the room.

"I don't want to bore you with my skeletons," he said, hanging his forlorn head low.

"Are you always this selfless?"

"I try to be," he answered.

Grace looked at his gloomy face. "I have the patience to listen without judging."

"Come here," Lance said, reaching for her.

Grace willingly went into his tender, warm embrace, each clinging tightly to one another.

"I was born with club feet, and my father was embarrassed by his newborn son. He wouldn't or couldn't play or care for his baby boy. Mother implored him to help, but he snubbed the very thought. To keep from seeing his deformed son, night after night, he would sleep at the office or sleep here at the estate."

Grace groaned within, and she summoned every ounce of strength within her to ask: "What did your mother do?"

Lance buried his face in her hair; Grace could barely understand his words.

"Around the clock, my mother took care of me. We were prisoners in our own home."

"Couldn't she demand your father's help?".

"No! No one could sway my father."

"But… he was a husband, father, and your protector."

"Perfection meant everything to my father," he spoke mournfully. "I was defective."

"You don't mean that," Grace muttered.

Lance shoved her away, cursing loudly. "I wouldn't lie," he roared. "I don't know why I'm telling you this."

Grace, looking vulnerable and uncertain, didn't know what to say or do.

"Speak!" he growled. "You think I'm a liar?"

"Lance, wait, let me explain…"

"I would never lie to you," he whispered.

"Somewhere between the emptiness of your embrace, I figured that out," Grace whispered back, raising miserable eyes to his.

"Every man isn't paternal," he said with his eyes downcast.

"Lance, I'm sorry," she softly touches his arm, and he pulls her back into his arms.

"It's foolish to continue about the ugly truth about my loveable family."

"It's not foolish; I wanted to know everything about you."

"In this very room, a decision was made by my grand-parents, whereas my father agreed," his hold tightens slightly around Grace while he imagines his grandfather saying:

They are an embarrassment to the family, and since Ava refuses to put the boy in an institution that would help him, leave them.

Grace looks up, confused. "But…but…you're here… walking normally," she stammered.

92

"Yes, but I hadn't met or seen my grandparents or father until three weeks ago," he snarled. "My mother and I were left with nothing, just the Worthington name."

Grace thought Mrs. Caroline Worthington to be a sweet, lovable, intelligent woman who had the best interest of her family. Why pretend? It didn't make sense.

"I'm sorry for your pain," she grieved.

Grace finally understood the painting was a threat, forcing itself upon him, striking a chord of disappointment, emptiness, and anguish. The roughness and unforgiveness in his voice took Grace's mind back to the troubling eyes she saw earlier in the painting.

Grace inhaled a deep breath. "Were you happy with your life after your father left?"

"We lived with my mother's parents, who happily took us in and provided the finest medical care and education money could buy. Mother refused to accept any money from the Worthington family but wouldn't give up Worthington's name. For years, she wouldn't sign any divorce papers. But my father lived a life free from all his responsibilities where my mother and I were concerned."

"Did you ever ask about him?"

"In my youth, I pleaded for information, but my mother's consuming wrath devoured her ability to talk to me about my father reasonably. Hence, I read every news article or magazine spread on Sterling Worthington. I discovered he loved traveling to exotic places. In retrospect, aviation became my conduit to be a part of the world he loved.

Becoming a pilot was inevitable."

"Do you feel it was all his fault?" said Grace.

"Yes! And I don't care if that makes me a monster." He pulled his tie loose as if it was choking him. "I wanted him and my grandparents to fight for me."

Grace didn't comment but cast her gaze down, focusing on her shoes.

Noticing her quietness, Lance turned to face her. "You may think I am a terrible person and unforgiving, but I would've sacrificed my own life for my son."

As he wrestles with his demons, Grace feels an undeniable sadness about him. Involuntarily, Grace leaned into Lance, and he gently tilted his head, his cheeks touching the top of her soft, scented hair. A lump caught in his throat, and he couldn't speak.

Cuddling her closer to his chest, Grace shifted, tipping her head back to see his face; his lips softly touched hers. Nervous, she lowered her thick eyelashes, trying to hide the emotions in her eyes.

"I need fresh air; let's leave this ice castle of white marble and sorrow."

"Where are we going?"

"Does it matter?"

"No,"

"Come, my sweet Grace."

CHAPTER 6
An Offer I Couldn't Refuse

G race was pleased to be leaving the estate. Lance took his grandfather's sports car and headed down the narrow, winding two-lane road from the estate to town. Driving at a steady pace seemed to lighten Lance's mood, and the couple lapsed into silence. With each bend, the landscape dramatically changed, revealing distant horizons and new seascapes as the road descended. Grace welcomed the warm heat from under the dashboard, cradling her feet. Grace turned to look at the man in the driver's seat; emotions flooded her brain. She found herself wanting to be a part of Lance's life.

"May I ask you about the portrait?"

"No," he hissed, glancing at her; the car's speed increased a little. "It brings nothing but pain. Grace, drop it."

She observed that he was a bit testy once more. For all his disdain and increased speed, she wasn't frightened. She wanted to know everything about him and his family.

"What hold does the painting have on you?" she pressed him. "Who are the people?"

"Grace?" Lance moaned.

Moments later, he pulled inside the median. The moon had disappeared in the sky, and the rhythmic ocean waves crashing against the shoreline created a mesmerizing atmosphere. Lance wanted to crush Grace in his arms and weep. Not thinking where they were, Lance exhaled heavily, took her hands and turned to face her.

"You won't let this go?" Lance asked.

"I want to know the good and ugly about you."

"Alright…in the portrait, the older woman is my grandmother, and the other woman was my father's mistress, whom he eventually married," he said, his tone bland.

Grace eyed him, knowing there was more, so she waited.

"It's funny, his wife wants kids, but my father's afraid of another mistake. To her, I'm a threat."

"You're handling the difficult situation fairly well."

He laughed arrogantly. "Listen to me, Grace, the night my grandfather died, he wept bitter tears asking for my forgiveness. Though he believed I forgave him, I still wanted to hurt those who stole my birthright."

Grace feeling bold. "You smeared the white paint on your father, grandfather's faces."

"Can I explain a few things to you?" Lance began, his voice almost inaudible. "Seeing my Worthington family for the first time and accepting my inheritance feels like a bad dream. However, I realize without reservation... one good thing did happen...I met you," he said and smiled.

"Why me?" the air she breathed was stifling.

Without another word, Lance put the car in gear and smoothly pulled out onto the lane.

Lance turned into a picturesque small inn. "Delicious pizza awaits us."

"Don't you think we are a little overdressed?" she giggled.

"There's nothing wrong in being a little rebellious now and then," his tone teased.

Efficiently parking the car, he came around to Grace's side, reached inside and gently helped her get onto the pavement. Lance stood close beside her, not giving her much room. He gazed at her disarming smile, which stripped his reasoning. Lance put both arms around Grace's waist and pulled her close. In his firm hold, she could smell his aftershave, and her heart skipped a beat. The warmth she felt was as if a soft blanket had been wrapped around her soul and heart.

"Have I told you how lovely you look tonight?"

"No," she whispered, lowering her head.

Lance lifted her chin, Grace looked into his eyes, and Lance looked right back. "Tell me, what do you think about kissing on the second date?"

"What made you think of that?"

"I was just thinking about your delectable lips. They were made for kissing."

"I thought we were going to eat pizza?" Grace said, licking her lips.

"Hmm," his thumb rubbing her back, Grace moaned. Unwillingly, her lips parted, breathing unevenly. Lance tightened his squeeze while his body leaned into her accommodating softer curves. Smothering eyes examined every inch of Grace's face. He tenderly captured her mouth with his. She melted in the sea of ecstasy, teetering on the threshold of total submission. Vigorously, Grace struggles out of his hold, her breathing ragged.

"Lance…I can't…we mustn't…" Her voice was shaking.

Confused, he reluctantly released her, holding her at arm's length. "I thought it was clear how I felt," he raised his voice. "How else can we know our feelings are real?"

Intoxicated from the kiss, she stood at the edge of a very steep cliff; falling off would mean either flight or obliteration. She beheld him so intently that he couldn't turn away.

"This isn't a causal relationship for me," Lance pressed.

"But I've taken the risk before and lost," Grace mutters.

He regarded her expression, knowing the parking lot wasn't a good place to continue their conversation. Lance clasped her hand and guided them toward the entrance of the inn.

"We will finish our talk inside."

An elderly man with twinkling merriment in his eyes under thick eyebrows escorted them to a red checkered-covered table in a dark corner. He smiled at them as he handed them a large one-sheet menu.

"Good evening. You have made a wise choice tonight. Our delicious pizza always brings loving couples together, and I can see a strong love between you."

The pronouncement effectively silenced both Grace and Lance; only the man himself was unconcerned. He seemed completely unaware of the turmoil he just caused. Lance made a swift topic change.

"Kindly give us a few minutes to decide," said Lance. The elderly gentleman bowed and rustled off.

Grace resolutely avoided Lance's eyes. In the stillness encircling them, Lance asked.

"Are we in love?

"I believe the gentleman repeats it to all couples. It's part of their marketing strategy," Grace replied, hoping that was the end of it.

"Shouldn't we discuss it?" said Lance flirtatiously.

She gave a half shrug. A few minutes later, the elderly gentleman returned to take their order.

"We will have the pepperoni special," Lance replied. "Water will be fine." Lance handed both menus to the elderly man.

While the gentleman set the water glasses on the table, Lance noticed Grace's distraction. Intently watching her, he saw the wheels of her mind turning, and he wanted to know what she was thinking.

"Talk to me; what are you feeling?" Lance whispered.

Unsettled about what took place in the parking lot, she carefully considers her answer.

"Tell me why you kissed me?"

Lance laughed.

"Don't you laugh at me, Lance. I'm serious! Tell me whatever possessed you to do that."

"I don't know."

"You must know," Grace reasoned. "How long have you thought about kissing me?"

"Actually, kissing isn't the only thing I think about. This morning, I fantasized about you as my wife," Lance admitted.

The moment the words were out of his mouth, Grace's eyes flew to him in surprise.

"I can't believe you said that," she gasped, shifting from one side of her seat.

Lance reached across the table, picked up her hands and rubbed them gently. Grace eyed him warily but didn't speak.

"You must know," he said slowly, his feelings on display. "If it comes to the point that I ask you to marry me, there will be no doubts.

Grace wanted to question him but didn't. His statement was entrenched in her mind.

"I'm interested in knowing everything about you, even your loss," he commanded faintly. "Are you ready to talk about it?"

She thought of the stories she'd heard…of silly women falling for the wrong man. Her heart racing.

CHAPTER 6

"In my second year of grad school, I met a pre-law student named Reese," she began.

Lance's collar felt as though it were strangling him, but he controlled his features as Grace told him the entire story. When she finished, she was drained of all her energy, but Lance was on the verge of attacking her with many questions, especially when he felt she didn't tell the whole story. Their order arrived, and the next half hour was dedicated to eating and small talk.

⁂

"We need to finish our conversation," Lance said to Grace as soon as their plates were gone.

"I'm afraid you will see me in a different light."

"I hope you trust me when I trusted you," Lance encouraged her.

On the edge of tears, Grace told him the dreadful end of her story. Lance dashed over to be near her. Shifting in his chair to see her expression, he gently stroked her cheek, whispering sweet talk.

"I'm so sorry you had to go through that," said Lance

"You're having a profound effect on me, requiring that I don't lose my resolve regarding you," Grace muttered.

Lance didn't speak or smile. The attraction between them was growing rapidly, establishing an unbreakable bond of their shared sorrows. Lance observed Grace before saying.

"Tomorrow, I'm leaving the estate, and the following day, I'm flying to London out of New York," Lance said glumly.

"I knew this day would eventually arrive," Grace replied seriously.

Without thought, Lance leans in and bestows several short kisses on Grace's sweeping, wet lashes. She anxiously wiggles away from him.

"Why did you move?"

Not knowing Grace's despair about being near him, Lance's brow furrowed in puzzlement over her actions.

"In this critical time of my life, I must choose between my relationship with God or pursuing loving you."

"You can't love me and your God at the same time?"

"No, Lance, we would be miserable together in such discord."

"I don't understand, Grace."

With the confusion on his face, Grace had no idea what to do or say. For a long minutes, she said nothing, then she had the answer.

"Lance, do you believe in God? Because if you don't, a believer can't be involved with an unbeliever. To do so would be in disobedience to God."

Lance, stunned by Grace's statement, could only nod. He couldn't believe a pretentious religious snob was rejecting him. Who is she to judge me? He required no more prompting; this date was finished.

❦

Riding back in an awkward silence all the way to the estate, the only word that came to Grace's mind was, wow.

The abrupt ending of the date came crashing down fast, leaving a trail of debris and dust in her heart. Her staunch belief in God shook Lance to the core, and his determined look told her *he was unprepared for her declaration. It's apparent he doesn't believe in a higher power. What she said didn't make sense; he had no idea what it looked like. Or maybe Lance was afraid to learn about God.*

Beneath the arch of the estate's breezeway, Lance sat in the car, looking at the sky. He couldn't release the heavy weight surrounding his heart. Yes, his pride was bruised, but in essence, these last few days were sacred to him. *What was he going to do? Confess and apologize for his bizarre behavior.*

"Grace," he turned toward her. "Please listen carefully; my feelings for you are real," he said in true humility.

Grace suddenly found herself once again at the edge of the cliff. *Would she disobey her Heavenly Father again, taking another chance for love?* Closing her eyes, she said, "Lance, my feelings for you are so strong, it frightens me. But I've already given my heart to an unbeliever and lost."

"So, what are you saying?"

"I'm falling in love with you," she whispered.

Lance's heart leaped up for joy; nothing at that moment could keep them apart. Staring down into her eyes of hope, he took hold of her face with both of his hands and let his lips touch her lightly. Lance mustered all his strength to refrain from taking hold of her in a passionate kiss.

"I am going to say something to you, Grace, that isn't normal for me," his eyes bored into hers. "I don't totally understand, but I will leave our relationship in the hands of your God."

"I promise to wait for your return from London," Grace said while hope bloomed inside.

❧

The morning of his departure, Lance made an excuse about why he wasn't having breakfast, but he assured his mother and grandmother he would see them before he departed. It was maddening to Ava that Lance chose to spend his last night with Grace. She had the impression Lance was going to see Grace, which drove her insane.

Alone with Caroline in the breakfast room, Ava was restless.

"Foolish man," Ava began to speak loudly. Then her discussion quickly escalated into venomous personal attacks and bitter accusations toward Grace, and her influence on her son. Caroline grew weary, and stood to leave, but before Caroline left, she told Ava her thoughts on the matter.

"Lance's an intelligent, smart young man. You must give him space to make his own decisions," she said, holding Ava's gaze. "Lance has my blessings to live his life without meddling."

"But...she isn't the one," Ava protested.

"Listen," Caroline said. "Your choices for Lance may be your ruin. Choose carefully, my dear," Caroline mumbled, departing the room.

Ava felt color creeping into her cheeks, her eyes threatening Caroline. *What gives you the right to meddle? You weren't the one*

104

keeping vigil late at night, rubbing his throbbing little legs so he could fall asleep. And you weren't the one who took him to doctor's appointments, working day and night until his small body healed. No! You have no say in this matter.

Fuming, Ava screams under her breath, like a cartoon, having smoke escaping out of her ears. *Ms. Forrester, you will never marry my son! I will go to hell and back to make sure it will never happen. This relationship is dead!*

Grace sat patiently on the settee in the Paris room, waiting for all the pleasantries of Lance's departure to finish. A contentment filled her heart, remembering the earlier scene in the Paris room.

In the stillness of the room, Grace turns away from the window and sees the man she had dreamed about. Standing tall in his pilot uniform, she swoons.

"Grace," Lance said softly, walking toward her. "I have looked everywhere for you; why are you hiding?" She willingly enters his embrace. Lance's heart clenched, feeling her tremble as she laid her cheeks against his chest.

"I couldn't bear saying goodbye to you with your family."

"I know we don't know much about each other, but our feelings are real, and there's no need to study or analyze it. But fear has arrested my heart, that when I return, you'll be gone from my life," said Lance, dispirited.

Grace lifted her head so she could see his face. "I will keep my promise to wait for your return," she whispered, her heart full.

He touched her shoulder, running his hand down the sleeve of her bare arm, lingering on her wrist. She gasped as though he knew his touch was burning through her skin. He laughed in delight, his attention refusing to stray from her widened eyes.

"Will you pray for me while I am away?"

"Every day," Grace purred.

His breaths quickened, and he gave her the most modest kiss he had ever given a woman. He left, with Grace staring at the closed door. Later, in the library, Caroline and Ava bid Lance goodbye.

It had been only twenty-four hours since Lance's departure. With the thought of becoming Lance's wife, Grace suddenly experienced a severe anxiety attack. For fear of probing questions from Worthington's family, Grace decided to avoid contact with them.

The morning turned out to be a battle between the will of God and her heart. When she finished praying and went to the study to work, Ivy had left a scrumptious breakfast for her. Grace found working on the painting difficult, and two nagging questions kept materializing. *Did she openly enter into another doomed relationship with an unbeliever? Had she released her heart to love once again?*

The morning was ending when Ava told Caroline she had decided to stay for two more weeks. Caroline listened in silent dismay as she wondered the real purpose of her visit. Ava insisted she wanted a chance to make up for lost time.

"Sterling and Betty will be here tomorrow."

"Care to repeat that?" Ava snapped.

"Ava, sit down!" Caroline waved her hand. "Sterling is my son, and like it or not, his wife is also my daughter-in-law.

Ava sat down in a subdued mood, wondering why Sterling was coming for a visit soon after Lance had departed.

Ava's interruption had stopped Caroline from completing her task at hand. She returned to finish addressing the last envelope, and then she buzzed for a maid.

"Rose, the thank-you notes are ready. Please make sure they are hand delivered."

Rose dutifully took the box and left the Paris room.

"Mother Caroline," Ava said sarcastically. "I don't have the energy to pretend that this news pleases me."

"You can leave today if you desire," Caroline said through pressed lips.

"Well, isn't that kind of you," Ava's mouth popped.

Exiting from the writing desk, Caroline stood in front of Ava. "I will summon Rose to help you pack," she stated.

"No need, I can assure you. I will stay in my room while your son and wife visit you., Ava explained while a storm of rage ravaged inside her.

"Very well; I will notify the staff you'll be eating your meals in your room while my guests are here."

Hearing her husband's dying words, she patted Ava's shoulder. "Ava," she whispered, "they're here for two days; afterward, we can re-discover one another." Caroline departed to meet her garden club in the garden.

Ava swiftly returned and entered her room. She wanted time to think. She concluded her ex-husband had a hidden agenda which she must discover.

What evil scheme has Sterling's mind concocted, Ava asked herself. He's trying to steal his son's inheritance.

Worthington Estate

The next evening, Caroline graciously requested Grace's presence for dinner to give her an update on the restoration. There was a palpable sense of trepidation in the air as if a looming threat was beyond the horizon.

Ava's face was so full of anger that she totally missed Grace, stating that the *restoration was half completed*. Amid the exciting news, Caroline noticed Ivy in the butler's pantry, frantically trying to get her attention. She nodded to Ivy to approach. However, from the corner of Ava's view, she caught a peek of Ivy timidly approaching the table.

"Ivy, what is it?" Ava inquired brutally.

Ivy faltered mid-way, gazing at Caroline. Not pleased with Ava's outburst, it took Caroline less than ten seconds to speak to Ivy.

"Ivy, what's the matter?"

Ivy resumed her stride slowly, her eyes locked on Caroline.

"Your son and his wife just arrived," she said, speaking just above a whisper. "They are in the Paris room."

"Please, show them to the dining room," Caroline announced.

"You can't be serious?" Ava shouts out.

Caroline turns to Ava, speaking intentionally.

"I understand you're not ready to see my son and his wife, but they are family also."

"Grace, it appears my son and his wife have arrived for their visit," she revealed calmly.

Moments later, Sterling greeted his mother, "Good evening," Sterling said, his eyes taking in his ex-wife and a stranger sitting at the table. Both he and his wife bent to kiss Caroline on the cheek.

"Greetings," Caroline responded, looking cheerful. "How was your drive from New York?"

Sterling smiled; "Fine, I hope you don't mind that we're a tad late?"

"Indeed not, please sit. If you're hungry, the servants are prepared to serve you. We just started on the second course," Caroline said.

Ava, weary of Sterling's constant supremacy, wanted to know the reason for his visit.

"Sterling, why are you here?" Her shrieking voice ran over Sterling's nerves as his eyes leveled hers.

"I've always been welcome in my parents' home," he said, drawing in a long breath. "I dare say I'm amazed you're still visiting."

"I have every right to be here as you do," she blasted.

Sterling, accustomed to his ex-wife's timid demeanor and obliging to his demands, took a moment to meet her fierce gaze. She was now a woman of strength and fortitude. Trying to erase that image gave Sterling much anguish.

The room grew quiet until Caroline tapped her wine glass with her butter knife. Taking a moment to look at her family and guest, she laid her hands flat on the table.

"Grace, forgive us for our ill manners," Caroline said softly, then turning her attention to Sterling and Betty. "It is my honor to introduce Ms. Grace Forrester from the Dupré Museum. She's repairing one of the portraits for the exhibit we are loaning to them."

"It's my pleasure to meet you, Ms. Forrester," Betty said passionately. "I can only imagine how fascinating it is to work in a museum.

"I'm mesmerized every day by the beautiful artifacts I have a chance to see daily."

"Do I detect a small accent in your speaking?" Sterling inquired, sipping a bit of wine.

"Why, yes!" Grace affirms, smiling as her cheek feels the heat. "Not many people can hear it?

"Grace, I absolutely missed your accent," Caroline admitted quietly.

Sterling, unaccustomed to not being in the limelight, gave a tiny laugh. How could this peculiar woman completely command everyone's attention? Strangely, a thought occurred to him: *did she meet his son?*

"How many languages do you speak?" Sterling asked.

"Three, Mr. Worthington."

"It's staggering that a woman of your background is proficient in any language but English," Ava snorted in contempt, pouring herself another glass of wine.

"Ava! That's enough," Caroline demanded. "I'm warning you, do not insult my dinner guest ever again. Do I make myself clear!"

Caroline turns to Grace. "I'm sure we're eager to know which languages."

"My parents are of Spanish and Scottish descent."

Betty, already captivated by the attractive young woman sitting next to her, desires to learn more about her.

"How delightful to speak several languages. Are you given opportunities to use those skills?" Betty asked.

"We visit my grandparents often."

The staff entered to serve the third course. Betty turned again toward Grace and smiled at her.

"How long have you been fluent in three languages?"

"Ever since I was a little girl. My brothers and I were taught at an early age."

Ava's eyes moved over the occupants around the table as

everyone gushed over Grace, which she deemed dirt under her feet. The fact that Lance sought Caroline's guidance regarding seeing Grace made her question Caroline's motives.

CHAPTER 7
Sweep Out & Weep

Not invited to the meeting the following morning with Caroline and Sterling, Ava stood in the alcove near the Paris room, dejected and depressed. Pressed up against the wall, she squirmed with a burning and intense gaze. She jumped at Rose's arrival, even startled by a note from Caroline requesting her appearance at the meeting.

Ava glanced at Caroline, then at the door, her brow tightening with confusion. Sterling's tardiness was rare—especially with Caroline, who made punctuality a virtue. Fifteen minutes ticked by in uneasy silence before the door finally creaked open. "What kept you? Caroline asked. "My time is precious."

"Mother, I will make this short," Sterling strolled in. Betty, not far behind, follows him to the sofa.

"So, it would seem," he said a touch dryly as he continued.

"Father made an unwise   decision in his will."

"May I ask in what way?" Caroline enquired boldly.

"Certainly."

"We're all ears," Caroline blurted.

Sterling took a moment to digest his mother's cool reception to his statement.

"Very well, Mother; I don't understand why Father changed his will in favor of his grandson."

Ava stood erect and roared. "Do you have any idea how willfully you disowned your son, and now you want to take his inheritance," Ava shouted.

"I didn't ask for your input," Sterling squealed. "Anyway, why are you here?"

"I wanted her here," Caroline stated.

"What do you suggest, Sterling?" Caroline implored.

"Divide the inheritance between father and grandson."

"That will never happen!" Ava shouted.

"Please, please," Caroline beseeches them. "Sterling, it can't be done; your father's will has a no-contest clause. You are entitled to a specific amount, but if you try to contest the will, you'll lose everything."

Sterling's love for money and prestige stopped him. He explained very gently that he would work with his son. Sterling believed once the Board recognized Lance's inexperience and youth, he would be disqualified as CEO, acknowledging Sterling as the rightful choice. Feeling that no more was needed to be said, he slipped out of the room, leaving his puzzled wife behind.

"It's okay," Caroline said quietly to her teary daughter-in-law. "Go and take care of your husband; he especially needs your encouragement," she added.

"Thank you, Mother Caroline," Betty said, "I'm sorry for all of this; I didn't know."

Caroline smiled and opened her arms, and Betty walked into them. For both of their sakes, Betty hoped Sterling would be happy with the situation.

The meeting hadn't gone well for Sterling, but Caroline believed she'd made herself clear concerning his father's wishes. She had no doubts that Sterling would continue to fight, but for the moment, the matter seemed settled. Both women retreated to their private quarters, seeking a moment of peace.

New York, New York

In the mass of people mingling at JFK International Airport, Lance's flight crew, for several years on the London route, were overjoyed to see their captain after his leave of absence.

"It's a pleasure to have you in the cockpit, my friend," said Perry Whitlock, the first officer known for consistently upholding high moral principles and admired by all for treating everyone with respect.

"I had my doubts about you returning once you had a taste of lavishness," said second officer Jason Miller.

As the men waited for the gate agent, Lance spotted Rachel Van Fitzgerald walking toward them. With catlike quickness, she threw her arms around Lance's neck. By kissing him, she flung him backward, where he bumped into Perry.

"Sorry, Perry," Lance said. Lance instructed the crew to check in and proceed to the airplane, saying he would follow shortly.

Then, he addressed Rachel. "Rachel, please," Lance's voice was shrill as he uttered her name. Despite the verbal rebuff and apparent annoyance, she lay her hands sweetly on his shoulders. Removing her hands off his shoulder, he led her to a quieter, empty gate area.

"Rachel, you had no business coming to the airport; you know I don't appreciate public display at my place of work."

"I truly believe you would be happy to see me after these long three weeks," she declared.

Lance gazed at her for an instant and then took hold of her hands and dragged her to a row of seats, pulling her down in one. Trained in the school of disasters, he knew how to speak in a low, controlled voice. "It may have seemed fine to come," he sighed, "but the trust of my passengers is very precious to me, and such displays are not professional!"

Rachel stared at him for an instant, startled at his outburst. Then she drew away toward the large window, lifting her chin a trifle condescendingly yet smiling indulgently. "Oh? Really?" she purred. "What has you in such a nasty state?"

Looking at his watch, realizing he must leave, he moved to stand next to Rachel and lowered his head. "This once, I'll excuse you," said Lance gravely, "When I return, we need to talk, particularly about us."

"Talk?" said Rachel, drawing her slim, plucked eyebrows in puzzlement. "Really, my love, what has happened to you?"

"I must leave now," said Lance firmly. "When I get back, we'll talk," he concluded and whirling on his heels, he disappeared through a security door.

Rachel departed the gate area, flashing a look of contempt at everyone in her pathway. Why should she be expected to wait for an answer from him?

London, England

Ten hours later, settled in a London hotel located on A4 Bath, Lance was mentally weary. He stood at the window of his hotel, watching large grey clouds drop rain onto the window sill. A singular car moving at high speed from Central London to Avon Mouth, broke the quietness of the carriageway.

Lance smiled thinking about Grace and wondered if she was always so charming. He had never considered marriage before, but lately, that's all he was thinking about. Yet, he wasn't sure who he would ask to be his wife.

Certainly, Rachel Van Fitzgerald offered things most important in his newly changed life. Rachel was from a wealthy, privileged background; her father has a high society position, and both he and his daughter enjoy spending time attending fashionable social gatherings.

As much as Rachel would be a fine choice for his new pivotal role in his family, there's sweet, intelligent Grace, whose father, famous in his own right and formerly a person of means. Who has raised his daughter with knowledge and refinement of art, cuisine, fashion, and a strong education.

Lance had not expected to meet a woman like Grace, who believes in God. Clear thoughts refused to form in his head, but he prepares to call Grace once more before he laid down to rest.

New York, New York

The past couple of days, Caroline had been busy getting acquainted with the board of directors and other executives within Worthington's company, leaving Ava alone. On the second night, after dinner. Ava noticed Ivy rushing toward the library.

"Ivy," Ava said quietly. "Why the rush?"

"Mr. Worthington is on the phone to speak with Ms. Forrester again."

A question swirled around in Ava's mind: what were Lance's intentions, calling Grace so much?

"Ivy, no need to disturb Ms. Forrester. Please take a message as before, and I will pass it along."

"What if…" Ivy interrupts Ava.

"I will make sure Ms. Forrester receives this message.

Ivy glanced at the new upcoming mistress and nodded. "I will take a message."

"That's kind of you,"

With tremendous courtesy, Ava waited for Ivy's return, and minutes later, she went directly to her suite.

Worried that Lance and Grace's relationship was in danger of becoming permanent, Ava felt a heavy weight on her shoulder. Lance has a huge responsibility to the company and the family. A union between them mustn't be permitted. She nicely tucked the message away in her jewelry case with the others.

The painting restored and Grace's departure from the Worthington Estates, Ava left sooner than she planned. She wanted to give her son a proper welcome. Pulling into her driveway, she entered her opulent mansion, which she'd worked so hard to attain. Ava, peering into the living room, saw visible dust; the new housekeeper had apparently whizzed through her chores. Ava intends to have a frank exchange with the housekeeper, on her views of cleaning.

Due to the mansion being closed for four weeks, the servants had opened all the downstairs windows to chase away the stale air. Oddly, Ava requested the fireplace be lit. Next, she furtively walked to the fireplace, dropping Lance's messages one by one into the roaring flames.

Then, she slowly sank into a plush chair, her feet hoisted onto the ottoman. Ava reached for the intercom phone nearby, her eyes twinkling with amusement, and a mile-wide smirk was on her face. With plenty of confidence, Ava alerted the kitchen staff that there would be three for dinner.

She wasn't certain what liberties Lance had taken with Ms. Forrester, but she wanted this relationship brought to a definitive conclusion. *Grace wasn't the woman for him.* Naturally, Lance was vulnerable at the moment, and it wasn't difficult to pinpoint his weak spot. Ava's scheme would shatter any fantasy Ms. Forrester had about her son.

Several moments later, in her bedroom, Ava grabbed her phonebook from the desk drawer. Shifting to a more comfortable seat, phone in hand, the room suddenly was filled with giddy laughter.

⌘

On Lance's last day in London, he realized Grace was the one. Desperate for answer, he knew he had to find her the moment he returns to New York. Lance concluded the cost of loving someone was high.

On the fifth of August, an agitated Lance fumbled to retrieve the logbook from the compartment. His co-pilots watched with concern. They remained quietly discreet while he speedily examined the post-flight checklist and signed off the logbook. Jason and Perry knew their friend was in a sticky situation. Lance left without a word to his fight crew.

Running from one terminal to the next, Lance remembered the pledge he and Grace had made before leaving. Checking the flights between New York and Penville he calculated the two-hour flight time and the time he had to spend acquiring a rental car, he would reach the Dupré Museum by three in the afternoon.

Penville, North Carolina

Thrilled to be home after restoring the painting, Grace stood with a clipboard in hand, blankly gazing at Worthington's list of artifacts and paintings for the museum's upcoming exhibit. After Lance left, she absorbed every bit of his one call, but waited anxiously for the additional calls he promised. However, no calls materialized, leaving Grace's heart aching to see Lance. The thought of losing him was almost more than she could bear. Grace wondered if she would sleep at all anymore; his enticing bluish-green eyes haunted her nightly.

Thanking the museum's greeter for directions, Lance bolted to find Grace. Hearing rapid footsteps approaching, Grace whirled around. The man she had been yearning about for days stood in the archway. Her beating heart wouldn't allow her to move from her spot. And as much as Lance frantically wanted to hold her in his arms, he stood motionless, gazing at the woman he needed. Glancing at him, Grace cast a despondent look, her eyes filled with worry. Lance, who wholeheartedly loved her, was unable to endure the pain of separation, so he proceeded to speak.

"Grace…are we alright?" he whispered.

"I'm not sure," she spoke softly. "Only you know."

Baffled by her answer and restlessness, he moved closer. "I've given many hours of why you didn't take any of my calls."

Abruptly, her eyes widened. "I only received one call."

Lance could not believe her words, but the urgency in her eyes worried him. Blood rushes to his head, and he groans within; why were his calls interrupted and by whom?

"Each time I phoned, I was told you couldn't be disturbed."

Grace now frowned in confusion, but Lance continued. "I left messages each time with a number where you could reach me."

Her heart pounded heavily, thinking how unreal everything seemed. "You do care."

Not able to stay still, he took the clipboard from her, laid it in a nearby chair, and crushed her in his arms. He kissed her ever so gently before moving back a little bit, reaching for her hand. He linked her small fingers with his own.

"You have my whole heart," Lance whispered.

"I missed you," Grace's voice fluttered.

"I'm staying in Penville tonight," he smiled tenderly. "I will be back at 5:30 p.m. so we can have dinner."

Nothing was more important than holding Grace close. The two talked for the next hour until Stella came looking for Grace. He promised that he would be back at 5:30 p.m. so they could have dinner and continue their talk. When she finally picked up her clipboard, she realized how much Lance had infiltrated her heart.

After spending three days in Penville, Lance returned to his apartment in New York. Easing into a chair, he leaned back, cherishing those days he had spent with Grace. Secure in the warmth of their affections, Lance felt happiness and fulfillment for the first time. Lance frantically glared at the phone on the desk, debating whether he should call his mother. Without warning, the phone rang.

"Where in the inferno have you been?" Ava demanded.

Lance sighed.

"I don't want to hear excuses."

"Mother, please… I wanted to see you, but I…"

"I'm waiting!"

"It's not an excuse, it's a fact."

"What did you do?"

His mouth went dry, unable to form words, it infuriated her the more.

"Lance! I'm still waiting."

Pausing for a few moments, he uttered. "I didn't do anything wrong. I went to Penville to visit Grace," he stated.

"I can't believe you went to visit that woman!"

Lance gripped the receiver, "Her name is Grace," he shouted. "And yes, I saw her, her family and friends."

"I wasn't aware you kept in contact with her."

Lance detected she was frantic with rage.

"There were a few personal things that concerned me that needed to be cleared."

"Personal?" The word knifed through Ava's heart. "I had a special dinner, especially for you. My guest was disappointed that you didn't show," she crooned.

"What dinner guest, mother?"

Silence. "It was Rachel," she snickered.

To Lance's surprise, he'd totally forgotten he needed to talk with Rachel. His three days with Grace and her family were so peaceful that he was still basking in their afterglow.

"I can't talk with you anymore," he said, his insides burning with anger.

"Don't you dare hang up!" she yelled.

Clearing his throat, "You can't make decisions about my personal or professional life," he exclaimed.

"Son! Your mind is cloudy at the moment," she pleaded. "Please listen; I don't want you to see her ever again."

"I will see her and her family whenever I please," he blurted. "Furthermore, her father is a famous NFL player named *Stonewall*, who, along with his wife, owns their own athletic and mental health clinic."

"Nonsense!" she howled.

Precipitously, Lance understood Ava's hostility toward Grace, and the answer to his mystery crystallized. It troubled him.

"It was you who intercepted my calls," he interjected. "What did you do with my messages?"

"How dare you accuse me of such an act," she said, breathing heavily on the phone.

"Mother! I will not tolerate you lying to me."

"You're not so powerful that I can't destroy you!"

Blood drained from his face. "I'm not your little boy anymore. Destroy me, that's a laugh, and you're deceiving yourself. I'm capable of making my own decisions," he proclaimed.

Ava couldn't stop the ravishing surge in her body. "You're naïve about power and true love," she mocked him. "But I know I was right in intercepting those messages and burning them."

"Goodbye, Mother," he said calmly and hung up the phone.

Ava held the phone away from her for several minutes, screeching, before slamming down the receiver. *It's appalling he went to Penville to be with that wretched woman and her family. I mustn't act rashly.*

Fifth Avenue Penthouse

Riding in a cab toward Rachel's apartment on Fifth Avenue, Lance recollected the day he met her. It was about two years ago when he accompanied his mother to a country club's dance and ended up dancing with Rachel multiple times. Her father, Mr. Paul Van Fitzgerald, was a very powerful man who owned numerous hotel chains in the United States and abroad, which gifted his only daughter a 5,400-square-foot penthouse.

Lance admitted to himself that he was drawn to Rachel's catlike eyes, framed by long lashes and long, straight sandy blonde hair. Overlooking her sense of entitlement and superiority, they became the golden couple within their circle of friends.

Emerging from the cab, Lance tilted his head to the intimidating building with its white-gloved doorman when a long, smart, shiny red car pulled up fast. Though driving a convertible, Rachel's flawless face seemed to glow. She greeted Lance with a confident smile and bold red lips showing her gleaming white teeth.

"Darling, sorry I'm late," Rachel crooned, throwing the keys to the doorman, linking her fingers in his, and swinging their arms back and forth as a child. "I have drinks on ice."

Lance didn't acknowledge her proclamation. Instead, he unlinked their fingers and walked behind her.

"Now, Lance, if you're going to be a bore tonight, there's no use of you staying," she demanded.

"Rachel," he snapped, "We need to talk."

The way Lance sounded, it was plain to Rachel that his mother was telling the truth; their relationship was in trouble.

"Really!" she said, turning around and appraising him with a wide, disagreeable stare. "How thrilling! Have I been a bad girl, my sweet Cheri?" Rachel beamed as she greatly enjoyed making a scene in the lobby.

Lance quickly moved to the private elevator, swearing under his breath. Thanks to his mother, Rachel knew about Grace. Their silence intensified while they rode the elevator to her penthouse.

Inside the penthouse, Rachel hustled off for drinks. She carefully dropped ice cubes into the cocktail, making them clink musically against the thin glasses. Lance stood in the living room, looking out the window at Central Park.

"So, now," Rachel went on, handing Lance a glass of rum and Coke, "I'm ready for the bad news," she giggled, sitting on the white sectional sofa.

Lance put his drink down on the three-circle glass table and faced Rachel. "I came here to tell you I met someone."

"What about our plans for marriage?"

"I've never proposed to you," he said, his voice implacably hard.

"But it was expected by our parents and friends." Rachel presented. "What about the many laughs and intimate nights together?"

"I tried to make this relationship work, but it just wasn't meant to be," he whispered. "Believe me, I'm sorry; I didn't want to hurt you."

Rachel crossed her legs, murmuring sweetly, "Cheri`, our love sizzled throughout the three bedrooms, not to mention a bathroom," she chimed in.

"I'd rather not talk about that, Rachel," Lance said, looking distressed. "I don't want to dwell on the past."

Rachel looked at him thoughtfully; she paused and slowly took a sip from her glass.

"Love, tell me, who's this wretched woman you intertwined yourself with?"

Lance spun around. "First, Grace is a vision of integrity and worth! And I want to be intertwined with her."

"Your mother informs me…"

"I know what Mother thinks about Grace," he yelled.

She laughed, circling the rim of her glass with her shining fingernails.

"I'd be embarrassed if I were you!" she ridiculed.

"You shouldn't be; she's a woman of intelligence and truth. She's sweet, pure, unspoiled, and modest."

"I bet," she giggled. "She isn't wild, daring and bold like Moi. She sounds boring; please don't tell me you love her."

Lance wondered how his attraction blinded him to Rachel's spoiled behavior. A great wave of dislike rolled hotly over him after seeing the beauty of unselfishness in Grace.

"Yes! With all my heart."

Her feelings of anger festered at his bold announcement, and her stance stiffened; she decided to modify her tactics.

"If you truly love this woman," she said meekly. "Consider your new status; you'll have to uphold a higher standard than before."

Lance turned his back to her and sighed loudly.

"I know it's hard for you to understand," he pleaded. "My love for Grace is real."

Rachel stood next to him and leaned her head slightly on his shoulder as they watched row boats from a distance on the lake.

"My sweet loveable Lance!" she said tenderly, rubbing his arm. "Remember that day we enjoyed a peaceful evening on the lake gliding across the water?"

Lance closed his eyes to dispel the image of them one moonlight night snuggling in a boat on the lake.

"You haven't forgotten we're the golden couple, and we can do so much more now."

"No, I remember everything we've shared," he groaned.

"Chéri," she said, gently guiding him to face her, "I can't believe your feelings for me have changed so quickly."

Shaken by the image of Grace, his chest clenches, and the color drains from his face.

"Rachel!" he frowns, "it's over between us," he said as he peeled her hands from his shoulder.

"Get out! ... Rachel flicks her hand dismissively. "Get out, you beast!"

"I'm sorry, Rachel."

"Sorry! Watch your back; that woman will be your downfall."

"No, she won't." He sprints to the elevator and hops in quickly as the doors open, with Rachel screaming, "Get out, beast."

Rachel watched the elevator's doors close slowly. For several minutes, she glared at nothing. Then, speaking slowly, she said to the air: *"Grace, you may have him for now, but I don't plan to allow you to get your little paws on his fortune. Lance Worthington, you will be mine. I stake my life on it!"*

Penville, North Carolina

Grace spent most of her work days diligently cataloging artifacts and paintings and assigning their locations. Lance's weekend visits made it difficult for Grace to concentrate on the execution of Penville biggest exhibit in just under two weeks. Engraved invitations were sent to all the Worthington family, colleagues, friends, and notable art lovers.

With the clipboard in hand, Grace views the replica of the painting of *the Last Supper;* the memory of Lance's first time attending a church service flooded her mind.

Lance entered the church doors with sweaty palms and hesitation. During the entire service, he squirmed in his seat like a little boy who felt trapped. It was heart-wrenching to see him suffer. Grace placed a reassuring hand on his leg, encouraging him to watch and listen, letting him know that it would soon be over.

Grace loved Lance Worthington, and seeing him trying to learn about God greatly endeared him to her. Her parents' mild rebuke wasn't far from her mind. *My wee one, your mother and I see your love for Lance blossoming, but we're afraid you'll find heartache at the end.* With a mental shrug, Grace continued cataloging until Stella tapped her on the shoulder.

"I'm sorry, Grace, but there's a woman from catering here to see you. She says it's about the menu."

"Thank you, Stella. Tell her to give me a minute."

"Excellent."

With the meeting behind her and the day coming to an end, Grace knew she was deliberately entering another relationship with an unbeliever; she forced herself to seize the moment.

CHAPTER 8
It's Over Before It Really Started

R eminiscing about his last visit with Grace, Lance settled against his pillow. He had chosen Grace For- rester over family and social obligations, notwithstanding threats from his mother and Rachel. However, having his grandmother's approval, arrested any doubts that he may have had.

Within a short length of time, his unexpected inheritance dramatically changed his life, generating his need to resign from his dream job as a pilot and prepare for his first board meeting.

Reaching for his robe, Lance sat on the side of the bed to stretch his legs. He paused, gazing for a long moment at an old photograph of Rachel. His heart celebrated as he removed the photo and tossed it in the trash.

A short time later, Lance finished his coffee, dressed, grabbed a handkerchief, and took his leave for his meeting with the Airline Union President.

Penville, North Carolina

Lance arrived at the home of Labella and Stone Forrester late Friday afternoon to spend another weekend with Grace. Grace, wearing a big smile, met Lance at the door.

"You're here! It feels like I've been waiting forever!"

"Come here," Lance commanded, holding his arms out to hug her.

Grace went into his embrace and hugged him right back, laughing until she felt weak. Still holding Grace close, Lance's voice became serious. "Have I told you how much I've fallen in love with you?"

"I think you just did."

Hearing footsteps emerging from the rear of the house, Lance kissed Grace's forehead and picked up her soft hand to hold.

"Lance," Stone said. "It's a pleasure to see you again."

"Do you mind if I steal Grace for a few moments before dinner? I need to discuss something with her."

Stone and Labella exchanged concerned looks but nodded. Rather fascinated, Grace was eager to hear what Lance had to say. The couple settled in the small study of the home. Lance had news to share, and even though their relationship was beginning, he wanted to include Grace.

"I turned in my resignation with the airlines this week," Lance announced.

"When will your last day be?" Grace asked, feeling saddened that he must give up his passion for flying.

"It will take about four to six weeks."

"I don't see how you can manage handling two jobs?"

"I will be required to fly at least eighteen hours a week. At the moment, it seems manageable."

The conversation went in all directions until they were called to dinner. Lance relayed the subject he had discussed with Grace to her family. Several things came to Labella and Stone's minds when Lance told them.

"Are you prepared for the enormous responsibility?" Stone couldn't help but ask.

"I have no choice."

"Will you continue to have a normal life, Lance?" Stone commented, his eyes focusing on Grace.

"I'm not sure that will be possible."

"No profession is worth separation from those you love," Labella whispered, a bit sad.

The sad note Lance heard in Labella's voice caused him to fall silent. It was a lot to take in for everyone involved.

During and after dinner, Grace remained silent. Lance said his goodbyes and confirmed their plans for the weekend. The moment Grace arrived at her small wooden cottage, an inner voice whispered a warning, urging her to reconsider her decision. *You're standing at the crossroads. Choose ye this day whom ye will serve.*

Worthington Steel Company

Lance's breath fogged in the morning air as he entered the underground parking garage for Worthington's Steel executives. Greeting the timid, middle-aged parking attendant, the new CEO handed his keys to him. Using a code to unlock the elevator, Lance stepped into a rich wood-paneled area with a glass ceiling and cameras at each corner. The ride to the forty-fifth-floor executives' suites was swift and smooth.

Nodding and greeting employees with inquiring eyes, Lance managed to crush any doubts about the new young CEO. He appreciated his maternal Grandfather Hastings' teaching about high-powered corporate business language and strict etiquette. Without incident, Lance met his grandmother in front of large frosted doors.

Lance walked through the intimidating doors, passing walls of pictures with Sterling Worthington, Sr., standing alongside presidents, state officials, and his ancestors of the company. On another wall was the company's logo, center stage, surrounded by numerous awards and plaques. Lance sat awkwardly at the head of the conference table with his black folder.

The room grew quiet. Caroline opened the meeting with the introduction of the new CEO. Lance reached for his notes and began the meeting, eluding his nervousness. For long minutes, he studied each member's facial expressions and liked what he was seeing, especially a teasing glint from the eldest board member. Cries of delight and gusts of laughter rose in the air as the meeting convened for a short break.

Entering his new office, Lance flinched, seeing Ava pacing back and forth. Without pleasantry, she relentlessly berated Lance's decision to spend all his free time with Grace and her despicable parents. Ava plunged ahead, demanding an explanation.

"What were the two of you thinking," Ava wanted to know, looking at both Caroline and Lance.

"I'm living my own life," Lance replied.

"What would the board think of their new CEO entertaining a trollop?" Ava jeered.

"Ava! That's enough," Caroline suddenly spoke, anxious to keep the outside office from hearing the commotion.

"I've your best interest at heart," Ava said in a no-nonsense voice. "You need my wisdom."

"Mother!" he snapped, audibly breathing through his nose. "You need to leave. I'm not going to argue about a closed subject," he turned to leave, and Ava tackled his suit jacket sleeve.

"You've broken your engagement with Rachel," she hollers. "Tell her you want her back."

"What...I have never been engaged to Rachel," he fumed.

"It was a given fact by our families."

The ruckus in the inner office begins to draw attention. "Ava, Ava," Caroline's soft, insistent pleading finally had a result. "You have spoken your peace; now let it go."

Ava's lips quiver, emphasizing the discoloration of her red lipstick. Brooding, Ava zips past them and out the door. Lance, unnerved, shook his head, needing some air. Caroline, mystified, slumped into the nearest seat.

Ava was sitting in her private chamber, profusely sweating; moisture covering her forehead, and her eyes cold and hard. She screamed. Dazed and detached, her mind rummaged through the last thirty years of sacrifices she endured for her son to be flawless in every way, then to have an insignificant person jeopardize all her efforts. This wasn't going to happen.

In all honesty, she assumed the relationship with Ms. Forrester would've been a one-weekend fling. Rachel Van Fitzgerald, with her flawless looks, money, and pedigree, was an exemplar of the perfect wife. In addition, both families were expecting a big society wedding in the near future. For those reasons, she telephoned Rachel, informing her of a plan.

Waiting until something better materialized, Rachel didn't care that she had been marking time with Lance. How delicious for her. Lance has become one of the most handsome and powerful young men in the world. Listening carefully to what Ava was saying, a faint little ripple of laughter thrilled her, and her eyes twinkled wickedly.

It was useless, Rachel thought, for Lance to think he could marry one of those clean, modest little creatures. *It's a pity!*

Why does he bother making a grandstand? We both know I'll get what I want eventually.

"Perfect!" said Rachel. "Now, tell me how you're going to convince Lance."

"Not to worry about Lance!" said Ava excitedly. "Once the plan is in motion, that hussy will be nonexistent."

Diabolical laughter rang out on both ends of the phone's receiver.

Worthington Steel Company, New York

From the moment he arrived at Worthington Steel Company, Lance stood out from all the other executives. The scope of his chest, bulging muscles through his suit jacket, made any man foolish to argue with him. Women's hearts skip a beat at the sight of him. Yet, at times, the intricacy of his role at the helm of this massive company baffles him.

Dictating a letter into the machine, he paused to mull over a correspondence he recently received from the board.

Mr. Worthington, we, the board, cautiously tread on this subject. As our new CEO, and being a single powerful man, it's imperative you review our core values, especially the first one: The company comes first; it comes before kids, wife, and friends. We hope you take the responsibility to accept and adhere to these values. We envision great things from the grandson of Mr. Sterling Worthington, Sr.

The correspondence so distressed Lance that he couldn't continue dictating. He began processing the implication this would have on his relationship with Grace. His life has taken on a new significance since Grace and Worthington Steel became a part of it. But another disruptive element has materialized. Last weekend, Pastor Young's message from Romans 10:2-3 left him speechless:

For I bear them record that they have a zeal of God, but not according to knowledge. For they, being ignorant of God's righteousness and going about to establish their own righteousness, have not submitted themselves unto the righteousness of God.

Turning the dictating machine off, Lance meditated on Pastor Young's explanation:

We become self-righteous when we try to validate our worth through our strengths, relationships, positions or actions. A self-righteous person thinks they can do no wrong and goes about with a holier-than-thou attitude, judging and scrutinizing everyone else.

Lance mentally tries to gauge how to ally with company, family and Grace. He tussled with, *Do I have the skills to be the ideal CEO, and should I expect Grace to renounce her faith for love?* He sighs heavily; he needs time to dwell on those questions.

Penville, North Carolina

On the last Saturday of September, Grace was at the Dupré Museum before sunrise for Penville most prominent event of the season later that evening. The museum will host influential people from the worlds of business, art and wealth.

The long hallways and high ceilings were supported by bright lighting. Historical pieces displayed Worthington's ancestors, were behind and under glass, and displays were roped off from public access. Artifacts stood on raised platforms and pedestals, with informational placards about various pieces and framed artwork decorating the walls.

Grace stops at each display in every exhibit hall, attempting not to think about Lance. While making minor adjustments to a painting, her eyes flew to the Worthington's portrait she had restored. She blushed, thinking about the moment she had heated words with Lance concerning it. It's difficult to relish in this wonderful event while Lance has been mysteriously silent in the last five days.

"Everything looks good," André greeted Grace as soon as he found her in one of the five exhibit halls.

"Really!" Grace smiled at the sight of him, his face alight with excitement.

"Oui," André smiled in return. "You've certainly done excellent work on the exhibit." Grace's face was flushed, and he thought she looked like a cute little girl.

"Thank you."

"Are we ready for this evening?" André jokingly said.

"Oui," Grace chuckles.

André smiled at her puzzled expression.

"Ma fille, tonight you'll realize your dream."

Grace nodded. In some way, she was still in disbelief. But she was pleased with his gentle push out of her comfort zone.

"You best hurry," he taps her shoulder.

"Oui," she whispered.

The biggest night of her career and Lance was nonexistent; only a three-word note was left: *see you tonight.* Not until that moment did Grace realize that it was only four months ago, when Reese acted strange before their wedding. Would she be able to cope with another failed relationship? She shook her head and prepared for the black-tie event.

Limousines and expensive cars queued up around the museum as attendees handed their keys to the parking valets. Women wearing gowns and glittering jewelry and men in tuxedos enter the museum on a red carpet. At the entryway, guests were greeted by hostesses, checking in coats and wraps, while the wait staff dressed in black and white mingles, carrying trays of hors d'oeuvres and champagne.

Immediately when guests enter the main entrance of the museum, they are struck by the sweeping, grand marble staircase that leads to the upper floors. The widespread mural commissioned in 1971 to illustrate the expansion of the museum surrounds the staircase. On each floor, a mural portrays a different historical event of the Museum of Art and Natural History of Penville. The story culminates on the third and final floor.

Poised and her chin high, Grace stood next to André on the lower level of the staircase. Lovely ringlets of curls trickled down her back. Grace's necklace and earrings, on loan from the museum, were studded with dazzling diamonds and fiery rubies, showcasing her classic red strapless evening gown. She was simply breathtaking. For a moment, Grace deferred her entrance, saying a prayer in her heart.

Father, I'm almost fearful of seeing Lance; something has changed, and my peace has been shattered. I knew from the start this relationship didn't have your approval. My continual disobedience... Grace couldn't continue, thrusting a hand to her throat. André lowers his head and whispers into her ear.

"I'm not certain what you're wrestling with, but tonight you look radiant."

Blowing out a long breath and smiling. "We'll have fun," Grace admitted.

"You'll be the darling of the party," Andre´ stated.

"I'm not so sure," she said, looking down at her shoes. Andre extended his tuxedo-clad arm.

"I think it's time for you to make your entrance."

Slightly shaking her head, Grace claimed his arm, and they descended the steps toward a sea of guests.

"Grace," Andre´ mouthed. "Tonight is yours; be your charming and gracious self." Before she could utter a word, he propelled her onward.

Grace looked back long enough at Andre´ until he disappeared in the crowd of men and women of untold wealth, sipping champagne. In between the glitter and glam, Grace gave the guests, details on each exhibit. It was comforting to answer questions till one question made her speechless.

"Did you have the pleasure of meeting the dashing grandson?" An inquisitive guest asked.

Mentally, avoiding eye contact, she nodded. Subsequently, the glittering jewelry, gowns and grins dissolved into a blur. Overhearing a random conversation, it appears the new CEO is on track to succeed, taking the company higher than his grandfather did. Unexpectedly, Lance comes into view at the opposite end of the room. Next to him was a striking, beautiful woman with cat-like eyes, her arm tightly interlinked with his.

Grace visibly stared. She opened her mouth and shut it quickly. All color drained from her face. She felt as if Lance had just thrown ice water on her. Needing to escape, Grace plasters a smile on her face. Spinning around in the opposite directions, she cringes as Zory barrels into her.

"Oh, Grace! you're mind-blowing; where's your handsome pilot or executive?" Zory, grasps for air.

"What about her hard work?" Nora inserted.

Zory gave her a forlorn glance.

"No squabbling tonight," Penelope remarks, trailing behind. "We're to support our friend, eat good food, and meet interesting new people."

"Where's Lance?" the friends asked in unison.

Grace looked thoughtful while the friends waited patiently for an answer, but none was forthcoming.

"Well, Grace," Zory said with vexation.

Grace's lips trembled a little, looking on the verge of tears, when she gave a nod in the opposite direction. Six pairs of eyes glanced in those directions, and an explosive gasp filled their lips.

"What's going on?" Nora exclaimed.

"I think I'd like us to forget about Lance this evening."

"We thought you were his date at this shindig," Zory badgered.

Grace's eyes strayed, and she raised a hand to her temple, rubbing it. "Forget it, please," pleading, unclear why Lance was with another woman.

"Who's the woman on your man's arm?" Zory barked.

"I don't know," she muttered, barely audible, swallowing past a dry throat and lowering her head in defeat.

Within forty minutes of interacting with high society, Stone and Labella were finding their footing. Several older male guests recognized the talented Stonewall Forrester of 1950. The conversation quickly turned from art to football. In his element, Labella watched with great attention while Stone demonstrated one of his famous tackle moves. But Labella reminds herself that they would need to find their daughter eventually.

Not anticipating another woman would be latched to Lance's arm, Grace was extremely nervous and couldn't relax. In a desperate attempt to avoid him, Grace and her girl-friends moved to the next exhibit hall, but she encountered her parents. Labella took one look at her daughter's face and knew that something was tremendously wrong.

Listening to Grace answer questions, Labella noticed her high-pitched voice and her eyes swimming with water. Zory, understanding that the Forrester would evidently see Lance with another woman, she deliberately moved Labella away from everyone. Confused by Zory's actions, Labella questioned Zory.

"Talk to me, Zory," Labella said softly. "What's wrong?"

Zory took a deep breath and shook her head.

"If you don't tell me what's going on, I'll be forced to pull Grace aside."

"Please don't," Zory blurted.

Simultaneously, everyone was thunderstruck by the entrance of a couple. Stone immediately ends his conversation with an elderly gentleman, and moving at a snail's pace, his eyes never leaving the couple, joins his wife, daughter and her friends.

For a moment, Grace couldn't find the courage to speak.

"Grace...?" Stone started.

"I'm sorry, Papi, I don't want to ruin the evening for you and Mami," she said, tears choking her voice.

The evidence of Lance's crime was for all to see, and the group reacted with barely audible whispers and disbelief. Stone's very existence was filled with righteous indignation at the injustice toward his daughter. Lance Worthington had courted his daughter for weeks. Punching a fist in his hand, Stone wanted to tackle him onto the polished floor.

"Do you all perceive what I'm seeing?" Stone asked. "I can't understand why Lance would do such a monstrous act to my daughter."

"It's shameful!" Labella proclaimed.

Upon seeing his baby girl hurting, his fatherly instinct kicked in, and he instantly shielded her with his broad shoulders.

～

All evening, Ava noticed Lance growing more agitated while they roamed the exhibit halls. Right now, she knew Lance's heart was in turmoil, and if she didn't handle the situation wisely, he would certainly quit this charade on the spot. She had to keep things light and professional.

"Rachel, I found a portrait that would interest you," Ava said meekly.

"Excellent, Ava," Rachel crooned. "Will I have the delicious opportunity to meet Ms. Forrester?"

"No, you won't," Lance spoke under his breath as he saw a few board members close by.

Ava saw Grace the moment they entered the Worthington family exhibit hall. Disrupting Grace and the small group, she almost shouted as she neared.

"Good evening!" Ava greeted them. "It's so nice to see you, Ms. Forrester, once again." Labella sees beyond Ava's façade, but Grace graciously intercedes.

"Mother and father, I believe you haven't had the privilege to meet Mrs. Ava Worthington, Lance's mother." Grace sounded calmer than she felt.

"Oh, Mr. and Mrs. Forrester!" Ava's teeth sparkled, "My pleasure to meet you, and let me introduce Lance's fiancé, Ms. Rachel Van Fitzgerald."

All heads shifted toward Grace with questioning looks. Knowing their thoughts, Grace knew it wasn't the moment to give answers when she had no clue herself.

"Nice to meet you…" Grace paused. Her stares never left Lance nor the woman who has curves and knows how to use them.

"Rachel," Ava joyously added.

"Nice to meet you… Rachel."

"She would've missed this night if I hadn't notified her."

Stone ignored the brassy women standing in front of him. His look corrals Lance. "Mr. Worthington, it appears you've forgotten to tell us one major development," Stone said softly.

Ava didn't care about his daughter's hurt feelings; her main concern was her son's tremendous obligation to the family, and she wasn't going to let Lance forget it.

"Yes, I do believe," Ava agrees quickly.

Lowering his head, Lance wanted to shout out, *I didn't want Rachel on my arm, and I don't need anyone to tell me who my wife should be. It's Grace.*

At the far end of the hall, Caroline was finishing her comments to several stockholders when she observed Ava and Lance talking with Grace, with a woman gripping Lance's arm. Caroline's gaze turned fierce at Ava; what trickery was she instigating? Caroline excused herself and hurried over.

Caroline was displeased with Ava's deplorable conduct. It was unacceptable, especially on such an important night for the family. Lance's foolishness in having Mr. Paul Van Fitzgerald's daughter as his date was not only hurting Grace but diminishing his significance as the CEO. Rachel was a stunning-looking woman, but she wasn't a woman of merit like Grace.

"Grace, my dear!" Caroline said, her back to the impertinent ones. "You have done a marvelous job; kindly introduce me to these lovely people," Caroline beamed.

Grace politely made the introductions to Caroline, disregarding the man she loved, his mother, and her guest.

"You have a very talented and beautiful daughter," Caroline said.

"We always believed it to be true," Stone replied.

"I'm aware you have had the privilege to meet my grandson. I'm sure once he has completed his responsibilities with his mother and guest, he will join you," she explained, nodding specifically at Grace. Lance didn't miss the command in his grandmother's voice underneath her softly spoken words. Caroline turned her challenging eyes on Ava, daring her.

In a voice she couldn't overlook, Caroline called, "Ava, we should depart and allow Ms. Forrester to continue assisting our guests."

"Yes, Mother," Ava said harshly.

"Enjoy the rest of the evening," Caroline said quietly. "Grace, I look forward to another chance to chat with your family and friends soon." Caroline moved off, not looking back.

Labella smiled. "I think I like Mrs. Caroline Worthington."

"Yes," Stone smiled back.

Grace did not want to dampen the group's spirit further. "I need to find a quiet place. Don't worry; love you all."

Stone gently patted his daughter's cheek, took his wife's hand and strolled away. Approaching a small alcove off the main entryway, away from the crowd, Labella turned to Stone so fast that he dropped her hand.

"I don't believe that was Lance's fiancé," Labella said ruthlessly.

"Lance didn't deny it."

Labella looked at him. "Aren't you angry," she demanded. "That...chica...had the nerve to lie and flaunt that woman in my precious daughter's face!"

"Calm down, Bella," Stone entreated.

"How dare you tell me to be calm," she exclaimed, throwing herself backward, her hand waving.

"Mrs. Caroline...cares for Grace," Stone stated.

Stone admitted he was quite annoyed with Lance, who was too cowardly to fight for the woman he loved. Grace doesn't need a weak man, especially an unbeliever. It rips their hearts to see Grace rejected once again by the man she loves. However, they left the museum, holding the delightful portions of the evening close to their hearts.

"Grace," Nora asks the moment they arrive in the banquet room. "Did you know Lance was bringing a date?"

"Not just a date, but a fiancé," Zory shrieks. "But I don't believe it."

Grace stood silently by one of the ice sculptures. She heard merely one word: *fiancé* and nothing else.

"I thought I had found true love at last. I don't know why this keeps happening to me."

"Grace, I don't believe a word of it," Penelope exclaimed.

"That was a dirty trick that old witch pulled," Zory said dryly.

"No name-calling, please," Penelope responded.

"There are evil people in upper society," Nora commented.

Moving over to the charming buffet table, Grace takes a glass of ginger ale and sits at one of the covered tables with floral centerpieces.

"We come from two different worlds," Grace noted, studying the chandelier above her. "Now he's rich and powerful."

"Correction, he's always been rich," Nora chimed in, "the difference is he's not just a rich pilot but a powerful eligible bachelor."

"Powerful but cowardly," they all said in unison.

Grace unpredictably laughs, releasing some frustration. Her friends grab a plate and begin to serve themselves. Sitting together at one of the round tables, they ate and chatted about how Grace was better off without him.

With choice words from his grandmother, Lance felt as if a bucket of hot coals was thrust upon him. His reluctance to defy his mother's wishes caused him to hurt the one person he cherished. With great resolve, he left Rachel and his mother in search of Grace. By the time he found her, he knew he'd caused her unnecessary pain.

"Can we talk, Grace," Lance spoke softly, bringing violent, angry protests from Grace's friends. Slowly, Zory stood, knife fitted tightly in her hand.

"What do you want?" Zory hissed.

His hands in his pants pocket, Lance blinks at the three women standing to defend Grace's honor.

"Please, Grace, look at me."

Grace knew she was going to have to face him. He had treated her so cruelly. If only he had told her that he was bringing someone else. With very subtle movements, she turns, trying not to sniff. Nora motioned the others to step away to give them a few minutes. Zory pointed her knife at Lance as they left the table.

"Grace." Lance's voice was lower than usual. He sat next to her, reached for her chin, turning her to face him. He held it, and she met his gaze with wide, tear-filled eyes.

"Do you know how much you've hurt me, Lance?"

Lance silently sighed at his lack of courage and his inability to stand up to Ava and Rachel.

"Whatever possessed you to bring Rachel tonight. I wish I

could understand and erase the image," her tears spilled over then, and Lance's heart broke for more than one reason.

Without permission, he pulled her into his arms, but she forcefully pulled away.

"No, Lance, I can't. What happened tonight was your own making."

"Please, Grace, I'm so sorry for this!" Grace raised her hand.

"In the beginning, you told me we came from different backgrounds; you were right."

"I was wrong," he said firmly.

"It's over, Lance; please go back to your family and your fiancé. I don't belong in your circle; you and I were raised differently."

His mind went blank, turning to her friends, who were gazing intently at him. However, when he spoke, it was from his heart. "Rachel isn't my fiancé," he stated and proceeded to leave. "It's not over with us," he said over his shoulder.

Grace shrugged, feeling miserably inadequate, but plastered a smile on and told her friends she must return to work. She entered the scientific exhibit area, and finding André, she tapped him on the shoulder.

André gazed intensely at her. "Are you alright?" He whispered, and Grace lowered her eyelashes. He slips his arm through hers. "The evening is almost over; stay close to me, and we'll finish together." Slowly, the corners of his mouth turned into a smile that lit up his face.

"Thank you, I like that."

André, her faithful mentor, heard the sadness in Grace's voice and knew she would share when she was ready.

CHAPTER 9
It's A Mess & I Made It

Penville, North Carolina

Ava and Rachel began their morning in the small café of the hotel they rented for the weekend. With menus in hand, they counted the previous night as a success, even in the face of Caroline's interference.

"What do you think?" Rachel asked Ava after their breakfast order was in.

"It seems Lance's little fling is over."

"So, you think the board approves of me?"

Ava gave a contemptuous laugh. "You fit the role of a CEO's wife."

Rachel didn't question her further, but she couldn't dismiss how graciously Grace received them and the news that the man she loved had a fiancé.

Nothing else was said on the subject, or any subject for that matter. On this particular morning, additional comments weren't necessary.

⚬⚬⚬

As usual on a Sunday afternoon, the town's plaza was filled with many people enjoying the outdoors. The grassy area was populated with people lying out on blankets, reading, eating, throwing a football, and playing Frisbee.

Grace and her friends sat under a large American elm tree, snacking from the appealing delights of their picnic basket. Seemingly happy couples embraced each other on park benches and blankets, laughing at the simple enjoyment of being together. It was only too clear to Grace's friends that she was miserable.

"Did Lance explain why he was with Rachel?" Nora inquired.

Grace nodded and said nonchalantly, "I didn't want to hear his excuses; his actions spoke volumes."

"Why should she?" Zory spatted. "To hear more of his lies, I don't think so!"

"So, you are not going to talk with him to find out the truth?" Penelope asked.

"He put Grace through hell," Zory's interjected quickly. "What more can he say? Nothing!"

Grace wrapped a curl around her finger. "I don't understand the reason for his actions."

"Do you believe his mother?" Penelope asked between sips of root beer.

"In truth, I'm not sure," she answered in a solemn tone. "Anyway, I knew God's teaching, yet I went into an unholy relationship with my eyes open. The best thing for me is to repent to God," she said, leaning against the tree trunk.

"You're correct, but can you control the heart where love is concerned?" Zory questioned.

"I loved Reese and Lance, both unbelievers," Grace commented. "And what did it cost me?"

"Heartache and pain," Penelope declared.

"Maybe it's best; you found out he's too reliant on his mother," Zory said with an exasperated sigh.

"True, but the damage has been done," Nora cried out. "Grace is in love with him."

"Could it be possible that God indeed chose him for you?" Zory asked.

"Do you realize what you're saying?" Nora whispered.

"Yes," Zory shouted, receiving strange looks from onlookers. "That could explain why they fell in love so quickly."

"Stop, stop it. I haven't forgotten Rachel's sneer. No more talking about Mr. Worthington; pleasing God will be my main focus," Grace declared.

The friends only nodded before changing the conversation to a lighter subject. Grace was looking forward to the evening, kneeling at her bedside, asking God yet again for forgiveness, and to give her strength to wait for his perfect timing. But now, memories of her phone ringing all night came flooding back to her. There was no bitterness, no regret, only a deep concern she wouldn't see Lance anymore.

New York, New York

In Lance's apartment, an eerie silence penetrated the area. Lance was dressed in his pilot uniform, but his whole body vibrated with dread. Anger swiftly rose within him; *I can't believe my stupidity! I just stood like a mannequin, watching my mother introduce Rachel as my fiancé; I'm such a coward.*

It was all such a mess. Lance hasn't had a chance to explain to Grace because she wouldn't talk to him at the event nor answer his calls. She's been avoiding him, and he admitted she had every right. It was painful to entertain that horrible moment two nights ago. *You're a fool, Lance Worthington, he told himself. You don't deserve her. She trusted you.*

While Lance was going through security and to the office to retrieve his flight itinerary, his single thought was how much he loved Grace. Forty-five minutes later, he boarded his plane, clinging to the hope that Grace would take his call when he returned.

"Why the forlorn look?" Jason asked the moment Lance sat in the captain's seat.

Lance stared at his co-pilot uttering a soft curse under his breath, and began the pre-flight check.

Never hearing his friend use that type of vocabulary, Jason pondered what had taken place so radically in Lance's world.

Soon, they were cleared for takeoff. After reaching cruising altitude, Jason breaks into Lance's thoughts.

"My friend, your face shows a sad story."

Lance glanced across the way at his co-pilot, and his chest lifted with a sigh.

"I did the unthinkable and lost the woman I love."

"You mean… Rachel?" Jason asked.

"No," Lance replied without hesitation. "I'm in love with Ms. Grace Forrester."

Jason sat silent for a long moment. "Who is Grace?" Jason questioned. "You know, Rachel thinks she is going to marry you."

"In truth, Jason, I never intended to marry Rachel."

Jason stared at his friend of several years, confused.

"Jason, what I feel for Grace, I never felt for Rachel. Rachel's rich in wealth, whereas Grace's rich in integrity."

Jason smiled at him. "My friend, you've got it bad, but I still don't understand your problem."

"During this weekend gala with the family, Mother arranged for Rachel to be my date. Then, she introduced Rachel as my fiancé to Grace, her family and friends," Lance fumed.

"Ouch!" Jason shot him a glance.

"Let's drop the subject," Lance declared. "I can't permit being distracted during a flight."

Jason nodded, hoping Lance would finish the story once they landed.

After returning from London and sleeping for over twelve hours, Lance awoke late Thursday afternoon—rested, clear-headed, and more determined than ever to win back Grace's love. Hungry, he made his way to the kitchen in search of something to eat. An hour later, he quietly went to his bedroom to make one more call to Grace.

Holding his breath, he dialed Grace's phone number, hoping against hope that she would answer. Within minutes, her voice came over the speaker. Silently groaning deeply, words hung in the air; he was speechless.

"Lance, is that you?" Grace asked in a tone of skepticism.

Foolishly, he shrugged. "I…didn't think you would pick up."

Feeling dismantled, it took her some time to speak. "It rather sounds like you were taken by surprise, that I answered."

Lance's voice was quiet and gentle. "I'm reluctant because I've caused you much harm. Your distress and pale face are very clear in my mind."

Grace silently agreed.

"I can't claim it wasn't my fault," he said, his voice cracking. "Yet, I feel sorry for myself for not being the man you deserve."

Grace was quiet and took more time to speak. Lance waited, his stomach churning.

"Lance, I'd hope you would be a tower of strength. I hated to see you coward under your mother's thumb."

Lance drew in a shuddering breath. "It's bad enough I hurt you, but to lose you completely is almost more than I can take," his voice caught.

"Oh, my," Grace whispered, her heart working to take it in.

His voice was toneless. "It never occurred to me we wouldn't be together. It's a fact that I'm a better person when I'm with you. Have I ruined it?"

"I don't know, but I do know I won't allow you to hurt me again," Grace mumbled.

"I beg of you, don't let my paralysis of indecision be the end. My love for you is real," he said, sniffling.

"I didn't hear from you for five days, and then you showed up with a fiancé; that's not love."

"Believe me, Grace, I love you and only you."

"How can I?" choking on her words. "You listened to your mother and not your heart. I appreciate you acknowledging your responsibility, but I can't do this."

"I can't let you go," A mixture of stillness and breathing ricocheted over the phone. "Please...Grace...Please."

"Lance," her voice fluttered, "I promised God; I wait on his answer, whether it's you or someone else."

The softness of her voice stopped him in his tracks. Here was the woman he'd fallen for. She was a woman who loved God, and he hoped that one day, he would become the man she needed. He let out a huge sigh over the phone.

"No one will ever take your place in my heart. Please don't leave me."

"I...goodbye, Lance."

The quietness of the phone left a dull ache in Lance's chest. It wasn't his intention to abuse their love. Nonetheless, his mother's persistent persuasion led him into manipulation and entrapment, effectively annihilating his relationship with Grace, which he wouldn't have otherwise done. Time will tell if he could once again possess such a rare beauty who left him breathless.

Worthington Estate

In mid-October, the hot and humid climate had surrendered to crisp air, with colorful leaves and a variety of outdoor activities. Having received an invitation for lunch with his grandmother, they were in the solarium, which brought bittersweet memories for Lance.

"Lance, how have you been?"

"I've been better," Lance said with saddened eyes.

"What have I missed these last couple of weeks?"

"Grace told me our relationship was over," he commented.

"Do you want it to be over?"

"No. But I've lost Grace's trust."

"I'm not surprised," her eyes bored into him. "Your mother used you, and you left Grace to fight alone."

After a moment of silence, his face stiffened. "Reading the letter from the board, I agreed with Mother's decision," he stated.

"Rubbish," Caroline snapped. "I helped create that letter; it explained whomever you married, must understand the life of a CEO."

"I didn't believe Grace could handle it."

"You didn't give her the chance to be in that role."

"But…" was the only word he could manage before Caroline continued.

"Grace's a very special woman compared to Rachel, who's just another self-serving person who put her ambitions above everyone else."

"You're right," Lance said, knowing she was speaking the truth. "I don't know why I thought Rachel was more suited than Grace," Lance's shoulders slumped in defeat.

For some reason, the statement, along with Lance's crumpled body, caused Caroline's voice to crack a little.

"Everyone, including the Worthington family, was thoroughly impressed with Grace's beauty, poise, and intelligence."

"What did they think of Rachel?" Lance asked quietly.

"Lance, listen, several board members and stockholders were flabbergasted by your choice of companion for the evening."

"Please, Grandmother, I know the seriousness of my position."

Caroline fell quiet, but it was brief.

"Do you? I hope you do," she said, still fighting back tears. "Because I want nothing but happiness for you."

"Why?"

"I loved your grandfather and my position as his helpmate. I believe Grace is your helpmate."

Lance studied his grandmother; he could read in her eyes that she truly loved him and wanted nothing but the best for him.

"Grandmother, do I have a chance with Grace?"

"I don't know, but if you don't try, it's your loss."

Suddenly flustered, Lance pushed his plate aside, leaving the table; he moved to stand by an overgrown orchid plant as Caroline was a few feet behind him.

"I regret not seeing you grow from a baby to a man. But now, my deepest desires are to help you. I'm here to help you succeed."

Outwardly calm, Lance nodded to his grandmother, but inside, he felt like weeping.

"Thank you, Grandmother. I will be fine," he assured her.

Caroline nodded. Lance's tired, confused face tore at her heart. Caroline thought...not for the first time... that Grace was meant to be Lance's wife.

The moment James, the butler, entered the solarium, he observed Caroline and Lance speaking in low tones. Therefore, he waited until he was noticed.

"What is it, James?"

"Madam, Master Lance has a visitor," James informed them.

"Thank you, James; please make them comfortable in the Paris room," Caroline instructed.

"Lance, it seems we must continue our talk another day."

Because Lance didn't know who his guest might be, he hugged his grandmother and departed with a little hesitation.

CHAPTER 10
The Fine Art of Awakening Out Of Sleep

Perry worked hard to keep his mouth closed as he was escorted to a room. The estate exuded the stateliness and charm of a castle. The details of the room included an oil painting he had once seen in a museum in France. Somewhat reserved, Perry remained standing, poised in a simple blue suit, until Lance entered.

"Perry Whitlock?" Lance said, astonished to see him.

"Come, have a seat," Lance invited. "How did you know I was on Long Island."

"A mutual friend informed me you might be here," Perry shrugged.

"What friend?"

"I had the profound privilege of working with Jason on a Phoenix flight earlier this week."

Lance chuckled. "What did Jason say to have you looking for me?"

"Problem with the heart, so I came to ask: how are you?"

Lance sat mute for several minutes, refusing to look at Perry.

"My heart and I are doing fine."

"Are you certain?"

Lance stared at Perry for a moment and then spoke softly. "I'm not sure what exactly Jason shared, but I'm sure it was about Rachel and Grace."

Halting their conversation, a uniformed servant brought in a cart with coffee and pastries. Perry marveled at how grand Lance's life had become.

"You look very subdued," Lance admonished.

"A little overwhelmed, I think."

"With me or the house?"

"Maybe a little of both," Perry regarded him. "I wonder if I could become accustomed to this type of living."

"I'm still in wonder," Lance admitted, casting his eyes around the room. "For many years, I wasn't aware that I was born into this. A few months ago, I couldn't wait to leave this place."

Perry wanted to say so much, but he held his tongue. The two friends grew comfortable in the silence. Perry didn't know how two women played in Lance's bruised heart. It occurred to Perry that Lance was carrying a heavy burden and needed to be rescued.

"Do you mind if I ask you about Rachel and Grace?" Perry asked. "Or do you find me pushy?"

"I don't mind."

"It appears you have lost something precious, and you are searching for answers."

"It's true," he said, his words punctuated by a low groan. "I'm cautious about seeking advice."

"What really happened, my friend?" Perry smiled.

Lance held himself rigidly in his chair without looking in Perry's direction.

"The damage was done the moment I agreed with my mother."

"How so?"

"Well, my mother lied, which brought humiliation to the woman I love; now, I have lost her trust and maybe her love.

"And that's…"

"Grace Forrester!" Lance answered boldly, sitting back in self-disdain.

"Lance, I'm sorry, you felt obliged to please your mother and have been hurt because of it…but I know a friend who can help you."

Lance suddenly felt very emotional, grateful to have a friend like Perry.

"Who's this friend? Can he produce results?"

"Yes," Perry answered, his face serious. "Jesus is your answer."

Perry, seeing Lance's shoulders sink, realized Lance was having some misgivings about his answer. In a flash, he asked himself what would help Lance at this moment.

"Lance, when I first started working for the airlines, my wife had just left me for another man, taking our two small children and moving to another state. Alone and betrayed, I found my survival kit in a relationship with God. It's been six years since I've seen or talked with my kids. They are now ten and eleven years old, and I don't even know if they're aware I'm their real dad."

This was the saddest story Lance had heard besides his own. His eyes slide shut for a moment. Finally, Lance opened eyes met Perry's eyes as he spoke.

"I'm glad you found a friend in God, and I can somewhat understand why you trust him."

Perry nodded and regarded Lance seriously. "Are you willing to let God into your heart and life?"

Lance hesitated, working hard to hide his feelings. "I'm not sure, but thanks."

Lance felt his pursuits, finances, and travels were the true meaning of his existence. He didn't see a reason to change now, but he knew he hadn't a clue; maybe Perry did have the answer.

The next morning, during his drive back to New York, Lance couldn't concentrate. It was useless. Ava's hatred for Grace was firmly rooted in her heart. However, it boggled his mind that two women from the same social hierarchy had very different opinions of who he should marry.

Ava made her sentiments clear. Ms. Forrester didn't have the qualities to live a life of wealth and privilege. However, Caroline believed quite the opposite. If the person you love lives in a stable home where money isn't an issue, that person would love you, not your money or status. Lance realized he had two choices: take his mother's advice or fight for Grace.

Lance considered all the facts before him and concluded there was only one choice: fight for the love of Grace.

Worthington Steel Company

Lance's loneliness marred his new fame as the finest CEO beside his grandfather. He eyed the paperwork on his desk as his mind centered on Thanksgiving's upcoming dinner with the family. Not in his wildest dreams would he have believed that four weeks had come and gone without speaking or seeing Grace. The urgency to regain Grace's respect was ever before him.

"Ms. Hall, please bring in my calendar for review," Lance buzzed the intercom for his assistant.

After Ms. Hall promptly educated him that the calendar couldn't be rearranged, Lance shrugged a bit. If he adhered to the demands of his calendar, finding time to win Grace back would be difficult.

Thanksgiving dawned with promises of joy and happiness. However, with Caroline's refusal to allow Rachel to attend the family's Thanksgiving, Ava was boiling with anger and disagreement. In the midst of the family going around the table saying what they were thankful for, Sterling stated he wasn't thankful since Lance stole his inheritance.

Ava already uptight, threw her plate of food at him, missing him by inches.

⁓

With the fiasco of the family's Thanksgiving gathering behind him, Lance had no desire to see his mother for Christmas or the near future. His desire to confess his love to Grace was constantly hindered by her refusal to see or speak with him. Meanwhile, he discovered his grandmother regularly talked with Grace.

Lance has been working on a new acquisition for a small steel company for far too long. In great agitation, he took deep breaths, cursing himself that he wasn't ready to present his idea to the board. With knitted brows, he walked to the credenza for a specific file. With his lips pressed together, Lance carefully searched file after file with no luck. Finally, in the very back of the file drawer, the file he sought came into his full view. Caroline entered, startling Lance.

"Lance, how are you?"

Lance swiftly turns around, dropping the file onto the floor.

"Grandmother!" he exclaimed, bending to grab the file.

"I'm okay," he said graciously. "Especially considering I get to see my favorite person."

Caroline's mouth twisted into a smile.

"Well, your desolate expression says something different, a sentiment shared by Grace."

Their eyes met for several moments while Lance strained to shake the swarm of butterflies in his stomach.

"Please tell her I send my love?"

"I certainly will."

"When will you talk with her again?" Lance asked his grandmother.

"In a few days, I have a meeting with Mr. Dupré on a possible loan to the museum here in New York.

Lance joined Caroline at a small sitting area across from his desk.

"I'm sorry she snubs your requests to see her."

"But why does she find my requests outrageous?"

"Well, considering Ava's influence prevails strongly, I don't think she will consider your requests."

Lance blinked in surprise at her firm tone.

"I have no idea what can be done about Mother. I have plenty of responsibilities at the moment, for one, this acquisition. Secondly, I haven't spoken to Mother since Thanksgiving.

Caroline suddenly laid her hand on his knee.

"I know you want Grace in your life again, yet I'm going to say something you must heed. I don't know if you have a future with her, but you must not rush this, and make sure you're ready to fight for her this time."

Lance nodded.

"Have I upset you?"

"No," he paused to meet his grandmother's gaze. "How will I know it's the right moment?" said Lance, his chest oddly tight.

"Your heart will tell you," Caroline said. "Don't fret; it will work out."

Lance's brows rose, but he didn't comment. He wasn't sure if he could trust his heart. Lance put a gentle arm around Caroline to lead her back into the outer office.

Alone in the office, Lance asked himself. *Are you so indebted to your mother that you will lose the woman you love? Don't you think it's time for you to figure out how to free yourself from this bondage?*

During the second week in December, Lance again looked at a new stack of work on his desk, sitting back with a sigh. His resignation from the airlines hadn't been approved, so he had no other choice but to continue working two jobs.

Sleeping at the office had become the norm, and today wasn't any different. Due to the constant criticism from his mother and the absence of Grace from his life, Lance succumbed to a deep depression.

Glancing at the corner of his desk, Lance saw the forgotten sandwich, which seemed to plead; *I've been waiting for you all afternoon. The stillness of the sleeping offices had created a ghostly feeling.* From the shadows of his office door, his assistant emerged.

"Sir, I was wondering, do you require my assistance further?"

"What time is it?"

"8:00 p.m." she smiled.

"No, Ms. Hall," Lance said. "I'm sorry you had to work so late these past weeks."

"Not to worry; I'll see you Monday."

"Stay warm this weekend and enjoy the snow."

"Thank you, sir," she turned to leave but paused. "Oh, I forgot, Mr. Worthington, your mother called earlier, but I informed her you couldn't be disturbed."

Knowing his mother was checking up on him, he waved a hand of thanks.

"Good evening, Ms. Hall."

Lance was now alone in his office, and even though he was tired, he knew he had plenty of work to finish.

Lance glanced around his office. He didn't imagine he would have an enormous office space on the 45th floor. The grand entrance to his office was dominated by a pair of magnificent wooden doors, which separated his office and the assistant's office from the main hallway. His desk overlooked a conference table with sixteen chairs next to a small seating area hosting two sofas and fabric chairs. To the left of his desk was a kitchen, and several feet away from the kitchen, a private bedroom with a bed, sink, and toilet.

To refresh himself, Lance went to the bedroom to splash cold water on his face. Knowing he couldn't waste time, he quickly grabbed a wet towel covering his face. Heading back to his desk, his face yet covered, Lance perceived a presence. Removing the towel, he took in a sharp breath and froze.

He watched in confusion as Rachel looked around the office and then at him.

"What are you doing here?" he snapped, numb with shock.

"Lance, control yourself?" she suggested in a normal voice, overlooking his rudeness.

"Has your mind turned into mush?" he raged.

"I don't believe this," she whispered. "I had hoped you would welcome me as a friend." Rachel was utterly delighted that he looked miserable. She fancied it was because of her.

"You've made a terrible mistake coming here. I can't help but wonder how did you know I was at the office?" Lance's voice was hard.

"I confess—your mother told me to come." Her voice trailed off as she moved closer inside the office. "She let it slip that you've been working late, and you might be hungry," she mocked him, showing him a picnic basket.

Without a moment of hesitation, he glared at her. "Mother is a user," he yelled. Rachel found herself recoiling a little.

"I don't think your mother is that kind of a person."

"What makes you say that?" Lance demanded. "Who knows what my mother would say or do to accomplish her goal."

Rachel didn't want to fight. In the beginning, she thought about letting him go…though Ava's promise was hard to dismiss. The first moment Rachel saw Lance, his charming way snared her like prey. However, now she doesn't love him, only his power and money, which she definitely plans to collect. Rachel stared at Lance's profile as he returned to his desk.

"Goodbye," Lance said, trying not to maintain eye contact.

Rachel's head fell back laughing. "I'm not leaving. I can't forget the numerous nights we spent together."

"You need a crash course in reality," Lance hissed. "We're no longer a couple and never will be again."

For a time, Rachel feared she was losing the war, but she wasn't going to give up.

"You're wrong," she answered with a bitter laugh. "You loved me once, and you will once more."

"Take your basket and leave," he demanded. "Tell my mother…it didn't work."

"You don't want me to stay, my pet?"

"You're forgetting something," Lance pointed out, rubbing one corner of his head. "I'm in love with Grace, not you!"

She lifted her chin. "Your mother will never approve of that marriage."

"Neither my mother nor you will stop me," he declared.

Rachel started to say something but checked herself. Seeing his eyes closing, leaning back, and rubbing his temple, she delicately sashayed to the side of his desk, lowering the basket quietly to the floor. With precision, she gently commenced rubbing the back of his neck. He froze, chills feathered down his spine.

"Trust me," she continued to knead his neck even more.

It's just a little massage, he told himself, as a low moan escaped and tension began to fade.

"I can see you're relaxing." Rachel sang, using her thumb to creep up the middle of his neck and hair.

Lance's face heated, and he closed his eyes, revisiting the missed intimacy, communication, solace, and emotions he shared with Grace. Little by little, he eluded the predicament in his heart.

A shuddering tremor ran through him. "I'm not a weakling," he protested too loudly.

"I promise... I will leave when I'm finished." Rachel slowly spoke as she moved her hands with smooth, caressing strokes along his lower back and neck.

She heard Lance pull in his breath.

"Do you want more like this?"

Lance felt intensely guilty. However, her touch sent a tingling sensation through his bones, and he felt as if his legs were going to fold under him.

"Please ...stop...please stop, I'm bound to Grace."

"But if you remain tense, you can't finish your work. I insist you let me continue."

"No..." Lance jumped away from her, unmindful that his desk had enclosed him. He couldn't escape Rachel's almost merciless look sweeping over him.

"Goodness Lance," she muttered. "You're a fool to deny you were enjoying it," she said as a flush rushed across her face.

"Oh, course," he flung his body around the massive desk. "Who wouldn't enjoy tension removed from their body?"

He glanced back at her; before he could stop himself from shaking, he saw the mocking little smile on the edge of her mouth.

"You shouldn't be ashamed of having feelings for me," she drawled.

"I don't," he denied; he found his gaze fixed upon the tight white winter sweater; he just had to avoid those sharp green eyes of the woman who knew his weakness.

He swung on his heels and strode away from the desk. He looked into her eyes, but they weren't mocking him. They had a look of yearning and need. He shuddered, remembering the many intimate nights with her.

"It doesn't hurt for you to give way to your emotions," she stared at him with her left eyebrow, arching into a slanting angle.

"I can't do this to Grace," he murmured.

"There are times when you curse self-discipline," she snapped her fingers dismissively. "Heed to your emotions."

He looked at her with surprise; how would she know about true love?

"Don't look at me with self-righteous eyes," she tossed back her long hair.

Lance turned his head away, too aware of her sultry look and the proximity of a bed.

"Look at me!" Rachel was suddenly standing in front of him, clasping the nape of his neck. "Shall I prove to you that we do have something?"

The pressure of her fingers around his neck was a warning, and his defenses were eroding; his heart raced at the mere thought.

"I...I'm aware that we once had something."

"We also have a natural need for someone who would

love us," as she spoke, her lips moved against the soft side of his neck, and he became intensely aware his body was responding.

"Please...Rachel...no!"

Her breath slid warm across his face as she drew even closer; his body stiffened as he was silenced into shock as her lips covered his. Unbelievably, he was kissing her...his mouth held hers, and she could feel him shiver in the embrace. The intimacy of it was incredible to him. He had no right to be enjoying it.

"Come," she whispered. Lance followed her into the sleeping room. The only light shining was over the sink, but Rachel was still able to see her way in. Lance pulled away, but as if his resistance made the deep-down savagery erupt in her, she knocked him down on the bed while she took a lounging position above him.

She laughed softly, unbuttoning his shirt and undoing his tie.

"You know you can't resist me because I'm in your blood. You thought your Grace could keep you?"

Her fingers float around the contour of his mustache, and then her hands slide down his chest. Lance's eyes widen, and his equilibrium is ripped asunder.

CHAPTER 11

Navigating The Scars of Guilt & Shame

L ance awakened in the early hours of the morning to the sounds of a vacuum in the outer office. Disoriented, he raised his head from his pillow, blinking several times, giving his eyes a few minutes to adjust to the dark room. Ruffled sheets and her scent lingered; obviously, Rachel had slept in his bed. Lance stared at the sheets for a long time, denying the evidence staring him in the face. What a fool he had been to allow himself to betray yet again the woman he loved.

He had clandestinely hoped God would honor his desire to have Grace as his wife. However, he recalled Rachel's last words before they... *Close your eyes and imagine Grace is in your arms.*

He murmured. *In many ways, love is blind; It comes from out of the dark recesses of ourselves, a spark that seeks the air so it can burst into flame.* His eyes dwelt upon the side of the bed where Rachel had laid. Where is Rachel? he thought. A groan escaped him before he noticed a note on the pillow next to him.

Please know I loved being close to you last night; I never wanted the moment to end. You're all I ever wanted. Leaving was very hard. Remember, I'm in your blood.

Love, Rachel

Perhaps last night was a dream, But the untidy room and note easily refuted that fact. So much for his foolish dreams of a family and love with Grace. Recognition dawned on his face, and he buried his face in his hands, bellowing, *what a jerk I am! That's it. I've lost Grace forever, and there's no one to blame but myself.* Grace, he mouths.

Ashamed, he threw his head back onto the pillow, his lifeless body slumped into the mattress. If a biography were published at that very moment, the pages would be full of pain, disappointments, mistrust, and betrayal, providing readers access to his empty heart.

For the first time in weeks, days of hope disappeared, and Lance Worthington's conviction that he was pursuing human decency was shattered. His eyes locked on the disheveled sheets, and immediately, his eyes flooded with tears. Leering at the sheets, he arched his eyebrows. Lance reached out and snatched the sheets away from his body, and at a slow pace, swayed onto the floor. In that instant, coldness squeezed around his heart.

The cleaning lady noticed the door to the private sleeping room was locked. She knocked twice.

"Mr. Worthington, are you there? Sir, are you decent?"

"No, please return later," he spoke softly.

"Very well, sir."

Lance fumbled to find his pants, thrown aimlessly across the room. He thought of his mother as his worst nightmare. Her threat to destroy him had become a reality, and she had given Rachel carte blanche to do whatever it took to destroy his love for Grace. How ironic, he caved in to a woman unparallel to Grace, and Rachel didn't care that she was being exploited.

Lance bent over and hooked his pants. Memories of his behavior wiggled their way out of the mud of his mind. His hand glided through his hair. He moved toward the door and entered his office. In the stillness of the early morning darkness, Lance left the office building, thinking he must locate and talk with Perry. He wanted to know more about the person Perry spoke about, who knows and loves him better than anyone in his life.

Lance didn't open his mail left on his desk Monday morning. Instead, he requested Connie Hall, his assistant, to arrange an impromptu board meeting. Though old fears die hard, he was stubborn enough to present his innovation.

For many weeks, Lance had proved to be a dedicated CEO who often worked more than required, ensuring success for the company. In less than thirty minutes, board members and top executives, in single file, had made their way inside the board room.

An hour later, Lance sat quietly at the head of the massive conference table, his back to the charts with his proposal. Without ceremony, the senior director spoke.

"You're sure about this, Mr. Worthington?" the senior board director asked after Lance's presentation.

"I won't tell you I'm a little scared, but we would be foolish not to jump at the chance. With this acquisition, we can increase our company's global footprint and market share in the industry."

The remaining directors had no reply to his answer, only exchanging looks with the senior director.

"Very well then, we will take a vote." The senior director spoke in his gentle, deep voice. "All in favor, say Aye." Each director, one by one, nodded, and with cool voices, they all agreed to the acquisition.

"The ayes have it," the senior director cheered. "We're all in favor of pursuing this."

Lance stood in awe, seeing the twelve directors voice their approval. It took him a moment to realize his first major proposal was accepted. Everyone was in high spirits except Lance; nevertheless, with composure, he cheerfully addressed each director as they left the conference room.

Holding up under the deep sense of shame, Lance trudged to his office. While standing at the window, questions without answers plagued his mind. *How will Grace react if she finds out?*

What are the potential consequences of my actions? A knock on the partially open door disrupted Lance's contemplation, snapping him back to the present.

"Mr. Worthington," Connie said, holding her notepad, "May we review the finalization of the new acquisition's budget?"

Lance sighed heavily. "Connie, I would like to be left alone." Lance turned his attention back to the window, his brow furrowed in concentration.

"I understand, sir, but we need to finalize the draft budget for the new acquisition by tomorrow."

"Connie!" his voice curt, turned to face her. "We will work late tonight if need be."

For a moment, Connie paused. "I apologize," she said softly, "but you gave me the afternoon off."

"You should've reminded me earlier," he said, his voice agitated. "I suggest you cancel your plans."

"I'm sorry, but…" Connie tried again, and without thinking, Lance took his frustration out on his assistant.

"Have you always been this unhelpful?" he suddenly asked.

Connie blinked in disbelief. "No, sir."

"You could've fooled me," Lance muttered as he ran his hand through his hair and closed his eyes.

Mystified by her normally kind and considerate boss, she held her place in the middle of the office.

What in the world has caused Mr. Worthington to turn into a jerk? I don't even know this man before me.

Working hard not to exaggerate the importance of the issue, Connie spoke steadily, though she wished she could stop shaking. "Sir, it's impossible to cancel; we are celebrating my parents' 25th wedding anniversary with dinner and a play."

"Connie, we can discuss this in thirty minutes," Lance said, defeated.

Not knowing what else to say, Connie nodded.

Hearing no reply, Lance turned around and looked at Connie, and for the first time, he noticed splotches of color on her face and neck, her lips shuddering. What he saw terrified him. He had scared her. He knew he needed to rectify the situation.

"Please forgive me, Ms. Hall," Lance pleaded. "Don't worry, I will have the final numbers for you in the morning. Go, you may leave at the agreed time at noon."

"Thank you, sir."

Lance deeply regretted his actions and was truly remorseful about how he had treated Connie. She didn't deserve his erratic outburst.

Meanwhile, Caroline waited patiently outside of his office, incredibly proud of her grandson for winning the board's approval. Beholding Ms. Hall's exit, Caroline inquired if Lance were available. "May I interrupt Mr. Worthington?"

"Yes," Connie gave a hesitant nod.

Bewildered by Connie's hesitation, Caroline quietly enters, finding Lance slightly slouched by the window, looking at nothing special. She straightway spotted devastation written on his face.

She swiftly said, "Congratulations!"

"Thank you, Grandmother," Lance dejectedly spoke.

Caroline couldn't understand his gloomy look. "Lance, are you feeling sick?"

"Sick within my soul," he said as his jaw tightened.

Like a pawn on a checkerboard, Lance moved away from the window to stand in the middle of the room to stare at the door that led to the sleeping area. Lance's hopeless look took on a whole new meaning for Caroline.

"What has happened?"

Not taking his gaze from the door of his sleeping area, he did not answer.

"You must know how much I care for you," she said.

Her statement did nothing for him, but he couldn't control his tremulous chin.

"Are you going to tell me?" Caroline pressed him.

"It's complicated," he said sharply, reminding himself she believed in him; he couldn't destroy her trust in him.

"I assumed as much," Caroline said, her voice not divulging her fears.

Lance glanced at her. "There's no point in my telling you."

"I see."

The office was silent for a moment, Caroline conceding that she would get nothing from Lance,

"Well, I guess there's nothing more for me to say, only that your grandfather would be proud of you," Caroline said. "You're truly a CEO," she said, exiting on that note.

Lance didn't move from his spot for a long moment. In the past, he had dealt with many unpleasant situations, but never anything like this. Gazing at the closed door, numb with coldness, a change of scenery was urgent. He departed, informing Ms. Hall not to wait for his return.

Forty-eight hours later, the Dallas flight crew was backing away from the gate at JFK International Airport. Once they received clearance from the tower, the MD-80 took to the skies. Once above the clouds, various shades of red, orange, and pink cradled the early morning sky.

Lance, who sat in the captain's seat of the cockpit looking over the instrument, called back over his shoulder to Perry, the co-pilot.

"Think we're heading into clear blue skies," said Lance.

It still boggled Lance's intellect that he was able to obtain the same route that Perry was scheduled to work. Lance agreed to work for another captain's route for the next several weeks. There had been no word of his resignation's approval, so he perceived it was safe to consent to the switch.

"Absolutely, perfect. It's going to be an enjoyable ride," Perry chuckled

"We couldn't have asked for a better day," Lance said, gazing out of his front windshield.

"What about a late lunch when we land?" Perry asked. "It's been a couple of months since our last visit; we must catch up."

Lance nodded. "I've been thinking something similar."

Three hours and 40 minutes passed before they inched up to the jet bridge at the Dallas International Airport. Lance and Perry worked in silence, completing the final landing checklist.

"Hey, do you want to try that new Mexican restaurant near our hotel?"

"Right now, I need a shower and a nap," Lance chuckled.

Perry hooted. "A pleasant idea. If Mexican isn't inviting to you, after our respite, there's a steak restaurant next to the hotel."

"That sounds great."

Strangely, Perry wondered if Lance was stalling. Together, they exited the cockpit.

"Thank you for being understanding," Lance said.

"My pleasure. We have all evening to talk," Perry responded, raising his eyebrows.

Alone in his room, Lance reflected on what the evening may uncover. He thought about the special kinship he had with Perry. True, Lance had never thought of religion in his thirty-four years, yet religion may be the answer he was seeking. He had never been this desperate.

Across the hall, Perry knelt by his bed praying, seeking wisdom and guidance, for the evening.

Dallas, Texas

Lance's hands fidgeted nervously with his watch. He debated within himself whether he should tell Perry everything, though it would make him appear a truly contemptible man. Nonetheless, the persistent feeling of shame was gnawing away at his ability to live as a decent human being.

At the agreed-upon time, they met at the steak restaurant next to the hotel. It had a forty-five-minute wait time. Not wasting any time, they crossed the street to a small bar and grill. Minutes after arriving, they were seated, and their order was in.

Perry understood that Lance wasn't ready to talk. Therefore, he quietly waited for Lance to begin.

"I don't know if I should tell you," Lance began moments later.

Perry folded his hands on the table and looked at Lance.

"I mean," Lance tried again. "I don't want you to perceive me differently."

"What is it?" Perry asked, his voice kind.

Lance looked at him with humiliation. "I'm so stupid. I've messed everything up. My relationship with Grace is dead," Lance hopelessly moaned.

Perry's eyes flooded with understanding and consolation. "What exactly have you done?" Perry questioned him.

"At my weakest moment, I allowed myself to be enticed, and I'm afraid if Grace found out, I may lose her forever."

Perry took a thoughtful sip of his Coke and said, "I don't know the details of your story. But I do know God is able to perform miracles."

Lance didn't even hesitate; his story flooded out in a whirlwind, including the ugly segments. Perry felt he learned a lot in a few seconds. Perry wasn't shocked, but he knew the strategy of the devil. He knew Lance's shame had cut him deeply, slowly killing his spirit. Perry's movements were totally composed, but he tended to nod. Did that mean he was appalled?

"Did I shock you with my admission?" Lance inquired.

"No...I want... you to know," Perry said slowly. "You aren't the first man to fall prey to a woman's charms, and you won't be the last."

Lance fell silent, thinking about what Perry had stated.

"Any chance your mother will tell Grace?"

"I'm going to tell her if she takes me back," pain stitched across Lance's face.

"Do you think telling her will remove your shame?" Perry asked.

"I must tell her to respect myself once again," Lance spoke calmly.

"But..." Perry was afraid to continue. "My friend, having respect for yourself is wonderful, but having a healed heart truly can only happen through God's healing hands."

Seeing the look of confusion on Lance's face, Perry quickly added. "We can't heal our heartaches," Perry whispered.

"I must say, it's difficult for me to accept what you're saying."

"Lance! You can forgive yourself, be healed, and you can trust God. John 5:6 (NIV) states, *When Jesus noticed him lying there helpless, knowing that he had been in that condition a long time, he said to him, "Do you want to get well?"*

"Perry?" Lance asked, leaning over the table. "Can this Jesus erase my grief and heartbreak and forgive me?"

"Without a doubt!" Perry said, secretly praying. "Without him, Lance, we are nothing. This weekend, my church is having an all-men's Christmas retreat. I'm sure you will find the answers you're seeking."

Lance was quiet for a few minutes, and Perry wondered if he had gone ahead of God's plan.

"Perry, I will attend," he said, his voice terrified.

"I will swing by your apartment around eight in the morning."

Perry laughed in delight and Lance smiled at him, discovering his heart felt lighter. Yet, Lance wondered if the reality of receiving answers for his problems could be an attainable goal.

Penville, North Carolina

The small bridge connecting Grace's rural community to Penville was flooded by heavy rain the night before. So, she had a day free from work at the museum. Her main objective for the day was to prepare the house for Christmas.

By evening, Grace was slumped in an oversized chair, her legs curled to her side, as she rested a hand on the chair's arm. The hypnotic flames from the fireplace and the cozy feeling from the fleece blanket lured her tired body into a limpness. Within minutes, Grace was fast asleep, dreaming about Lance, as small raindrops hit her window.

In her dream, Lance had come to the church looking for her, but the church's doors were bolted. Suicidal, he camped out on the steps, repeating over and over, "I must pay for my crime." Suddenly, he stood, staring down from the top of the stairs, weaving back and forth, until he cast himself down the stone stairs.

The slap of coldness from the dormant fireplace awakened Grace. Her heart was throbbing. She felt cold air nipping at her feet and legs. Slowly, she sat up, shivering as the cold air threaded its way through her pants leg. She glanced around and saw her blanket had fallen to the floor.

Reeling from the explicit graphic of the dream, she took several deep breaths of air to steady her troubling mind. She remembered every detail of the dream, but she shied away from the very thought of what it may mean. Still feeling groggy, she swayed to the fireplace, opened the damper, and carefully raked the existing embers together.

With a heavy heart, Grace reached for her bible, her hands trembling slightly with each movement. When she opened the bible, it fell open to the book of Psalm 46:1.

"God is our refuge and strength, an ever-present help in trouble.

Meditating on the scripture, a quiet voice drifted to her ears. *Lance frantically needs your forgiveness.* Grace's hand flew to her throat, and she promptly began to pray.

Later that evening, she took a shower, using the nozzle full force, trying to remove the feeling of dread. Grace wasn't sure of the extent of Lance's probable assault, but she only knew he would beseech her for mercy.

Ava sat in the backseat of her car, wishing Lance would appreciate her sacrifice, of loss youth and true love. This new journey meant she and Lance was finally accepted by the Worthington family, and she knew Lance was willing to throw his inheritance away for Grace Forrester.

"Madam, we're almost home, Jenkins stated, his voice intruding on Ava's thoughts.

"Thank you, Jenkins."

Ava sighted the car of Sterling, Jr., parked in her circular driveway. For many years, she regarded him as a dead man. But since the death of her father-in-law, she has had to deal with him and his family.

Ava discovered Sterling sitting in her living room, looking manly and capable. Wearing a dark periwinkle blue pinstripe suit, Sterling imparts an aura of superiority that Ava has hated for years. She meets his bluish-green eyes that no longer affect her.

"Well, it's about time. I've been waiting over an hour for you," he said, his voice thunderous.

"Pardon me," Ava laughed. "You do have a reason for being here?"

"You can't use that teasing tone. I won't stand for it."

"Oh no, this is my house, not ours," she bursts out.

Confused by her ex-husband, Ava glances over her shoulders and sees her maid nearby.

"Please bring a tray of fresh coffee," she instructed Lucy.

Taking her seat, she mocks him by shivering. "Your growling has improved, though I'm not frightened by you in the least.

Grunting and uncrossing his legs, Sterling looks at Ava. "I thought you might want to know what our son has done."

Ava smiled a little but took the hint. "Do tell," she deliberately gave a backward wave.

Sterling cursed softly. "Lance has rescheduled the board's weekend meeting to attend a religious event."

"Lance wouldn't do such a thing," she snarled. "Who told you that lie?"

"You don't understand," Sterling stood. "I received word from his assistant that the weekend meeting will convene next week."

"Wait a minute, Sterling," Ava said, her voice shrieking. "But who told you about that religious event?"

"Lance's assistant!" he spit out. "Plus, a few newspapers announced a two-day statewide Christmas meeting for men."

Ava was angry at Sterling's accusation, and she decided she needed a distraction. Lucy arrived minutes later, and Ava pretended to help Lucy with the tray.

"Something tells me you think Lance is in trouble," Ava spoke up.

"Yes! What are we going to do?"

"Nothing," she sighed. "Caroline is the chairwoman of

the board, and it is apparent she approved his request. Relax, there's nothing to worry about."

Sterling saw Ava's hand lay firmly in her lap and her expression serene. He did as he was told.

CHAPTER 12

Pleasing The Tornado

P erry, a minister within his church, worked closely with the leaders of the conference. Unbeknownst to Lance, Perry's position enabled them to gain seats close to the stage in Madison Square Garden. Since God was not part of his vocabulary, he was mystified by thousands of men in attendance. Lance always believed everyone had the power within to be a moral, respectable person.

The morning services opened with prayer, singing, and breakout sessions on such topics: *guarding your mind, understanding financial woes, and a life full of roadblocks.* Lance listened carefully to each speaker, thankful for the detailed outlines provided. He found the speakers very helpful and was excited about how each session covered points that reflected his own life. Throughout the three-hour lunch break, Lance marveled at the men, who had forgotten their life's problems and were looking to a higher power for answers.

The night service was magical; Lance gazed around the stadium utterly flabbergasted, thousands of men holding their hands upward, praying, singing, and worshipping in unison. Peace and joy were inundating the place. It took everything within Lance to maintain a closed mouth and rationalize what he was experiencing. Never knowing anything about the bible or God, this single moment held great power, revealing to him the beauty of knowing God.

At the end of the worship service, two men from the audience were introduced. What happened next baffled Lance. Each told his story, how, since accepting Jesus into their lives, they have received answers to all their dilemmas in life. Before Lance could digest the testimonies, the main speaker of the evening, dressed in jeans and a white tieless shirt, walked up to the podium. In addition to his greetings, he solemnly admonished all the men to open their bibles to the book of Revelation, chapter 3:20:

Behold, I stand at the door and knock; if any man hears my voice and opens the door, I will come into him and will sup with him, and he with me.

Relieved the verses were on the big jumbotrons, Lance read along with everyone else. Smiling, the speaker looked out at the gathering of men and asked a question.

"Have you answered the knock?"

Lance stroked his furrowed brow and glanced around to

see if anyone else was puzzled by the question. The speaker continued. "At one time, I was a young man who was sure of my abilities. Then, one day, my wise father urged me to study Jesus's invitation diligently. Initially, I dismissed the invitation from Christ until my life started to unravel, becoming empty and purposeless. My own beliefs became filthy rags."

"This verse signifies Jesus standing at the door of your heart, knocking and waiting to be invited in. It tells us Jesus wants to have a close relationship with you. But he isn't going to force himself in, and you must choose to open the door and let him in. It's alarming to think Jesus is standing outside your heart knocking. You mustn't be smug in your beliefs and leave Jesus standing in the cold. Living by your rules is foolish."

"Let's read Romans 3:23-24." *For all have sinned and fall short of the glory of God and are justified freely by his grace through the redemption that is in Christ Jesus.*

"Without exception, each of us has committed sin and is therefore unable to reach God's perfect standard on our own. But through God's grace and the sacrifice of Jesus Christ, we can be declared righteous and forgiven. Brethren, have you answered the invitation, or are you wondering if you should? Do you persist in trusting your self-worth, or are you bold enough to place your trust in Jesus and open your heart's door. 1John 1:9 tells us,"

If we confess our sins, he is faithful and just to forgive us our sins, and to cleanse us from all unrighteousness.

"Anyone who accepts the invitation will have a new life that defies human explanation."

Lance twisted his body side to side in his seat. Both what he heard tonight and what Grace's pastor had said—the ideas were identical. *Being self-assured and trusting in myself was another way of being self-righteous.* Lance hung his head down and sighed. *I am tackling my problem with Grace wrong; should I turn my life over to God?* Lance's face clouded with torment. *What will my family say and think?*

Near the end, the worshipping team took the stage and began to sing "Amazing Grace." Lance glanced around the stadium, and he noticed hundreds of men dressed like the speaker were moving and standing in different locations of the stadium with open arms.

"Are you ready to answer the invitation? If your answer is yes, our prayer warriors are in your section, waiting for you to open the door and let Christ in."

Lance wistfully wanted to walk to the front of the stage to have someone pray for him, but his feet were immovable. Intensely, he watched the stage area fill up with men until he couldn't tell where the stage began. Lance knew God was his answer, but he simultaneously justified why he shouldn't move from his seat.

The color drained out of Lance's face while he watched men jumping for joy; contentment spread through them, and tears flowed down their faces. Lance pivoted to his left and faced Perry, his face blooming with hope.

"I will walk with you to the altar," Perry whispered

A teardrop fell down Lance's cheek as he shook his head no.

Perry touched his friend's shoulder and quietly prayed for him.

Finally, the services ended. Perry excused himself for a moment to speak with his pastor, who was on stage. Lance remained in his seat waiting for his friend while men surged to the stage to meet the speaker and praise team. Suddenly, a group of men came toward him.

"So happy to see you!" a lawyer introduced himself from Atlanta.

"What a powerful move of God," said another, a bank president from California who introduced himself.

Other men were approaching Lance to convey their delight in the retreat. These were men who worked professional and nonprofessional jobs from around the world. Somehow, when it was all over, Lance felt, in some way, he identified with each of them as they shared parts of the experience at the retreat. It was a strange feeling, better than when he received his pilot license to fly large aircrafts.

Perry spent the good part of the drive to Lance's apartment recalling the previous days and nights of the retreat. Lance listened attentively while he studied Perry. It was clear how different they were from one another, yet they grew to be good friends.

The Sunday meal after church services was progressing as it usually did. Grace was at her parents' home for dinner, surrounded by her brothers, Wyatt and Edmond. There was one major difference this late afternoon: Lance was the main topic at the table.

"Would you like more rice and beans, Grace?"

"No, thank you, Mother, I've had enough."

Grace fell silent then and continued to look at her plate of food. Her parents exchanged looks of concern while her two brothers were working on a second helping of fried chicken with red beans and rice.

"Grace, you look preoccupied," Stone commented, while Labella served him another serving of food.

"Father, I do believe you saw him. It's incredible, Lance attended a men's retreat," Grace said with wonder.

"There's no conceivable reason why he shouldn't attend."

"True. But father, you saw his reluctance to know God during his weekend visits."

Stone chuckled. "I still believe that God can change Lance, don't you?"

Grace's eyes focused on her father for a moment. "Yes," she replied in return, trying to dispel the feeling of doubt.

"Why the doubts?" Labella asked.

"I had a dream that Lance is in dire need of help."

It wasn't easy for Grace to denounce her love for Lance. She was still thinking, wrestling, and asking God for help when her father interrupted her.

"My wee one, let's be clear. Lance needs God's help, not yours," Stone explained. "I will admit, seeing Lance at the retreat altered my assessment of his character."

For the moment Grace decided she would continue asking God for strength to wait on his perfect timing.

Monday afternoon, Perry stood in front of an imposing building in midtown Manhattan. Determined not to be intimidated by the considerable accumulation of plaques on the exterior, he felt anxious. Within minutes, Perry was upstairs in the building and immersed in the culture of corporate power.

A moment later, he was escorted into Lance's office and was welcomed with open arms. Perry's gaze went to the enormous conference table full of Italian food. Joining Lance at the table, Perry's laughter rang out.

"You can laugh, my friend, but I acted the same way a few months ago," Lance said good-naturedly. "Do you want to be served?" Lance continued teasing.

"No," Perry chuckled. "Thank you for the lunch invitation."

"You're welcome," Lance smiled. "Perry, please give thanks for the feast before us." Perry did so, and then told Lance how happy he was to share lunch with him.

While they ate their delectable lunch with great attention, Perry and Lance engaged in small talk.

"Do you want seconds?" Lance checked with Perry.

"I don't think I can eat another bite," Perry groaned.

Both men laughed at each other. "I believe between the two of us, we ate like an army," Lance joked.

"Lance, I was truly delighted to have your company at the retreat."

"Oh," Lance rubbed his chin. "It was really different for me."

Perry searched his friend's face; not lost from his memory was Lance's heavy breathing during the altar call, yet, he sensed Lance's yearning to join in.

"Really different…Lance? How *different?*"

His tone was suddenly so serious that Lance stared at Perry.

"I think," he began uncertainly, "because God was never a part of my upbringing."

"I respect that, but how do you feel after Saturday?"

"I want you to know, Perry, I spent a lot of time observing the people and the environment to understand the dynamics."

"What was your conclusion?"

"I haven't been able to talk to anyone, not even my family. There was a sense of peace I felt that day, and I can't stand that I'm not a part of it," Lance softly said.

"Lance, my belief in him is a choice I'm happy with."

"How can I have that kind of relationship?" Lance inquired. For the first time in months, he felt he could forgive himself with God's help.

Perry wanted to shout hallelujah but now wasn't the time. Perry's voice was gentle, and he answered. "Admit you're a sinner and confess your sins. Romans 10:9-10 says," *That if thou shall confess with thy mouth, the Lord Jesus, and shalt believe in thine heart that God hath raised him from the dead, thou shalt be saved. For with the heart, man believeth unto righteousness; and with the mouth, confession is made unto salvation.*

A heavy silence fell between them, and Perry prayed silently, asking for patience from God. He didn't want to say things that would drive Lance further from the truth. *You're not the one who saves,* Perry said to himself.

Lance's gaze went to the painting of his grandfather on the wall facing him. He had been tempted to confess his sins but changed his mind. He was vaguely aware of Perry watching him and waiting. Lance had become a part of his world, and now he was indecisive and fearful.

"Well," Lance smiled, looking at his watch. I'm obliged to attend a staff meeting in a few moments," Lance announced.

"No worries."

Each man stood up. Perry couldn't resist hugging his friend, an embrace Lance gladly returned. With a prayerful heart, Perry's long legs ate up the distance from the table to the door.

Lance sighed. *Why do I feel as though I've lost out on a great opportunity? One would be tempted to try this man Jesus.* Lance couldn't help but wonder if that was why he felt that Perry was a better person because of his beliefs.

Before the end of the day, Lance opened his mail; his termination papers from the airline had arrived with one stimulation, he must complete ten hours. As for his future with God and Grace, it wasn't yet known.

1981 London England

Just two days before Lance was to leave for London on his final flight, he called his mother and grandmother to inform them. Sitting in the cockpit, Lance quietly contemplated the fiercest opposition he would encounter if he accepted Christ. He decided his only way out was to give up on this religion thing.

Successfully landing in London, he was an alternate pilot of three for a flight from London to Auckland, New Zealand. After the required rest period by the airline, Lance joined his new crew the morning after the New Year.

Mid-way to Auckland, one of the pilots awakened Lance for his shift in the cockpit. The plane was cruising at 37,000 feet with 248 passengers and 15 crew members on board; everything was going as planned. Around 10:42 p.m., south of Jakarta, Indonesia, the number four engine began surging and then flamed out. A minute later, engine number two also surged and flamed out. Then, simultaneously, engines one and three failed as well.

The engines had ingested volcanic dust from the erupting Mount Gallunggung, a 7,115-foot stratovolcano located in West Java, which had melted the inside of the combustion chambers, cutting off the airflow and shutting each engine down. The large 747 started to glide, and the flight crew immediately turned the plane toward Jakarta while they went through emergency procedures. Lance calmly made an announcement:

Ladies and gentlemen, this is your captain speaking. We have a small problem. All four of our engines have stopped. We are doing our darnedest to get them going again. I trust you are not in much distress.

His statement was an ironic twist to how the passengers reacted to the announcement. At 13,500 feet, the flight crew was finally able to get one engine restarted, and, soon after, a second. Eventually, all four engines were running, and they began to regain altitude. However, the number two engine again began to surge, so the crew shut it down, and the aircraft remained at 12,000 feet.

On approach to Jakarta, the windshield of the plane was completely sandblasted by the volcanic dust, and the airport lights were barely visible. With God's help, the plane landed safely without injuries. It seems the airplane had kissed the ground.

After the plane was repaired, the crew flew it back to London for further extensive repairs. More than a little shaken, Lance had no doubts about the decision he had been wrestling with.

Penville, North Carolina

The sun had gone down sharply, leaving the mountains in a dark purple haze. The air was radiant with lovely lights. In the valley off in one of the fashionable neighborhoods, the Forrester had no more than finished their Sunday dinner when a still coldness settled down over them.

They sat on the edge of their seats, and everyone's mouths opened. *60 Minutes* News was reporting on a recent brush with the disaster of a 747 plane over the Indonesian Ocean. Grace shuddered, grappling with their preliminary announcement. For several consecutive minutes, she sat, her eyes cast down, but her overwrought mind kept jerking back to the news. Horrified by the reporter's news, Grace could barely comprehend what had happened. She somehow knew that Lance had been involved in this episode. Then, she heard the newscaster confirming her fears:

Lance Worthington, CEO of Worthington's Steel and former pilot of New York, lost all four engines but was able to restart three engines to land the aircraft safely.

The sounds of the doorbell shattered the stunned observers. Stone arose, leaving the room without any disturbances.

"Zory," he greeted her. "What brings you out tonight?"

"I've been calling Grace with no success," she said, her mind on the task of finding Grace.

"Really, now?" Stone smiled, letting Zory inside.

"Is she here?" Zory asked, wanting to scream Grace's name.

Stone was silent for a moment, and Zory wriggled under his watchful eyes.

Urgently, she spoke again. "Mr. Forrester, is she here?"

Stone chuckled. "I don't believe anything could change your impulsiveness. Follow me."

Zory blushed at his true statement. Preparing to follow him, she heard voices from the living room. She scurried past

Stone and approached the family, gawking at the TV set.

"You'll not guess what I heard," she proclaimed, her cheeks flushed.

Blank faces glared at her. It dawned on Zory that Grace was unresponsive, and her body was angled in a way so that her face was turned completely away from the television screen. Uncertain of what mess she had stumbled upon, Zory faced Labella, whose expression showed agitation. By contrast, Labella usually tolerated Zory's impetuous outbursts, which usually created problems. But today was different; she didn't want to waste her time explaining to Zory that she needed to be quiet.

"Zory," Labella said at last. "You're certainly focusing on getting everyone's attention. I take it you think it's important."

Put so bluntly, Zory hesitated but eventually nodded.

"In that case, I need you to take a seat and keep quiet."

Zory's face paled at these words. Sitting down on a chair near the doorway, she wished she had turned off her enthusiasm.

Several moments later, Labella spoke. "I didn't mean to be so harsh," she said, putting a hand on Zory's shoulder.

"I'm glad," said Zory. "But I have some incredible news for Grace."

Stone smiled, "Let it fly, Zory."

Zory relayed the exciting news told to her by her co-worker who attended the same church as Lance's friend, Perry. Lance had accepted Christ. Zory's explanation of how and when Lance accepted Christ left her out of breath, and everyone was shocked. Shaken by the news, Grace was feeling anxious and wanted to be alone with her thoughts, to process this incredible news. She informed everyone that she needed to go home.

"¿Qué Pasa?" Labella questioned her daughter.

"Yo necesito estar solo."

"Grace, gather your things. Your brothers and I will take you home. Your car will be delivered tomorrow," Stone said kindly.

"No, Father, it isn't necessary, I assure you."

"Go along, now," he said softly, his eyes watchful.

Grace moved to gather her things without another word. When she was ready, she bid her mother and friend good night, promising Zory, she would call her soon. Riding in her brothers' car, Grace listened to Andrae Crouch's gospel songs on their eight-track tape until she reached home.

A half-hour later, Grace was relieved to be home, yet her mind scrambled with many questions. Soaking in a hot bath, she had a long talk with the Lord. By the time Grace climbed into bed, she acknowledged that she wasn't the one in control. At the moment, she was very glad.

New York, New York

Lance stood outside his apartment building, pulling up his windbreaker collar, preparing to take his short run in the nearby park. The crisp winter air resulted in fewer crowds on the streets while the cleanup crews were busy removing the festival remnants from the holiday season. His mile run came faster than he anticipated, and he soon was back at the apartment.

Lance wasn't certain how Grace would receive him, but after talking with his grandmother, he made a difficult decision that could win Grace back. Lowering himself behind the desk, he wrote a letter.

Dear Grace,

I'm sorry I haven't written to you prior to this time. It was difficult to express my sincere apologies for my unspeakable cowardliness, which prevented me from fighting for us. I deeply regret my actions and understand the impact they had on you. I take full responsibility for my behavior.

Surrendering my life to Christ has forced me to examine every facet of our past relationship. Grace, loving you was easy. I need you to trust me once again. My dreams of you being my life mate haven't changed. A letter from you would be welcome. I am hopeful you can forgive me and give our relationship another opportunity.

Please take care. I love you.
Lance

A couple of days later, Lance hungrily opened the personal mail, his assistant laid on his desk. The return address indicated it was from Grace. Breathless, with nervous hands, he opened the letter.

Dear Lance,

Thank you for your letter. I could sense it wasn't easy for you to write. I pray for you daily, and thankful for your new life in Him. These months have been a time of reflection for me. In the short time we were together, you became very dear to me. But I'm genuinely skeptical about opening my heart again too soon. God has a plan for our lives, and we must be willing to wait for his lead. If we wait on his timing, it will teach us patience while we trust and rely on him. Please write again. I love you.
Grace.

It was brief but enlightening. He tipped his chair back, repeating over and over the last six words of her letter. He urgently wanted to discuss the letter with his grandmother.

"Ms. Hall, please check to see if my grandmother is available."

Ms. Hall raised her eyebrows, her face lit with a smile. She wasn't sure what caused his elation, but in the last week, Lance's character had vividly changed, emitting an oasis of serenity amidst the bustling within the office.

Leaving his assistant's desk, Lance did a little dance step, receiving a jaw-dropping look at his merriment. It didn't occur to him how startled his grandmother would be by his unannounced summons to his office until she entered wide-eyed with trepidation.

"Lance?" she questioned him without thought. "What's wrong? Are you having trouble with the executives about the acquisition?"

"I apologize, Grandmother; I didn't mean to upset you. I just need to divulge to you, a bit of good news where the plot thickens."

Caroline took a moment to calm her nerves, then uncharacteristically dropped heavily in a chair, causing Lance to laugh.

"You gave me a fright," she admonished him, shaking her finger at him.

"I must admit, I enjoyed seeing my graceful grandmother flop into a chair."

"What's the good news?" she winked; her curiosity awakened.

"I heard from Grace," he replied. "She still loves me!" he flung his arms up in the air.

Lance didn't realize until that moment how delightful it was to have such an understanding and loving grandmother behind him. She was the one who encouraged him to pursue Grace, and he was extremely happy about his newfound love for God.

"How does the plot thicken?"

His voice softened. "She wants us to wait on God's timing and to write again."

"My son, do what Grace instructed," Caroline smiled. "Writing to each other is another way of courting. Be patient, and you'll be rewarded."

He grinned, delighted at the new special relationship that had grown between him and Caroline. Lance curled his arms around his grandmother, hugging her to his chest. Her heart was full of joy, and Caroline floated out of his office. She knew Ms. Grace Forrester would soon be her new and only granddaughter, a lovely addition to the family.

CHAPTER 13
Stolen Tomorrow

Long Island

It had taken quite a bit of tactful negotiating, but Lance and Caroline had accepted Ava's small, intimate Valentine's Day luncheon. After his near-death experience, Lance had called her several times in the last four weeks. However, she had a gnawing suspicion she couldn't shake. Looking elegant in a ruby red and gold hostess dress accented with slim satin pants, Ava welcomed her guests with open arms.

When lunch was finally ready, Lance opened the conversation.

"Mother, I believe in God now."

Ava looked at Caroline and then her son with honest confusion.

"Lance, this world is full of fools who believe in a higher being. But you were taught to believe in your superior intellect."

Lance looked at her, troubled. "I found out I was a sinner who needed a savior. Our sinful actions are sometimes so mute we are ignorant of the need for God."

Ava was still looking at Lance as though she had missed something, but her mother-in-law was delighted.

"I don't have time for this. Our meal will get cold."

Lance remained quiet and recited in his mind James 1:5."

If any lack wisdom, let him ask of God, that giveth to all men liberally, and unbraided not, and it shall be given him.

Lunch had been over an hour, with Ava constantly chattering. With a heavy heart, Lance squirmed in his seat. Caroline had noticed his discomfort, and opted to start the conversation again on religion.

"Lance, I would love to hear more about God," Caroline stated.

"If you are going to talk about that nonsense, I'm leaving," Ava's voice was high-pitched.

"Ava, sit; what harm would it do to listen to your son?"

Ava had little choice but to agree. She wondered if that was why he accepted her invitation.

"Please, Mother, I would love to finish our conversation."

Ava nodded.

Lance continued, "It all began when I attended a men's retreat with my friend, where I discovered I lived a life only for myself. But now I am living a better life having God a part of it."

"Your life is now pointless if you don't denounce this foolhardiness. You'll humiliate yourself and the family. Stop this now, before it's too late," Ava wailed.

"I disagree with your assessment, Ava," Caroline said quietly. "He's better for it."

Ava just stared at them. She would have continued doing so, but Lance reached across and took her hands.

"Nothing else in my life had value until I gave my life over to God."

Removing her hands from his clasp, she snapped. "You have attached yourself to a fanatic group."

"No, Mother, I have a personal relationship with God," Lance said. "I was introduced to the promise of everlasting life. John 3:16 shows me.

For God so loveth the world that he gave his only begotten son, and whosoever believeth on him shall not perish, but have everlasting life.

Ava left the room without another word.

"Ava will see reason, Lance," Caroline wasted no time to say.

"Thank you, Grandmother, for understanding my new life."

Penville, North Carolina

The afternoon dawned beautifully. Grace was sitting on her porch, speechless after reading Lance's latest letter.

My dearest Grace,

It never struck me that we could communicate this way, expressing our most profound emotions, desires, and dreams. But I want to thank you for the gracious manner you've received my letters. We have answered many hard questions and learned from them. Above all else, I know we have grown closer, though we're apart. My love for you hasn't vanished, it flourishes every day. Though we couldn't be together on Valentine's Day, remember, I believe we belong to one another, and soon being together will be a reality.

Love, Lance

It didn't matter that she hadn't heard or seen Lance in months, but she felt better receiving his letters. She could have questioned the meaning behind his last letter. If the words *soon to be a reality* could be trusted, she would see Lance momentarily.

Tired from a hard week at the clinic, the Forrester family was preparing for an evening of relaxation. They were startled to see Lance on their front porch. Stone quickly understood that Lance was there to discuss an urgent matter. Knowing Lance was now a believer and after the exchanging of letters, he couldn't dismiss the love between Lance and Grace. But marriage possessed a very delicate balance for him and Labella.

Although Lance and Grace were in God's hands, yet a union with the powerful Worthington family brought certain emotions to the surface for the Forrester. Stone, in particular, felt misgivings in view of Lance's past treatment of Grace. Stone and Labella went to the living room where the boys had taken Lance.

"Good evening, sir," Lance stood to shake Stone's hand.

"Please sit down, Lance," Stone replied. "How are you?"

"I'm all right," Lance smiled at everyone as Labella, Wyatt, and Edmond followed behind Stone.

Lance sat in the lone chair near the window, his hands gripping the chair's arms as all eyes were gazing at him.

"Tell us about this visit," Stone urged.

Lance anxiously informed them of his reason for being there. Labella realized in an instant how much Lance cared for her daughter. She should have been thrilled he wanted to marry Grace, but she wasn't. Labella had gone white as a sheet, and she couldn't forget his mother's stunt during the exhibit.

Stone was concerned by his wife's expression; with both of his hands, he grabbed her hands and lovingly laid them in his lap.

"I know you're afraid of my family," Lance said feebly. "But I love your daughter very much. Having Christ in my life has given me courage and clarity."

"It's good to know you realize our fears and doubts," Stone said honestly. "I take it you haven't spoken with Grace yet."

"Guilty as charged," he replied. "I'm here to ask your permission first to have your daughter's hand in marriage," Lance said humbly.

Full of concern, Stone asked, "Will this marriage be built in Christ?"

"Yes, sir, we are taking it very slowly."

Everyone was subdued in the room, and Stone and Labella wondered what Lance was thinking.

"Well, son, when do you plan to ask Grace."

Lance was so filled with wonderous joy that his mind wouldn't focus. He knew he couldn't wait much longer to have Grace as his wife, but he was going to face it with Jesus Christ by his side.

"I'm staying the weekend in Penville; I will call on her tomorrow."

Watching Lance twiddling his thumbs, Labella invited him to stay for dinner. Before leaving, Stone prayed for Lance and Grace's pending marriage.

Father, we ask you to give Lance and Grace wisdom and patience and that they keep you first in their life and marriage. Afterward, Stone and Labella hugged him tightly, shocking Lance speechless.

It's been a full week since Grace said yes to Lance's proposal. She avoided her usual Sunday dinner with her parents, going straight home after church. Alone in her kitchen, sitting on a stool, Grace was musing about her future. She wasn't ashamed to be Lance's wife, just desiring as little publicity as possible. The desire for solitude and the beauty of knowing she belonged with him was enough.

Grace was astonished she had received the approval from Worthington's matriarch, Caroline Worthington, who reminded Grace the importance of understanding her position as wife to the CEO of the Worthington dynasty. Caroline suggested that Grace must, like her, become a pillar of quiet strength for Lance.

Grace was dreading tomorrow's paper announcing their engagement. She was afraid of what Lance's mother would say and react. Grace's soul cried out: *Stop it!* She laughed softly. *Get a hold of yourself; how did you think life would be, married to Lance? You are so easy to falter at the sign of conflict.* "I am not!" Grace yells, but her voice lacks all conviction. *Where's your faith? God loves both of you, so stop letting the devil win.*

⁓

Ava had found her chat with Lance at the Valentine's luncheon emotionally taxing. Leaning against the fluffy headboard, she leisurely focused on the delicious breakfast the kitchen staff had prepared. Ava looked up in disbelief when her maid interrupted her solitude.

"Lucy, what's the meaning of this," Ava's voice hurled.

"Madame, I thought…" Lucy rooted in the doorway.

"Child! Spit it out." Ava sucked in a long breath. "Lucy, you're not a two-year-old, or are you?"

Lucy doesn't make eye contact while she speaks. "Congratulations, madame, on your son's engagement."

"What in blazes are you talking about!" Ava's voice cracked raw, slamming her utensils against the fine China plate.

Lucy lifted the paper in the air. "The paper states... he's getting married to a Ms. Forrester."

Ava rocketed from her bed, knocking the tray to the floor. Lucy ran to clean the mess while Ava snatched the paper from Lucy's hand, knocking her down. Ava read through the society page, and in bold letters:

The most eligible bachelor is going off the market. He is engaged to the beautiful Grace Forrester, the only daughter of the famous NFL player Stone Walled Forrester. Sorry, ladies, he's taken.

"No! No! No!" she yelled, the words vibrating the room. "Tell Jenkins to be outside in twenty minutes."

Lucy stands, brushing the remnants of eggs from her uniform's hem, vacantly staring at her mistress.

"Snap out of it!" Ava snapped her finger. "I said, go quickly," Ava yelled, breaking the spell. Lucy ran like dynamite had dropped in the room.

Ava couldn't envision being the mother-in-law to Grace Forrester. Dressing in record time, she was standing outside the front door waiting for Jenkins to drive up. Glancing at her watch every two minutes, hysterical, Ava was sure she was going to die of total annihilation from society.

The helpless feeling Ava was experiencing brought pain to her chest. She was totally absorbed in her anger. Jenkins studied his generally prudish boss, but now all her social norms had vacated. He steered his employer in the direction of New York. Jenkins noticed Ava's normally thin lips seemed to have disappeared into the folds of her mouth.

The sky was becoming gloomy, like her mood, when Ava entered the Worthington office building. From every corner of the offices, people gawked at her. Even though her head was throbbing, she continued to Lance's office. She wanted to make her position clear to Lance about his engagement. Before reaching his office, Caroline emerged, smiling extensively and stepping lightly. After Ava made a brief phony greeting, Caroline continued on her way.

Lance was relishing in the enchanting idea, that God had tremendously blessed him in such a short time. In addition to reclaiming Grace's love, he had successfully purchased the small steel company, and his preference for a wife endeared him to the board of Directors.

He was preparing to leave for a business lunch when Ava stormed past his assistant, bursting into his office. Deeply upset by the disturbance caused by Ava, he waved his hand to his assistant, saying, "Come in, Mother, this is a nice surprise."

Ava growled at him through clenched teeth. "I was under the impression that I'm your deceased mother."

Not knowing if Ava would accept the news and perplexed by her reprehensible attitude toward Grace, Lance couldn't bring himself to tell her the news. Hence, he confided in his grandmother.

"It seems you have a problem with me," Ava said rather coldly.

Lance hesitated before he spoke. "Mother... you prefer I would marry someone other than Grace."

"Disobeying me doesn't suit you," she told him.

"During my early life, I needed your guidance, but now I'm following God's guidance."

Ava clenched her fist and suddenly slammed her purse on Lance's desk, her voice rising.

"Did I hear you correctly?"

"Yes," Lance responded, standing up. "Please excuse me; I have a lunch commitment to attend."

Lance's impertinence was wearing on Ava's nerves, and it took a few minutes to regain her composure. "I was wondering when you would mention that God business again."

"God is a gigantic part of my life."

"I can see that," Ava stated, her face showing dread.

"I don't believe you do, Mother."

"Okay," Ava said, telling herself not to look at Lance. "This idea of you believing in God is inconceivable."

Lance nodded, but Ave returned that nod with a frown.

"Well," Ava began, her gaze taking in Lance's firm resolve, thinking any wrong word right now might permanently destroy her relationship with her son. "I'm just hurt you didn't come to me first."

Lance did not look convinced.

"Mother, I love Grace, and there's no other woman for me."

Ava was finding it hard to fight with him any further due to her exhaustion. Mortified, she soberly reached for her purse and stood, looking at Lance.

"Just the thought of you marrying Ms. Forrester makes my heart stony."

"Your heart will find a way to love Grace," Lance spoke with confidence.

Lance hugged his mother. "Mother, I love you," he said softly.

"Same here," Ava said, meaning it with all her heart.

Ava followed Lance out of his office while he gave instructions to his assistant. She waited for him in the massive waiting area. By the time Lance reached Ava, the rain had burst from a cloud. Lance leaned over and kissed his mother. "Mother, your car has been summoned," Lance said. "I'm sorry, but I must leave you; we will talk soon."

Ava looked at his loving eyes and told herself to drop this absurd squabbling. He will either survive on his own or be destroyed. Lifting her head high, she headed out to her waiting car. For long moments, she sat in the car, her eyes focused straight ahead, staring at nothing. Ava's head was pounding, and she wanted nothing more than to lie down, but an hour later, she was on her way to see her ex-husband.

Lance met up with his father at the bar of the men's club. Sterling had not spoken to Lance about his engagement, though Ava demanded he do so several weeks ago. Sterling didn't know what to say when Lance invited him and Betty to his engagement party.

"Father, I am ready for a change in our relationship…as much as I'm able to discern, like myself, you also have battled difficulties these past months. I'm committed to repairing our broken relationship and desirous of you to be a part of my life. Grace and I would be honored if you and your wife would attend our engagement party. We'd love to have you there."

He could hardly argue with Lance's truce. *And who knows,* Sterling thought to himself. *This could be a new beginning for him and his son.*

⁂

Caroline was elated to host Lance and Grace's engagement party. Arrangements had been made to have Grace, her family, and friends stay in the west wing of the estate. Chauffeur-driven cars were scheduled to pick up everyone at the airport and bring them to the Worthington Estate to spend the weekend.

Grace's family wasn't accustomed to such flaunted wealth. Arriving at the estate the second Friday of March, the Forrester imagination couldn't have prepared them for the ambiance of the Worthington's Estate. Exchanging looks, the family gazed at the road of lighted trees on the pathway to the estate.

"At any point, do you think we'll fit into this world?" Stone whispered to Labella.

"I honestly don't know."

"Grace, do you believe you're suited to be a Worthington?"

Before Grace could answer, Labella intercepted. "Absolutely, our daughter will enlighten every one of them," Labella chuckled.

Stone stared at his wife, gauging whether he should be concerned about his feisty Latin wife. "Bella, you will behave this weekend," Stone stated.

"Let God be in control," Labella groaned at that statement.

Several miles later, the Forrester gazed at the most formidable mansion. Stone wasn't the only one awestruck as the chauffeur opened the doors. Minutes later, all the guests were escorted inside an entryway fit for royalty. Stone, a man who likes a challenge, was sure his family were up for the job.

Caroline and Lance, alongside several maids and a butler, greeted their guests, inviting them to dine with them in an hour. The guests thanked their hostess, as it was the beginning of an enjoyable evening of meet and greet.

***

The next morning, the estate was filled with excitement. Caroline had arranged a day of sightseeing, shopping, and eating, returning in time to rest for the evening festivities for the engaged couple, family and friends.

The staff had worked hard to make Caroline's vision a reality. The long white tablecloth, adorned with hurricane lanterns, was filled with white lights and purple and pink flowers, highlighted by the 24-karat decorated porcelain dinnerware and crystal stemware. A string of lights cascading over the solarium provided illumination, focusing attention on the garden plants and the flowery-covered lattice in the adjacent rose garden.

Later that evening, in the enclosed rose garden of Worthington's Estates, Sterling held a shot glass of scotch and soda. His wife, Betty, was confounded by his impertinent expression and indifference.

"Sterling!" Caroline started when she walked into the enclosed garden to check on the hors d'oeuvre trays. "Please make sure the bar has supplies."

"Anything else?" Sterling asked.

"Nothing at the moment," Caroline said and motioned Betty to follow her into the solarium.

In the solarium, Rose, along with a few staff were adding the finishing touches.

"Beautiful," Betty and Caroline both said.

"Do we need to do anything else?" Rose asked, stepping back to permit the lady of the manor to examine their work.

"No, but have the cook bring out the cake."

Smiling with pure contentment, Rose responded, "Yes, my lady."

Moments later, the guests entered the enchanted garden. Caroline took the liberty to introduce Lance's father, step-mother, and mother to Grace's family and friends.

Lance and Grace haven't made their appearance yet, but the parade of maids and butlers buzzed around the guests while music serenaded everyone. Moments later, the honorees arrived, and the merriment began. But Zory wasn't feeling the cheerfulness; the opulence of the estate was comical to her. Zory, her face red, covered her mouth to muffle the sounds of laughter.

Penelope looked at Zory's face. "What so funny?"

"This," she said as she waved her hand. "Not to mention that Grace will be married to this."

Even Nora's voice was vague. "I wonder if Grace will ever properly fit into this family?"

"It's possible that she'll be a beacon of light for the family." Penelope chimed in, a distinct glitter in her eye.

"Good heavens, do you really believe Grace will be a suitable fit?" Zory snorted.

"Now, calm down. This is Grace's engagement party, and I know she wants this marriage to work," Nora said sternly from her place near her friends.

Socializing with the ultra-rich wasn't new to André since he was born into wealth. However, it took some time for Stone and the others to bypass Lance's parents' air of supe-riority and snobbishness. Thanks to the kindness and respect shown by Caroline, the evening was enjoyable.

Thirty minutes later, and after many shots of scotch and soda, Sterling dropped his snootiness and talked football with Stone and the men. Lance and Grace chatted with their friends as the older women talked among themselves.

Tapping his glass and receiving everyone's attention, Sterling held up his glass.

"We are here to celebrate the union of a lovely couple and two families. My son was fortunate to meet the most captivating woman, who agreed to be his wife. Raise your glasses as we honor the happy couple."

Everyone took a sip from their glass, and Caroline announced that dinner would be served shortly. Ava Worthington had been unusually quiet during the entire cocktail hour.

CHAPTER 14

From Bliss to Brokenness

When the cocktail hour was over, Caroline led her guests into the solarium, instructing them to look for their assigned seats. Soft guitar music floated into the room. Disregarding her son and daughter-in-law's prior pretentiousness, she was looking forward to a delicious meal. Immediately, the servers bought out the first three courses of a seven-course dinner.

"Please…allow me to apologize to everyone for the additional ten pounds or more," Caroline smiled while laughter roared around the table. During the serving of a fruit sorbet to cleanse the palate for the next course, an enchanting feminine voice drifted into the solarium.

"Lance…Lance…where are you…Lance…"

Laughter and friendly conversation around the table

abruptly ceased, and all heads turned in the direction of the voice. Sashaying in the room with Arthur close behind was Rachel, ignoring his calls.

"Ms. Van Fritzgerald, please…please wait."

Caroline frowned. She hadn't even thought about Rachel upsetting the evening. Taking one look at Rachel's revealing dress, she thought she might actually hate her.

"My lady, she wouldn't…" Arthur began…Caroline turns to Arthur, "You may be excused; I will handle this."

Arthur found it easy to leave the nasty woman to the lady of the manor. However, Lance hastily stood up without glancing in Grace's direction but placed a firm hand on her shoulder. Grace gave a faint smile, trying to keep the sudden pounding of her heart at bay.

"Rachel!" Lance screeched. "What are you doing here?

"My love," Rachel cried in delight… her eyes not missing the leers. "I came to congratulate you, but your grandmother's butler treated me obnoxiously."

Lance roared. "To put it frankly, you weren't invited." All eyes riveted from Lance to the sultry woman.

"Oh, don't be silly…your mother invited me. Plus, I couldn't miss your engagement party," Rachel hissed.

"Ms. Van Fitzgerald…" Caroline said kindly, "Please forgive my breach of manners, but I wasn't expecting you, as you can see," she said, nodding toward the full table. Caroline rises from the table with a respectful bow of her head. "Then, she turned to her guests… "Everyone, continue your dinner. I have no idea what the evening will bring." Caroline looked directly at Grace… "No need to worry."

The group watched in surprise as Caroline snatched Rachel's arm, literally lifting her off the floor as they departed.

Ava, all smiles, stood to follow them when Lance exploded. "Mother…how could you?" Lance, gagging on his words, said. "It was wrong for you to invite her without Grand-mother's or our approval."

"I see… it's okay for Grace to have friends, but not your friends."

"My dearest friend is here," he motions to Perry.

"But Rachel is also a dear friend; you couldn't let her miss this auspicious occasion."

"Rachel has never been a dear friend, and if you continue interfering in my life, you will never see me again. Do I make myself clear?"

Ava hesitated. She detected Sterling's smirk, and the others were ready to launch an attack on her. She slowly sunk into her chair.

"Allow me to re-introduce Ms. Rachel Van Fitzgerald, whom you met briefly at the exhibit event. Everyone, please let's try to finish this delicious meal," Caroline said cautiously. She instructed Rachel to be seated directly to her right while Arthur and Rose brought an additional chair and plate setting.

Stone heard himself groan within; his hand went to the back of his neck, rubbing at the pain there. He knew being a father, he wanted to take his rattled daughter in his arms. But there was no point; Lance was perfectly protecting Grace.

Grace had not planned on fighting with Rachel. In fact, this was the second time she had encountered her. She had been fairly contented in her state of euphoria. But when Caroline returned, she didn't want Rachel to spend another moment at her engagement party. Grace's tormented thoughts set her on edge. On the contrary, Rachel sat almost regal in her bearing, like an adversary or a queen about to seek vengeance upon her prey.

"Lance, I foolishly hoped it was going to be our engagement."

"I must tell you," Ava wasted no time in saying, "I've never gotten over Lance breaking off with you."

"That's impossible!" Lance responded. "I've never given you the impression we would be married."

"Lance, you shouldn't treat your guest curtly," Rachel meowed. "Have you forgotten your upbringing since you turned religious? I remember we used to have so much fun together. I pictured us enjoying our very own engagement party."

Rachel watched his chin propelled in the air, and his eyes raked her.

"That's enough, Rachel," Lance said, his voice sizzling.

"Since you found God, you think yourself somehow superior to me," Rachel said, agitated. "You never believed

230

in God before; why now? It's nothing but fallacies. The Bible is just a collection of mythical literature. That's what we were taught in college."

"Don't start hurling accusations, making yourself feel better. I've told you and Mother that I've a relationship with God and that both of you need him, too."

Rachel had the good refinement to look ashamed.

"Rachel, I think it's best you leave," Lance offered, praying that her social grace would dictate her leaving.

"I'm sorry, Ava, I really must be off. I just wanted to honor my invitation and offer my congratulations to Lance."

Not a soul in the room believed her, but no one wanted to chance the ordeal being prolonged, so there were no replies. And thankfully, it was over. Ms. Rachel Van Fritzgerald came to her feet and graciously said her goodbyes. Arthur, standing nearby, saw her out.

Forgetting the remaining courses, the room emptied except for Lance and Grace. They looked at the entryway before turning to each other.

"Are you alright?" Lance asked.

"Why wouldn't I be?"

"Maybe the past, painful memories played in your mind this evening."

Grace's look was indecipherable, and Lance wondered if he'd hit close to the mark.

Several moments passed until Caroline poked her head back into the solarium.

"We are going to finish our dinner in the garden; come and join us when you're ready. Incidentally, your mother had the decency to leave, too."

"We will," Lance replied without hesitation.

Lance took his fiancé's hands, kissing them tenderly, desperately wishing he could explain his mother's behavior. With no desire for the rest of the evening to be ruined, holding each other they joined the party.

On Monday morning, Lance found his office inundated with calls from Ava. His mother was in her definitive role of meddling, and viewing how it hurt those he loved, he silently prayed.

Father, my mother has done something that I can't forgive. I have tried to respect her, but what she did at my engagement party, I could've slapped her in the face. At that moment, I hated her. I can't help it. She did an awful thing that is unforgivable. I love you, Father, but this is so hard to bear.

Perry's message from Sunday on Ephesians 4: 31-32 bombarded Lance's mind.

Let all bitterness, and wrath, and anger, and clamor, and evil speaking, be put away from you, with all malice: and be ye kind to one another, tenderhearted, forgiving one another even as God in Christ forgave you.

His grandmother's advice was also a confirmation. *Don't get trapped in your mother's web, you will never find someone like Grace ever again.*

Meanwhile, perched on a lounge chair outside her Woodland courtyard surrounded by bushes filled with flowers, Ava was thrashing herself in a frenzy over her unanswered calls. Several moments later, immaculately dressed, Ava let, a low growl escaped her throat, demanding Jenkins to bring the car around. Minutes later, she was headed to downtown New York.

Reaching her destination, Ava hurried ruthlessly to the private elevator in the apartment building. Within minutes, the doors open, and like puppies wagging their tails at arriving guests, Rachel and Ava smiled with conviction.

While sitting on an L-shaped sofa, their heads joined, they whisper for no apparent reason. When Ava dared to look up, Rachel tentatively bent Ava's head down once more. They knew that they must not pause, not till everything was said. Once the plot was planned, Ava rose promptly and skittled to the elevator. She mustn't linger or look back. Ava raced into the elevator where Jenkins was waiting with her car.

Ava felt deadly weary without being sleepy. Her body was filled with exhaustion, but her mind was moving out of control. Rachel was her only hope to attain her goal. She let her eyelids droop over her tired eyes, and a few slow tears welled up from the depths of her misery. Choking them down, she slipped into a deep sleep. When she awakened, Jenkins had opened the door.

⁓

Friday brought warmer temperatures, turning the leaves to vivid reds, yellows and oranges. The mountains surrounding Penville were overflowing with the song of spring. Filled with excitement at the thought of seeing Lance, Grace was stunned to receive a note she had a visitor waiting in one of the exhibit halls.

Believing Lance had arrived early, Grace nearly ran. Stopping hastily inside, Grace couldn't collect her thoughts nor rationalize the reason why Rachel Van Fritzgerald stood several feet from a painting. Hearing a loud gasp, Rachel turned slowly around, confronting her enemy, as a great wave of queasiness roars inside Grace.

"What do you mean coming to my place of work, Ms. Van Fitzgerald."

"You and I have some unfinished business to discuss."

"We have nothing to talk about, and the only business I see is you leaving at once," Grace lifted her chin high.

"Oh," Rachel said lightheartedly. "I'm surprised; Ms. Perfect has claws."

"I will not tolerate your insubordinate attitude," Grace spoke with authority. "You are chasing an unattainable idea, Ms. Van Fritzgerald."

"I'm delectable and curious. Did Lance tell you we weren't just friends, we were lovers?"

Grace hesitated before she spoke. "Yes, he did."

"You're lying!" Rachel spit out.

"I have no reason to," Grace snickered. "Our mutual intimacy can't compare to your tryst."

Rachel stared brazenly into Grace's eyes.

"Don't get ahead of yourself," Rachel crackled. "You're simply not on my level, darling."

"You're right, I'm superior to you…darling."

The workroom pulsed with raw, crackling energy; the air thick with Rachel's seething anger. A low grumble thundered from deep within Rachel's heaving chest. The once primeval blue dress she wore now seemed to rise and fall from the intensity of her fury toward Grace.

"You're unworthy to have a man like Lance."

"Funny thing, I'm wearing his ring," Grace responded. "Apparently, I am worthy!"

Rachel's mask had received a direct sting.

"Days before you became engaged, Lance and I enjoyed a passionate evening," Rachel fluttered.

Grace didn't flinch. Without a word, she turned on her heels and walked out, leaving a dazed Rachel behind.

⁓

"Have I told you," Lance began, catching Grace in the kitchen that evening, "How much I love you."

Grace smiled as his arms went around her and looked into his eyes. "I needed to hear those words."

Lance cuddled her close and said, "Glad I could help." But hearing a soft sigh of weariness, he reached down, lifting her chin to look into her eyes. "Anything I need to know?"

"You wouldn't want your dinner spoiled," Grace said just before the doorbell rang.

"We will finish our talk later," he kissed her.

Obvious to everyone at the dining table, Grace was troubled. She had worked steadily to avoid recreating the dialog regarding her unwelcome guest. Labella couldn't tolerate another minute of Grace's fixation on her silverware.

"Can we help you, Mija?" Labella sweetly offered, seeing Grace's obsession with her fork.

"Well, Rachel visited me at the museum today.

"Her reason?" Stone asked.

"I wasn't acceptable to marry into the Worthington family," Grace murmured.

Around the table, faces masked by calm, now contorted into sneers, veins bulging everywhere, as eyes narrowed to burning slits.

Lance sighed deeply. "Tell me exactly what she declared to you."

Grace didn't like revisiting her conversation with Rachel; nonetheless, she held her place, her shoulders high, and conveyed the information. She only moved once to take a sip of water for her parched throat. Grace watched her parents and the man she loves become frustrated.

"Mother is behind this?" Lance spoke with conviction and then conveyed his mother's words to him.

Whatever the cost, I will not lose my dream of being the Matriarch of Worthington's fortune. Even if it means destroying you in the process.

They fell silent then.

"I need to rest, Lance."

No one replied but immediately left the table for the sofa.

"What will we do?" Grace asked.

Lance answered immediately. "If necessary, we will get married promptly."

Stone was pleased that Lance was taking responsibility and believed this was the perfect timing to talk with the young couple.

"After the incident at your engagement party, your mother and I wanted to impart a piece of wisdom to you both. Hearing today's encounter, I'm clear we are doing the right thing," Stone said, his intense gaze holding the couple for a moment.

"Love is a tremendous gift and burden, and marriage is more than just hope and luck," Labella explained.

"Your mother is right," Stone interjected. "Marriage requires enormous work because it's a living entity, needing everlasting attention."

"It will push you, bend you, and test you beyond your wildest dreams, and if either party is not prepared for any of that, it will shatter one or both parties," Labella added.

"But doesn't being in love make all the work easier?" Lance questioned.

"To a degree," Stone chuckled. "The hard work doesn't eliminate the problems that will arise. Remember, my son and daughter, sacrifice is a requirement to survive the pains and heartaches you may encounter."

"Lance, we have come to appreciate your love for our daughter," Labella said, "But be aware, we have entrusted you to take care of our daughter with your life."

"I promise to love and care for Grace with all my existence."

Their work done, Stone and Labella told the couple goodnight. They could tell Lance and Grace wanted to talk alone. Stone and Labella rode home in quietness, trying to understand what God would take them through next.

The Worthington Estate

As March gave way to the first Friday of April, Labella and Grace arrived at the Worthington Estate to meet and work with the wedding coordinator Caroline had hired. They have been busy all morning in the Paris room, rummaging through tons of books and magazines. In view of Ava's accusations and hatred toward Grace, she had no part in the planning of the wedding.

"Have you any news on Ava?" Labella asked.

"Not lately, and I prefer that it stays that way."

Labella didn't comment on Grace's statement. Indeed, Ava's absence was beneficial to everyone.

The coordinator declined lunch due to a pressing appointment. Caroline made her genteel goodbye, and the women entered the breakfast room for lunch.

"Grace, you were wonderful with the coordinator."

"Thank you, Caroline," Grace whispered as the two embraced, taking their seats.

Caroline found the Forrester to be a kind and understanding people. She had hoped Ava would accept them. Regrettably, anyone Ava deemed unworthy received only her wrath.

"You're worried about Ava, aren't you?" Caroline accurately interpreted her look.

Grace gave a reluctant nod.

"You needn't be. Lance, your mother, and I will not let her continue bullying you."

Grace sighed, and Labella chuckled. A moment later, Lance entered, announcing he was starving.

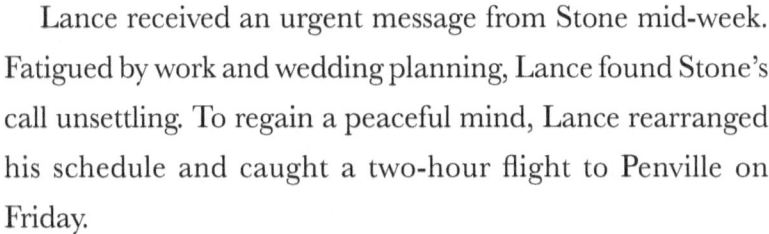

Lance received an urgent message from Stone mid-week. Fatigued by work and wedding planning, Lance found Stone's call unsettling. To regain a peaceful mind, Lance rearranged his schedule and caught a two-hour flight to Penville on Friday.

Lance, his mind racing, scrambled to leave the plane and pick up a rental car. Finally arriving at the Forrester's home, he scurried by Labella, looking for Grace.

"Grace, Grace!" Lance called nonstop until he reached the family room.

Lance was sweating with his heart racing; he had a sense of terror while standing in the doorway.

Grace's expressionless face knocked him off balance. Stone, with a deep scowl across his forehead, stood next to Grace; Lance nodded at him.

"Will someone please tell me what's wrong," he asked.

Sitting next to Grace, Labella shook her head in frustration.

"Oh, please, darling…" Grace shook her head in obvious pain, shocking Lance in the process. "Please…is there anything I can do?"

Stone took Lance by the shoulder and moved him to the loveseat opposite where Grace and Labella sat.

"Sit down, son."

"Lance, Grace has been systematically harassed since she and Labella stayed at your grandmother's," Stone's voice was tinged with irritation.

"Stone," Lance asked in fear as he looked toward his fiancé, having seen thunderclouds on Labella and Stone's faces. "How?"

"She was followed from work on several occasions. A couple of nights, she heard footsteps outside her bedroom windows."

"One night… someone attempted to get into the house," Labella said, upset. "At that point, her brothers brought her home."

"Once she moved back home, the phone calls with heavy breathing at the museum and letters of intimidation started to arrive," Stone said with compassion.

Feeling as though he could be quite ill, Lance's eyes slid shut. He had not anticipated this coming. He hadn't truly understood what his mother or Rachel was capable of doing in the name of love. Grace was near hysteria; even her cheekbones were hollow. A sob broke in his throat as he moved to hold her in his arms.

"Son, this can't go on; what are you going to do?" Stone asked.

The situation became clear: they couldn't wait another two months to have a big wedding. It would be inconvenient to lose their deposits or to have the wedding of the century. None of that mattered right now; all that mattered was that he married Grace.

He turned to face Labella and Stone. "We can't wait!" Lance said.

"What's the plan?" Stone asked.

"Labella, can you get in touch with Grace's friends who attended our engagement party?"

"Yes," Labella answered.

"And I will do the same, minus my parents and Rachel."

Lance continued to lead the conversation, part of his heart in turmoil and part in peace, thinking this was the right and only choice for their happiness.

CHAPTER 15
A New Life Amidst A Gathering Storm

New York, New York

Exactly one week later, Stone Forrester's heart felt like it was going to erupt as he led his only daughter out of the judge's private library. Grace, a vision of loveliness in a snow-white long dress embroidered with pearls and a short veil accentuating her lovely midnight wavy curls, coasted toward Lance.

Stone was proud to call Lance Worthington his son. He loved how Lance proved himself worthy of Grace the previous week. Over several months, Stone watched Lance transform from a wimpy man to a Christian man of valor. His heart swelled when he considered how much Lance and Grace loved each other. If their marriage was going to survive, he knew that they must keep God first.

Assembled in the judge's private office chambers, Labella Forrester sat on the front seat next to Caroline Worthington, along with Stella Hastings, André Dupré, Martha and Harold Henderson. Special wedding licenses and small floral arrangements were permitted to adorn the judge's private chambers, beautifying the walls full of law books and the symbol of justice.

With great joy, Stone handed Grace over to Lance, giving her cheek a quick kiss, before moving to sit in the empty seat next to Caroline. Lance's hand immediately sought Grace's, and he turned to smile into her eyes.

Standing up with the couple were family and friends. Lance's best man was Perry, his former colleague; groomsmen were Wyatt and Edmond, Grace's brothers. Grace's maids of honor were Zory, Penelope, and Nora.

As far as tears went, hankies were used during the enchanting, intimate ceremony. With genuine best wishes from family and friends, all adjourned to a small reception at a café on the Upper East Side of New York. The owner, a dear friend of Caroline's, closed it down for the entire day.

Three long tables were arranged into an open square, covered in lilac tablecloths, and christened with floral centerpieces. Dainty lilac bows tied with white baby's breath decorated the back of chivaris chairs on one side of the tables. For guests to admire, a buttercream wedding cake trimmed in gold sat on a decorative round table in the middle of the open square.

Lance led his bride on the dance floor to set off the reception to soft, timeless love songs. Labella stood watching them, whispering a prayer of thanks and hope. Ava and her co-conspirators would no longer have a reason to bully her sweet daughter. Labella thought the small, intimate ceremony far outweighed the pretentious one they had originally planned.

"You look exquisite," Lance's eyes tenderly appraised her.

Grace leaned in close. "You're not so bad yourself," she laughed.

Labella now watched as Stone claimed Grace for a dance, and Lance followed suit, taking her hand to go around the dance floor. Moments later, guests joined them. Caroline was most contented with Lance's choice of a wife and the people he lately had surrounded himself with. Ava was a fool to put social status above the needs of her child. She thought to herself, you can't demand the heart to love someone. Your heart knows the one it needs to bond with for life.

"It's customary for a grandson to dance with his grandmother." Lance's voice broke into her thoughts. "Grandmother, may I have this dance?"

Caroline beamed up at her only grandson and allowed him to swing her onto the floor for a waltz. The word *Grandmother* made her positively giddy; smiling from ear to ear, she swirled on the floor as a teenager at her first dance.

After a honeymoon of four days and nights in San Francisco, Caroline stood in the baggage claim section of the airport, eyeing each passenger shuffling through the automatic doors for a sight of Lance and Grace. Caroline had taken it upon herself to meet them for their arrival home. A moment later, the happy couple walked through the automatic doors, laughing. Seeing Caroline, they roared and charged her with hugs and kisses.

Twenty minutes later, Caroline sat on the opposite side of the couple in the day limo, and listened to their animated account of their honeymoon. Grace was thrilled to ride down the crookest street in the world. They climbed Nob Hill and tasted the wonderful seafood at Fishermen's Wharf. Caroline was drawn into their adventures.

From time to time, Caroline's gaze would drop to her grandson, who found his wife enchanting, and she delighted in their enjoyment of each other. When Caroline was able to get a word in, she informed them that she had a surprise for them. She went on to speak of Ava's meltdown the day after their wedding and the article that appeared in the social column, *Secret Wedding of the Year, between the handsome CEO of Worthington Steel and the lovely daughter of former NFL player Stonewall Forrester.* Rachel Van Fitzgerald left for Europe for an extended stay. Lance asked about his father and step-mother. He had regretted not inviting them, but at the time, he thought it was best.

An hour or so later, Charles passed through iron gates decorated with the emblem "W" and continued down a short drive, pulling in front of a large imposing house.

Grace shifted so she could better speak with Caroline. "It's lovely you picked us up at the airport, but we're too tired to visit with anyone," Grace spoke softly, missing the emblem on the gates.

"No, my dear, this is my surprise…welcome to your new home," Caroline gave a small laugh.

"It can't be possible, we don't understand," Grace said.

Charles was opening the door to help them out.

"I can see how this is overpowering…" Caroline said as she stepped out of the car after Grace and Lance exited. "You can always sell it if you don't like it," Caroline said businesslike. "But I do hope you like it."

Grace whispered, *what's not to like… the stone, Roman columns…. windows letting in the sunlight … its stately manor exudes every essence of luxury, elegance and comfort.*

Lance smiled at his wife first and then at his grandmother. "This is the most wonderful gift of love anyone has given me," he said, his voice rough. "Our thanks aren't enough for this lovely manor in South Hampton, Long Island."

"I wanted you to be minutes away from the estate," Caroline said, smiling. "Do you want to look inside?"

The couple shook their heads in disbelief.

"Yes!" they said in unison.

South Hampton, Long Island

During the first few days in the house, Grace was finding it taxing to get acquainted with her new lifestyle and running a huge house with staff. She recalled the stories her father told her, how he once had an abundance of money. However, one false move on the football field instantly changed his life forever. Her parents taught Grace the value of using money wisely, but she wasn't prepared to live a life of endless wealth.

The staff hired by Caroline was swiftly growing to love the young lady of the manner. On the morning just five days after moving in, Grace sat in the library behind the Georgian writing desk, which her girlfriends had gifted her. Janet, the maid, and Bently, the butler, their arms full of packages and letters, enter quietly, not wanting to disturb the new mistress, deep in thought. She was surprised by her family's weekend visit the previous evening. Though her younger brothers teased her constantly, it was hard to maintain a certain decorum as the lady of the manor.

Wyatt and Edmond graciously took over the mortgage on her cottage, moving away from home. Lance leased his apartment to one of his new junior executives with a wife and baby on the way.

"Good afternoon, my love," Lance said, bending down to kiss her.

"Could it be you taking a break from reading your father's proposal?" Grace asked.

"Yes, where are our guests?" Lance inquired.

"Caroline has summoned them for a day of sightseeing and shopping," Grace said, teasing.

"Tell me why you didn't go?" Lance requested when he sat in one of the two armchairs.

"More gifts arrived, and I wanted to open them with you. Plus, I'm expecting furniture for the great room and patio."

"I thought you were planning to furnish the house gradually," Lance chuckled.

"Your grandmother is very persuasive," she explained, shrugging her shoulders.

"Do I hear doubt?" Lance watched her closely. "What's on that pretty mind of yours?"

"I was just thinking of how different my life is going to be and wonder if I will ever fit in."

Lance, too, was wondering how she would respond to her new surroundings. He knew Grace loved him deeply, but he realized that this life could be immensely crushing at times.

"I fear it will take some time for me to adjust," Grace suggested.

Lance, still watching her, had the impression that Grace would not only fit in, but emerge as a woman of influence like his grandmother. As with any newlyweds, the two sat planning a future together.

Grace turned around in circles, admiring the elegant room from every direction. Called "the great room" for its size, it was impressive even to her. An ornate fireplace with a carved oak mantel was the focal point of the room. The room was filled with abundant light pouring through the large windows. Taking a breather, she sat on an oversized chair, gazing out at the patio through the French doors, inviting her to step outside and enjoy the warm sun. The space was almost perfect; the only thing missing was a loveseat she had eyed a few days earlier.

Known for walking without shoes, Grace had the habit of taking off her shoes the minute she entered the house. The beautiful wood floors and silky Persian rugs were too tempting to resist, even though she knew the lady of the manor shouldn't. Grace was startled when Bently announced she had a visitor. Gathering her shoes, she promptly requested Janet to set up the patio for her guest. When André arrived on the patio, he began speaking the moment he stepped outside.

"I'm here with my wedding gift!" were the first words Grace heard.

"Thank you," Grace said, noticing no package in his hands. "Oh, it's so nice to see you."

"How are things going?" André inquired.

"Just fine. Trying to find my sea legs."

Fidgeting with his coffee cup, he looked like a kid ready to spill the beans.

"Spill it!" Grace said, causing them to both laughs. He knew that Grace would be elated.

"In two weeks, I'm opening another museum in New York. My younger brother, René, will take over the museum in Penville. No need to look for another job; I want you to continue to work for me and Stella right here in New York!"

As Grace absorbed the news, her mind was still processing the implications, leaving her momentarily speechless. "How…" she whispered.

"Stella's daughter just had a baby girl. Being the first granddaughter in the family, her daughter wants her to move closer. And I don't want to lose my talented art conservator."

They sat for several hours, with André doing much of the talking. Grace found herself thinking she was saying goodbye to Penville and the simplicity of living in a quaint rural town to work and live in New York permanently. Was she ready?

It's been weeks since the board accepted Sterling's new proposed acquisition for another company, believing Lance had approved it. Lance learned too late that the new company was near bankruptcy. To avoid being forced to liquidate its assets, a bidding war had started. Lance was upset that his father superseded both Caroline and his authority, and now his only recourse was to find a solution for Sterling's mistake.

"Do you have any idea what time today you will leave work?" Grace asked her standard question for the last three days. The couple tossed the remnant of their lunch in the trash can of Grace's new office. "If you're working late, I need to arrange transportation with Jeffrey."

"I'm sorry, my love, I'm working late," he groaned. "It seems I have no other choice," he dryly said as he proceeded toward the door.

"Having lunch with you these days has been magnificent, but I miss you during dinner," Grace said sadly. "You've missed two nights coming home."

Lance held her gaze as long as he dared. The temptation was strong not to stay in town tonight working, but he fought it. "It will be okay," he said to his alarmed wife, holding her close. "Once I have an answer, we will have our life back."

"Oh Lance, please come home tomorrow night," she begged.

Lance smiled and kissed her tenderly. Finding a solution had been far harder than he ever expected. He kissed her again, squeezing the breath out of her with his pent-up emotions. His embrace slithered away from Grace, leaving her feeling vacant.

Sagaponack, Long Island

"I'm having so much fun," Caroline told Grace on a Saturday afternoon as the two women were leaving their fifth antique shop in town.

"I love the history of antiques," Grace said excitedly.

"It's fair to say you're having a good time," Caroline declared.

Grace looked at her teasing eyes and told herself what a relief to have Caroline in her life, if only to fill the void of not having her mother-in-law's blessing.

What happened next was hard to recount later. Without warning, Grace felt unsteady, and her speech slurred. Suddenly, she collapsed in Caroline's arms, her eyelids fluttering, dropping her bags of purchases.

"I want to lie down," Grace said in a strange voice. Reaching wildly for Caroline's hand, she slumped onto a nearby chair in the store.

"Grace!" Caroline whispered her name, leaning close, "Grace, can you hear me?"

Fretful of his employer's overdue return to the car, Charles entered the last antique store the women had visited, only to witness a crowd of people in a circle. A lady rushed past him with something in her hand and broke through the circle. He saw Grace slumped in a chair and Caroline bending over her and calling her name.

"Grace," Caroline tried again, moving the curls from Grace's face.

Her lids fluttered for a second and then opened. Her surroundings were fuzzy, but there was no missing Caroline's distressed face, and a strong smell of ammonia made her gag.

"What... what... happened..." Grace struggled to speak clearly.

"You fainted, my dear," Caroline whispered

"That's impossible," Grace said.

"But true."

Grace's smile was weak. "I'm all right now; I just want to go home."

Caroline didn't say another word but gathered all their bags while Charles lifted Grace into his arms, and they advanced to the car. Climbing into the car with Charles' assistance, Grace leaned her head back against the leather seats.

"Grace, maybe we should go to the emergency room."

Grace patted Caroline's hand. "I'm fine, Grandmother."

Caroline could've wept for joy, hearing the word "Grandmother." However, anxiety overruled.

Caroline only waited until Charles was behind the wheel.

"Charles, go to the hospital."

Charles turned around to look at Caroline. "Charles, Now," Caroline ordered in a tone he'd never heard. Even Grace blinked.

"Food and rest are all I need," Grace protested.

"We are going," Caroline stated, her eyes straight ahead. "I don't want Lance angry at me."

Charles did as he was told. Minutes later, he pulled into the parking lot outside the emergency room.

Grace tried not to think about her nausea. She wanted nothing more than to lie down, but with the help of Charles, she climbed out of the car and started inside. She wasn't going to argue with Caroline, so she allowed the hospital attendant to meet her with a wheelchair.

"You're pregnant," the doctor said about two hours later. "Nothing to worry about, but you need to see your doctor soon. No more long shopping sprees, plenty of rest, and cut-out rich foods for a while to combat the nausea."

"Doctor, are you sure?" Grace blurted out. "I've only been married for a month."

"Mrs. Worthington, it can happen after one month," he smiled. Stunned, Grace didn't hear the remaining instructions.

Caroline and Grace were quiet on the way home. Grace was not sure how to tell Lance the news, and Caroline was planning a baby shower.

Not knowing the reasons for Grace's odd phone call, Lance left work early and waited for her arrival. Several hours later, Grace assured Caroline that Janet would take care of her, so Caroline wished her a happy evening. At a complete loss, Grace took herself straight to bed without knowing Lance was home.

Lance was unsettled learning that his wife had been home for an hour. Genuinely concerned for his wife's welfare, Lance knew he couldn't rest until he spoke with her. Leaving his paperwork on the desk, Lance went upstairs to their room, easing the door open. He saw a light was on in the bathroom. Debating whether he should enter, Grace came from the bathroom and found him standing in the middle of the room.

"Hi," Grace spoke softly.

"Are you all right, Grace?"

"I'm not sure."

Lance anxiously watched her slowly walk toward the bed.

"Come, talk with me," Grace said as she sat on the edge.

Lance lingered a minute while Grace scooted over so he wouldn't be at the end of the bed.

"Tell me what happened today?" Lance said, waiting for her to look at him.

"I'm not sure how to tell you."

There was a brief silence. "My love, nothing you say will change my love for you," Lance said.

Grace swallowed. "I'm pregnant."

Lance wasn't certain he heard correctly. "Pregnant?" he questioned her.

Grace stood. "Yes! Lance, pregnant."

Without thought, he jumped up, clasping Grace. "I'm going to be a father," he yelled. Grace found herself being jubilantly twirled. For the next hour, in each other's embrace, they discussed the unexpected news.

Despite her exhaustion, Grace pondered the thought of becoming a mother. It didn't escape her that Lance's parents might feel threatened by a new heir. Finishing the milk Lance ordered for her, she nestled once again in the cradle of Lance's arms. She wasn't sure about God's tiny gift, yet she hoped it would unite their families.

A week later, Ava didn't bother asking the typists in the outer office the whereabouts of Lance. To give herself some privacy, Ava positioned herself by the huge pillars that led in two opposite directions. Sitting in a comfy chair, Ava tapped her foot impatiently. The hallway was wide open to the outer office; therefore, Lance had no problem spotting his mother. Considering they hadn't spoken to each other for a month, Lance approached her quietly, gently tapping her shoulder as soon as he was near.

"Why was I summoned?" he heard Ava say.

"Mother, it's nice to see you," he said, bending to kiss her and standing aside for her to follow him to the inner office.

There was no point in making a scene before the low-level staff, so Ava came to her feet, barely glancing in Lance's direction. She gave more than a grunt. Crossing the threshold of the inner office, she refused the offered chair and remained standing.

Lance nervously laughed as he sat at his desk. He had the impression this conversation would be more difficult than he had anticipated.

"Actually, Grace and I have some exciting news."

"You look as though you're afraid to tell me," Ava mocked him.

"I am," Lance answered. "Grace is pregnant."

Ava's gaze intensified as she lowered herself into the chair facing his desk. It's obvious that Lance was excited, and she tried to understand this, but it didn't change her concerns about his marriage to Grace.

"Why didn't you tell me sooner?" was the first question Ava asked.

"We just found out Saturday, and you had shut us out of your life."

As much as she didn't want to admit, Ava was sorry she missed her son's wedding and now was on the threshold of losing her first grandchild. Ava kept her hands very still in her lap.

"I might not understand your love for Grace, but just humor me for a second. She's now a Worthington carrying my grandchild, and I don't want to repeat history."

"I thought you might not care to know."

Ava wasn't offended that he didn't trust her. "Do you have a problem with me getting to know my grandchild?"

Touched by her words, Lance stared at his mother for a moment, skepticism looming. The whole episode hadn't upset him only surprised him.

"I just want to know that you're going to love Grace as much as the baby."

Recognizing she would've preferred someone else as his wife, Ava contemplated this for a while. However, she knew that she must make an effort.

"I want you to do me a favor," she stated.

"What's that?"

"Give me time to adjust to all of this, Grace, marriage, baby."

"I will tell you what," Lance said. "We are having family and friends over this weekend to make the announcement. You're invited."

To decline the invitation wasn't an option. Ava would accept the invite without any agitation on her part. Ava didn't try to detain him any longer. She nodded and followed him to the door.

Grace's condition had endeared her to the entire staff. Working steadily for days, the staff wouldn't allow their mistress to lift one finger. Though the company's financial crises were still looming, Lance had cut back on his hours at work, riding home with Grace each night. Out-of-town guests arrived the night before the party, lending to sounds of laughter and mirth late in the evening.

Bright sunlight arrived for the announcement party. The highlight at Worthington Manor was Lance's parents apologizing to the Forresters for their obnoxious behavior toward them. Grace and Lance were joyful that their prayers had been answered. The weekend's gathering was one that Grace and Lance knew they would cherish. In the blink of an eye, their baby had inherited four aunts and uncles, three grandmothers, two grandfathers, four great-great-grandmothers, and three great-great grandfathers.

Secluded in the comfort of their room, husband and wife bowed their heads in prayers of thanks for all he had provided them. Putting his wife to bed with her milk, Lance realized there were no holes or gaps in his life; God had filled them all. Silently, Lance lay beside his sleeping wife with pleasure and the warm serenity of God's goodness and prayed for them and their unborn child.

CHAPTER 16

Truth Doesn't Change Your Lies

On July 3, Grace stood alone, licking her lips to battle the nausea. She was disappointed that they couldn't attend her family's annual July 4 barbeque. Finding a solution for the failing acquisition had taken over Lance's life. Three nights a week he slept at the office, and the other two nights, Grace was already asleep when he arrived home. Massive loss of revenue lurked in the shadows for Worthington Steel.

For weeks, Grace witnessed Lance becoming distant, and at times, short-tempered. Being petite and eighteen weeks pregnant and alone for many nights, she was lonely, sad, and often nauseous.

One Friday evening, Lance surprised Grace by coming home for dinner. He didn't detect anything was wrong until he saw Charles, his grandmother's faithful driver, parked outside his front door. Lance ran up the stairs, rushing into the slightly ajar bedroom door, but Caroline blocked him.

"Lance," she whispered, "follow me."

Standing in the hallway, Caroline was all business.

"Grace called me earlier to come quickly. When I arrived, the doctor was here, and all the servants unconsolable for their mistress."

"You're going to tell me why her doctor was called," he said, disappointed Grace didn't call him.

The doctor suddenly appeared and looked at the disheveled husband before him.

"Mrs. Worthington experienced spotting, dizziness, and fatigue. She's fine now, but we must limit her activities."

"What must I do, doctor?" Lance inquired.

"Pamper her, lots of bed rest, and absolutely no stress."

"Thank you. We will make sure your prescription is followed."

The doctor left without another word, Caroline in his wake. Lance felt shaken over the chat. He wondered how much more he could take, feeling worried about his wife and unsettled and uncertain about the future. He went in to see his wife.

A week later, Lance pulled into the driveway. Lance found Grace in the library reading. Sitting next to her, he pulled her into a light embrace, and Grace laid her head on his broad shoulders, feeling cherished.

"You're home early," Grace raised her head.

Lance sighed. "I needed to be home and to tell you how much I love you."

"Oh, Lance, I love you."

Just hearing her sweet voice warmed his heart. Grace looked utterly vulnerable, so he asked God to help him be the husband she needed.

"My love, I need to discuss something with you," Lance said in a hushed tone. "I've already given this much thought."

"I'm listening."

"My mother called today."

"I gather she had a good reason," Grace said quietly.

"Yes," Lance paused. "She feels you shouldn't be alone all day while Grandmother and I focus on stabilizing the acquisition."

"I'm not alone, Lance; I have the staff."

"Listen, my love," Lance said softly. "I'm feeling disquieted about you and the babies' well-being. Mother thinks you should stay with her."

While Grace considers his statements, Lance wastes no time to add. "I haven't completely disregarded your feelings, but darling, you can't travel, and your parents are at a business conference."

Grace remained silent. Her heart was in an upheaval. Since the baby's announcement party, Ava had been a model mother-in-law.

"It's noticeable your mother is trying," Grace said.

"Mother sounded sincere in her offer, but it's your decision."

Before the couple retired for the evening, holding hands, they decided God had taken care of each of their needs so far. And they believe he would give them wisdom on which next steps to take. They also believe that nothing in the world could darken their love for one another.

Rachel arrived mid-morning. She had returned from her vacation and was raring to start a new assault on the bride. She was ushered to the small sitting room while Victor summoned the lady of the manor.

"Do you wish a glass of cold lemonade, Ms. Van Fitzgerald?"

"No," Rachel screeched. "Just inform your mistress I'm here."

Victor nodded and scrambled off to notify the lady of the manor.

Ava sat stunned, her hand covering her mouth at Victor's announcement. For a moment, she wasn't sure what to do.

"Victor, please tell our guest I will be there shortly," she concluded and began to stand.

Ava buried her face in her hand, thinking how unfair she had been to Grace. The past two weeks, she has seen the vast difference between Grace and Rachel. Only one had the characteristics of being loveable, respectful and kind, and that was Grace Worthington. Ava had an uncomfortable feeling Rachel wanted to make more trouble.

Does Rachel's visit signal more heartbreak for Grace?

Ava headed downstairs to greet her guest, determined today was the perfect time to define Grace's position within the Worthington family.

"Why have you kept me waiting?" Rachel accused Ava.

"Don't get yourself overwrought, my dear," Ava added.

"I don't know how you come to that conclusion," Rachel's voice held bitterness.

"Please… have a seat, darling,"

"I've been home for a week," Rachel's voice was firm.

"I hadn't…heard…" Ava began, stumbling a bit. "I guess I have been busy."

Seeing Ava look uncomfortable, Rachel immediately tabled her plans, to scold Ava's for her lack of enthusiasm.

Grace chose that moment to waddle toward the sitting room, to feel the warmth of the sun, while she ate her French fries and drank her orange juice. She heard voices from her place outside the room. They weren't raised in anger, but something wasn't right. Grace was able to come inside the door without being seen, but the sudden appearance of Rachel made Grace almost drop her food, spilling a little juice down her dress. She was perplexed; *why was Rachel visiting Ava?*

"I need to ask you one question," Rachel said quietly.

"All right."

"Why haven't you called me?"

"I'm sorry, Rachel. So much has happened since you left."

"Have I done something to upset you, Ava? I feel as though you don't trust me, and I won't leave until you tell me?"

Ava took a moment but eventually began to speak. "My priorities have changed since you left."

Rachel fell silent, rising from her seat. Exasperation covered her features. She didn't understand the cold reception from her co-conspirator.

"Changes...? No worries, I have a new..." Rachel stopped in midsentence when Grace suddenly stepped into view. A shrieking sigh escaped from Grace's mouth that was shattering as Rachel's gaze went past Ava's shoulder, and ceremonially, her nemesis was in view.

"My...my...what do we have here?" Rachel grunted... "I hope you hadn't gotten the ridiculous notion you've won," Rachel gloated, casting her eyes on Grace.

Ava zipped around and looked helplessly at Grace, mouthing. "I'm sorry."

Both Rachel and Ava watched Grace's retreating back, her head down. It was a posture that Ava normally would have enjoyed, but no one had ever made her regret her actions like Grace.

"I don't understand you," Rachel exploded in anger.

"Rachel, please, I must ask you to leave."

"I certainly will not until I know what is the meaning of that woman being here."

Ava took in her flushed features and doubted if Rachel would ever accept her answer.

"Can we talk?"

Rachel took a breath. "Talk!"

"Please try and understand; Lance made his choice. I know what a shock it must be, but I'm thinking of the babies, as well as Grace."

"How could you betray me?" Rachel whispered. "All this time, I thought you cared for me."

"I can't begin to explain," Ava went on. "I've actually heard Grace praying for me. No one has ever shown me kindness like Grace."

Rachel's link to Lance was gone. She slid her eyes shut in agony. Both women were astonished as water slipped from beneath Rachel's closed eyelids. She promptly stormed out of the room.

⁂

Upstairs, a part of Grace wanted to scream and ask Ava why she would invite Rachel. Grace soundlessly sat on the bed; Lucy rushed in and made her comfortable in the bed, beseeching her to forget what happened downstairs and rest. Lucy sat in a nearby chair, subtly humming a melody her mother had sung to her. Slowly, her young mistress closed her brown eyes.

Ava frowned at the frustration she was feeling. She needed to explain everything to Grace. It took several minutes to control herself, tapping Lucy's shoulder.

"Madam, Mrs. Grace is sound asleep."

"Thank you, Lucy," Ava said. "I will sit with her now."

"Yes, Madam, I will check on the two of you later."

A short time later, Lucy found both Worthington's women asleep. She was content that her mistress had changed dramatically in the last few weeks due to her daughter-in-law. The manor had become a haven for everyone.

Close to midnight on that hot night, Ava finally made her way to bed. Terrified by her visit with Rachel; a feeling of alarm hung over her when Grace fell ill and despondent.

The following morning, while Ava outwardly expressed calmness in speaking with Labella about Rachel's visit, Labella could sense a subtle but discreet dismay in Ava's voice. Arrangements were made for a driver to meet Labella at the airport and drive her directly to Grace's home.

At the beginning of the following week, Labella told Grace as she hugged her, "I'm so glad you're feeling better."

"The doctor insists that you stay in bed for a few more days," Ava tried to reason with Grace.

"I'm sick of lying down; I want to stand up," Grace spoke to both of the older women, who didn't respond.

"Please…you must rest," Labella said.

"I will ask Janet to prepare a pitcher of cold orange juice," Ava said.

Slowly, Grace elevated herself against the pillow to rub her stomach. Her recent cramping had the doctor and family concerned.

"I'm worried about the babies?" Grace's voice was fretful.

"Don't worry, little one," Labella assured her.

With Janet's help, Ava brought a small tray of fresh fruit and orange juice. Keeping Grace's recent cramping in mind, Labella insisted Grace take a nap.

"I'm not sleepy," Grace protested.

"If I didn't know better, you would like us to leave," Labella commented.

Grace chuckled softly. "Don't be ridiculous. I love having two overbearing mothers."

A new beginning had been created with an unbreakable bond between the Worthington and Forrester families. The more the Worthington family spent time with Grace and her family, the more they saw God moving in their lives, which increased their desire to learn more about God. Dismissing Grace's protest, Labella covered Grace with a light blanket; she was too tired to fight her mothers, so she closed her eyes and fell into a deep sleep.

Frantically searching for a solution to his father's bad investment, Lance was spending more time at the office. In the past couple of months, despite his concern for Grace, he relied on the family to assist in caring for his sick, pregnant wife.

An unexpected summer storm in the middle of August echoed, rattling his windows. Apart from his last-ditch effort to negotiate with the construction company to accept their investment's bid, he received a mid-day call from their lawyers. Worthington Steel had lost the acquisition, costing the company millions. The mood around the office mimicked the dreary, wet day.

Lance, ducking his staff, left work, checking into a men's club. His head down and posture sagging, Lance unsuccessfully sought solace in his faith. Powerless, in his prayer, he questioned God, *why had he attained advantages and cumulative grief in a short period?*

Meanwhile, with Janet's help, Grace sat in her favorite chair by the window in the great room. Nothing could have prepared her for Lance being away the entire weekend. Frightened by the Sunday newscast, which revealed that *the young golden CEO of Worthington Steel has fallen.*

Grace whispered a prayer: *Lord, please take care of my husband. I need him now more than ever. I'm cramping again, and the doctor is concerned. Maybe he's ashamed…but I love him no matter if he's a pilot or CEO. Send him home, father.*

"How are you, my lady?" Janet asked, knowing her mistress had several rough nights.

"I'm a bit tired," she answered, missing her two mothers.

"Do you want anything?"

"Nothing at the moment, thank you."

Grace wasn't sure when she would see her husband, and she had no idea how she was to maintain her sanity.

"Are you really sure, my lady?" Janet asked, fidgeting and ready to call Mrs. Ava Worthington to return.

"Yes," Grace said with utter confidence.

I can feel my temptation to beg you, Father, and I must not. You know the reason why I haven't seen or heard from my husband in eight days. Nevertheless, I thank you for this tribulation and for teaching me to keep trusting you for Lance and our future. Grace continued, talking from her heart until Janet came to check on her.

"Are you ready to dress for breakfast, my lady?"

"Please."

Appreciating the reliability of Janet's help, Grace good-naturedly obliged her.

"Do you wish to speak with the staff about the upcoming Labor Day weekend?" Janet asked the eighth day that Mr. Worthington hadn't been home.

"Mid-afternoon will work."

"Very well. Should I notify Mrs. Worthington?"

"No, I will inform her when she comes down for breakfast."

Janet smiled as she escorted Grace downstairs for breakfast.

The morning was warming swiftly. Flowers were in riotous bloom on the patio, a sight Grace enjoyed until Ava made her arrival.

"Lance didn't call last night?" Ava asked at the end of Grace's prayer.

"No," Grace said quietly, trying not to rip Ava's dignity.

Ava sat with her head down.

Grace's throat tightened, thinking what Ava would do if Lance never came home. For several moments, Grace wasn't sure what to say.

"I get the impression we've both been crying," Grace began, "but I understand he's hurting and ashamed."

"Ashamed to come home to his wife and unborn babies?" Ava asked next.

Closing her eyes, Grace said, "I don't know, Ava?"

"I'm going to bring him home," Ava stated without preamble.

"Please, don't, Ava," Grace's voice was breathless. "He should desire to come home."

"I must," said Ava, standing to leave. "Lance has responsibility to you, not just Worthington Steel."

Please...please... don't go," Grace begged Ava, grabbing her hand, becoming nearly hysterical. Grace sobbed uncontrollably, unable to speak.

"Don't cry," Ava whispered, wiping her face with a napkin.

Ava thought about how unfairly Lance was treating his wife. His absence wasn't good for either of them.

CHAPTER 17

Fire of Hell

L ance listened with a hurting heart to Ava's description of his lapse in judgment for not being home with his wife. Also, his fears of being a failure, and unsure if his unborn boys would inherit his deformities, kept him away.

"Are you finished, mother?" Lance asked.

"Yes, I'm here to take you home."

Lance frowned. In the past, Ava always seemed self-absorbed. Not today. Today, she was there for another person.

"Your actions are upsetting your wife."

"You understand, I can't go home until I make restitution for father's mistake."

"What about your commitment to your wife and unborn babies?"

"Grace understands."

"No. I believe Grace is on the edge of losing you and the babies. Don't make the same mistakes as your father."

"I haven't abandoned Grace; I'm still her husband," Lance said.

"You haven't called or seen your wife in over a week," she roared. "Do you plan to miss your family gathering for Labor Day?"

"I thank you, but mind your own business."

"Your wife isn't a goddess made of stone on a pedestal, but flesh and blood with feelings."

"I guess you, too, feel I'm a failure?"

"Not true! When your father left us, I almost lost my mind. We survived because of my love for you. It's time to go home. Grace needs you more than this company."

Lance saw none of Ava's power-hunger maneuvering, only her love for his wife. He believed his top priority was to solve the company's financial distress. Unfortunately, he is unsure if his way of thinking may prove to be his downfall both at home and at the office. With conviction, he discusses Grace's needs with his mother.

Labor Day weekend arrives full of laughter, music, games, and delicious food, and her husband. Grace couldn't ask for anything more. She decided not to inform her family of Lance's lack of judgment but locked the memory of what could've been a monstrous loss in the vault of forgiveness.

Grace relaxed on the terrace all weekend, letting the older women take charge. Sterling, on the other hand, was disheartened that the bar wasn't stocked with liquor. Yet, before the end of the weekend, he was enjoying camaraderie with the other men in her life.

The last day of the weekend came much too soon for Grace. Her goodbyes to her guests were filled with raw emotions. She hoped they would have this event every year.

At the start of a new week, Caroline received an ominous phone call. When the call ended, she was jolted to the very core of her beliefs. Immediately, she summoned Sterling to her office. Baffled by the summons, he was shocked, seeing her jaw tightly clenched as she delivered her message to him with precision and authority.

"You must know I'm embarrassed and hurt by your actions."

"What are you talking about, Mother?"

"Less than thirty minutes ago, I received a call from a board member about your secret meeting."

Sterling struggled to breathe, twisting his wedding ring. "Do tell… Mother…what have I done?"

"You had a meeting with the stockholders to replace Lance," Caroline lamented.

"It's simple, Mother," Sterling said. "I think you should accept that father made a mistake in choosing Lance over his son."

"I'm speechless at your coldness toward your son," her voice quaked.

"You shouldn't be surprised," Sterling argued. "I wouldn't allow my right inheritance to go to a son I never wanted."

Caroline tried to contain herself while anger filled her eyes. She had never wanted to raise a thankless son. For years, she had yearned he would change.

"So, you're deliberately destroying this family, especially your son."

"It's too late for Father to atone for his sins by denying my existence!" Sterling cried.

"Your father didn't deny you! But Lance is your son!"

"Only by DNA," Sterling snidely said.

Caroline never considered that Sterling would make her sick to her stomach. His kindness to Lance was counterfeit. It was all a lie.

"You purposely lied to the board that Lance and I agreed with the latest acquisition, knowing the company was going bankrupt."

Sterling was silent.

"Answer me!" she said, livid.

"I see you're highly upset by my business practices." Sterling wasn't shouting…his voice was level, but he was going to have his say. "Our business was thriving, though I question why you and the board so easily accepted Lance as the CEO."

Caroline was so flooded with rage that her mind tried to take it all in. She finally said, "First of all, your father knew your superiority complex would be detrimental to the company.

He was right; because of your folly, the company has lost millions."

Sterling's mouth tightened a bit, his face red as beets.

"What are you going to do?" Sterling asked in a teasing tone.

"This is no game! Mark my word, son; I have the power to discharge you on the spot. Only my love for you and Betty hinders me."

"Do whatever you must do," Sterling said, rising from his seat and giving a backhand wave.

In the following days, Caroline campaigned for Lance to remain CEO. The controlling stockholders wondered if Lance was too young for such an important position and wanted to override the board's decision. At the end of the week, Lance conceded that the stockholders may win because of his father's trickery. Impulsively, Lance wrote his letter of resignation.

Mortified by being a failure, Lance went home conflicted. *Was it time to resign?* Finding Grace asleep on the chaise in the study, he didn't have the heart to tell her of his father's unscrupulous behavior; she wouldn't understand. Lance stared at the letter in his briefcase, clinging to the scripture, Exodus 14:14: *The Lord shall fight for you, and ye shall hold your peace.*

"Hi, Father, can we talk?" Rachel asked…making herself comfortable in his office.

Mr. Van Fitzgerald had been on several conference calls, discussing his new hotel in Paris, slated to open soon. "Can it wait?" Paul asked furiously the moment she walked in.

"I promise," she crooned, "I won't stay long."

Paul smiled a smug, complacent smile that caused Rachel to giggle.

"You have five minutes."

"I want you to give the new hotel in Paris to Lance Worthington."

Mr. Van Fitzgerald snorted. "As if I don't have sense enough to know who to hire!"

Rachel dashed around to his desk, placing an affectionate kiss on his forehead.

"Are you sure you won't hire him?"

"Rachel, your man just lost millions for his company. He's too immature to run my newest hotel."

Rachel lifted her chin as an ungrateful child. "That wasn't his fault."

"Well, that doesn't make him qualified," her father reasoned.

"Even if I tell you, I want him."

"How would that make a difference?"

Rachel pouted, her lips out while her manicured finger stroked his thinning hair.

"Father, please, I love him."

Paul's heart went out to his daughter, even though he was

convinced Lance Worthington wasn't the man for his hotel. Forgetting Lance was a married man, Paul knew he was definitely the man for his only daughter. The Worthington's name would bring a feather into the cap of the Van Fitzgerald's.

"Promise me you'll let me handle this," his voice grew a little gruff. "This must be done with skilled diplomacy."

"I promise." Rachel smiled.

"See you tonight at the country club," Paul told her, and with that, Rachel was gone.

Known for his ruthlessness in business, in his opinion, bending the rules was wholly justified. Joining his family with the Worthington would be a delight. Lance's marriage to someone else was only a minor detail.

◦◦◦◦

After much consideration, Lance decided against resigning, but with each passing day of heated debates with the board, Lance lost hope in retaining his position. By September 11, sitting at the head of the table, Lance accepted the board's decision. Carline grabbed his hand while each board member quietly exited the conference room.

"It's only a two-week suspension," she whispered.

"I can't believe this…"

"It was clear to everyone," Caroline said. "Sterling was the essential element of the company's loss."

"It's not normal," Lance told her. "Companies don't tend to give their CEO a suspension, but walking papers."

"Not to worry, this will give you a chance to spend time with your wife.

Lance politely explained to his team the board's decision and packed up his office with the anticipation of returning soon.

The reputable Worthington name was being dragged through all the news outlets, including the scandal papers. Headlines stated that the *current CEO, Mrs. Caroline Worthington, has dismissed her son and put her grandson on suspension.*

Reporters from all over the country camped outside each of the Worthington properties. Outraged at her ex-husband's humiliation to the family, Ava remained out of the public eye. Lance roamed around his large house like an animal in a locked cage, his behavior growing more unpredictable.

Each day, the newspapers brutally ridiculed Lance, calling him a bonehead. Day by day Lance's self-worth was being obliterated by reporters. During the nights, Grace felt useless and cried out to God, repeating the Lord's prayers.

CHAPTER 18
Laughter In The Grave

Standing on the terrace downhearted, Lance wasn't pleased that September had come and gone, and he was yet on probation. Caroline's call informed him that a few stockholders were holding out to reinstate his father in the position. That piece of news didn't improve Lance's state of mind. He clearly didn't like the idea of waiting another week or two, but he would try to be patient.

"Grandmother, I'm without a job," Lance stated.

"You will be back soon."

"How will I support my family?"

"Lance," she said quietly. "You're not destitute."

Lance chuckled a little, not able to help himself.

"You're not able to view this objectively," Caroline said.

Lance sighed with irritation. "I'm a great disappointment to everyone."

"It's not true; hold on to your faith, and one day, I will visit your church."

Lance hadn't opened his bible since the failed acquisition. Retrieving it, Lance went to the nursery and sat in the rocker. He read the story about a man named Job who had lost his wealth and kids, yet Job trusted God. Lance couldn't imagine losing everything in an instant.

With sudden passion, Lance knelt on his knees. *Oh, Father, distress has clenched my soul. Forgive me for not trusting you. Help me to put my trust in you and not man. Help me to believe in your word and your promises, Lord; please take care of my wife and babies. Amen.*

Lance eventually climbed into bed his heart yet praying. The rustling of the sheets and his movement awakened Grace.

"Lance," Grace scooted close, gazing lovingly at him. "I love you and believe in us."

Lance leaned over, tenderly kissing her and said, "No matter what happens, we have each other and God by our side."

Grace took his hand and positioned it on top of her stomach, and one of the babies kicked at that moment. Lance smiled widely.

"I believe you're carrying football players."

Grace could only nod, thanking God for the miracle he had given them.

Lance grasped very little of the evening's conversation with Paul Van Fitzgerald. His mind was so centered on what Grace would say, that anyone could have set his hair on fire, and he wouldn't have noticed. All he gathered *it's a job—a golden opportunity for you and your wife to work and live in Paris.*

The night was still young when he finished his call with Paul. Lance found himself alone in the study, mulling over the job offer. He felt nervous, thinking about living in Paris. The thought of giving Grace her lost dream was very exciting but also a little scary. Questions plagued his mind: why did Paul choose him? Could this be God's plan?

As much as he wanted to share the job offer with Grace, under the circumstances he would need to keep it a secret. Wringing his hands, he left the study, heading upstairs with a firm resolve not to rush into accepting the offer.

"If you're not tired? I was hoping we could read the bible," Lance said.

"Was the call about your job at Worthington Steel?"

"No, my love," Lance answered, his voice calm. "It was a business call, but not from Worthington Steel."

"You weren't disappointed?"

"No, I wasn't," he said, talking fast and a bit flustered. "Let's read our bible."

"I'm sorry I asked; let's forget about it," Grace murmured. "We can read about Jacob and how his mother tricked his father into giving him the family blessing."

Lance's surprised gaze flew to Grace's grinning face. Lance, laughing in delight, his conversation with Paul Fitzgerald was forgotten. With the bible open and Grace snuggled against his chest, they read for the next forty-five minutes until Grace was nodding off to sleep.

Anxious over Grace's suggested Bible story, he didn't let it trouble him. Lance easily rationalized it by thinking that not telling her was prudent for Grace and the babies' safety. With a soft-spoken prayer over Grace, he made his way to change and join his wife in a peaceful slumber.

The following morning, Grace rose slowly with no energy and was experiencing nausea. A few moments later, Lance appeared in his dark blue three-piece suit and starched white shirt, wearing her favorite blue tie. Standing by the bedside he was seized with indecision. Grace was on the verge of asking where he was going when Lance spoke.

"I have a meeting this morning regarding the business call last night."

"Oh," Grace's voice was calm, but her mind was racing. "What time do you think you'll return?"

"Hopefully before the evening commuter traffic."

Lance suddenly noticed Grace's questionable expression.

"Nothing is wrong, and I promise to tell you everything this evening."

Grace watched him move over to her, plant a kiss on her cheek, and leave.

"Lance," Paul spoke as he approached. "Welcome; it's been such a long time since our last encounter."

"Yes, it has, sir." Lance shook the older gentleman's hand, concealing his surprise over his invitation.

"It's my pleasure you've accepted my invitation to come here." The older gentlemen searched Lance's eyes. "I hope it means you're interested."

The lavish Van Fitzgerald hotels are famous for their oasis of catering to the rich and famous. Lance didn't think there could be any more opulence until the elevator's doors opened to an entrance of pure extravagance. Lance knew there was more to Paul's offer. He quickly decided to be gracious and uncover what Paul truly wanted.

"I am interested, sir, but I warn you, if this offer has no merit, I will leave without a word of explanation or apology."

Paul didn't care for the note of superiority in his visitor's voice, but still, he nodded in agreement. The ninety-minute meeting was an appealing offer that Lance had never envisioned. Paul offered him a two-year hotel management contract for his newest Paris hotel, La Château de Delicatesses. It included cash compensation, a sign-on bonus, benefits, compensations with perks, plus a confidentiality agreement. However, there was one stipulation: the contract could be terminated if the hotel's performance was poor after one year. Termination fees were attached.

"Is there a problem with the contract?"

"Not exactly," Lance told him as Paul pulled out a pen for his signature. "It's just that I must speak with my wife and family. How soon must we move to Paris?"

The fact that Lance was married was irrelevant to Paul. Once the trap was activated, he wouldn't be married but speaking with divorce lawyers.

"I'm more than willing to wait after your wife has her baby, but Lance, I will need you to travel with me to Paris in a few days to review the property."

"I'll have an answer for you by tomorrow evening."

Paul smiled and stood to shake hands with Lance. "I look forward to our partnership."

Filled with enthusiasm, Lance shared everything with his grandmother in the Rainbow Room restaurant. Appalled by Lance contemplating accepting the offer, Caroline worried that if the offer were ever revealed, the board would automatically vote against Lance. Yet, she couldn't deny this amazing offer would appeal to any newly married couple.

"I thought you loved working with the family," she commented,

"I do, but how long must I wait before I'm allowed to return?"

"It appears you're leaning toward accepting Paul's offer."

"Yes, but I won't sign a contract before talking with you."

Caroline nodded; sitting before her was a powerful man facing a major decision.

Already dressed, Lance watched a sluggish Grace squint into his smiling face. She groaned, shifting herself up against the headboard, and took the glass of milk from his hand. Lance captured her free hand and pressed a kiss to her palm. They were silent for a moment, and then Lance spoke.

"Grace," Lance began, "I wanted so badly to tell you last night, but you were asleep when I arrived home. Now, I'm almost afraid to admit this to you: I met with Paul Van Fitzgerald about a job."

A minute or two of silence passed before Grace spoke in a voice of wonder. "Isn't that Rachel's father?"

"I hope you'll hear me out first," he pleaded, "before passing judgment."

Grace drew a great breath. "This job...tell me about it."

Lance relayed his entire conversation with Paul. Listening quietly, she didn't feel quite so sure about this job offer, though living in Paris would be a dream come true. Could she move so hastily after the babies were born, leaving her support group of family and friends? How could she take the babies away from their grandparents?

When Lance finished, he probed his wife's face. Grace wasn't totally on board with the idea. Anger was swiftly filling Lance and dampening his appreciation for her willingness to listen.

Shifting a little to compensate for her hurting back, she stared at her husband. She realized Lance was responding to the needs of his family. It would be petty to quibble over its being Rachel's father. "I don't wish to sway you from whatever you believe is best for us."

Lance thanked his wife sincerely, and he told her his decision. Grace took little notice that it wasn't a definite yes. However, her heart was in turmoil over him being in Paris with Rachel and her father.

Later that evening, after dinner, Lance, Ava, and Grace gathered around the phone to call Grace's parents. Once Lance was finished with his news, they heard a loud gasp. Neither parent considered his decision to be a good one, each voicing their concerns.

Before making his final decision, he planned to go to Paris in three days to check out things. Ava volunteered to stay with Grace until Lance returned on Sunday.

Paris France

What had seemed like speculation now was a reality for the Worthington and Forrester families. Grace stood mournfully at the front door, waving goodbye to Lance. Ava, having a thorough understanding of Grace's brooding all morning, spent hours trying to distract her.

Friday evening, Lance disembarked from the Concorde at Paris Charles de Gaulle airport. With his head throbbing, Lance walked outside the terminal, hoping to hop into the car sent by Paul. But a long delay in the arrival of the car caused him a lot of frustration.

By the time the driver finally showed up, Lance had almost decided to return home. Paul's driver had arrived without any apologies for his lateness. Ignoring his rudeness, Lance leaned his head against the back seat, closing his eyes. Periodically, he opened his eyes to see the magical romantic city.

After a while, Lance noticed they weren't heading to a hotel but were headed toward the countryside. Immediately, he questioned the driver. Though the driver was polite, he was evasive. Having no other choice, Lance questioned the driver again: *Where are you taking me?* This time, the driver didn't even turn around. For the remainder of the drive, Lance's neck was stiff with rage. The driver didn't speak until they reached a large country estate blocked by tall hedges. The huge windows permitted a spectacular view of lush green rolling hills.

For the moment, Lance was delighted to reach his destination finally. Weary from his travel and with a dull headache, he just wanted to lie down.

"Sir, welcome to the home of Mr. Van Fitzgerald," said the driver, opening the car door. "Mr. Van Fitzgerald is waiting."

"You've got a wonderful home," Lance verbalized when he arrived in the elaborate vestibule.

"Thank you," Paul replied.

Lance followed along with Paul while he began to explain his reason for having him stay at his estate. Lance was escorted to a private wing on the east side of the estate. He was expected to join Paul for dinner in fifteen minutes. Lance knew no matter how tired he felt, he must be cordial to his host.

The dining room was warm and comfortably furnished. Paul sat at the head of the table, and Lance to his right. Too little food and too much weariness made Lance famished. Lance was very pleased that he was eating five minutes after settling in his chair.

Unexpectedly, Rachel walked in without acknowledging their guest; she glided over to her father, kissing his right and left cheeks. Without batting an eyelid, she dilly-dallied to sit on the left side of her father, giving all her attention to the meal before her.

"Daddy tells me you've accepted his offer," she meowed.

"I'm still weighing my options," Lance stammered.

"Tell us what's keeping you from committing?" Paul asked.

"I would love to say yes, but I have responsibilities, one to my wife and my grandfather. I don't even know if …"

"It's painful for you?" Paul questioned.

Lance hesitated and then went on. "On my grandfather's dying bed, I promised to uphold the Worthington legacy, and I'm feeling that I'm letting my family down."

Paul's brow was knitted with confusion, so Lance continued softly. "The board of directors promises to make a decision momentarily."

This fact was obviously new to Paul, so Rachel carefully asked. "Are you prepared to leave your family and move to Paris?"

Lance took a breath to calm the frantic beating of his heart. He didn't know how to answer, and Paul and his daughter didn't say anything but continued to eat. Lance followed their lead, hoping for an opportunity to escape to his private room. Unable to call Grace, he wondered if it was a mistake to agree to stay with Paul.

⁂

Early Saturday morning, Caroline strode into the great room smiling, but it slowly turned into a frown seeing Grace wrapped in a blanket, her shoulders sagging and her face dull and wet.

"I can see I arrived at an opportune time," Caroline announced. Ava stood nearby in anguish.

"I have good news," Caroline spoke as she laid her purse down on the sofa. "Come now, where's Lance?"

"He isn't here," Grace said in a hoarse whisper.

"I don't understand," Caroline's hands moved helplessly in front of her.

"He left for Paris," Ava related. "We thought you knew."

Caroline paled and moved to Grace's side. "He told me about the offer but not about going to Paris."

Grace nodded, and Caroline reached for her hand.

"Listen," Caroline said to the two women. "The board has approved Lance's reinstatement."

Grace's lower lip trembled. "How?"

Caroline's gaze embodied both daughter-in-law and granddaughter.

"My investigator uncovered, Sterling had purchased information on the acquisition and knew the company was near bankruptcy when he suggested it to the board. The board and stockholders all agreed that Lance was unaware of the situation and tried his best to find a solution afterward."

Grace grabbed onto Caroline's arm, "You did it!" Joy rushed through her.

"What will happen to Sterling?" Ava asked.

"The board had wanted to press charges, but I suggested they remove him from the board of directors and reassign him into an innocuous post, using his salary to pay the company back."

Ava's shrieks of laughter were louder than the wind. "When can Lance return?"

"Monday, if he wishes, or later. He's the CEO with all its benefits and power."

Grace's thoughts were entirely different. She prayed that Lance would be watchful and prayerful. She intuited that something much larger was behind the offer from Mr. Paul Van Fitzgerald.

Paul and Lance were greeted by Madame Sofia, Director of the Executive Level of La Château de Delicatessen. Rattling off a string of sentences in rapid French to Paul, Lance raised an eyebrow as Paul replied in French.

"Bienvenu," Sofia nearly crooned. Mesmerized by the sight of Lance's beautiful blueish-green eyes smiling at her. *It would be delightful to work with him.* "Please follow me."

"Thank you."

Paul and Lance followed her; Lance noticed this level was the beginning of a hotel within a hotel. A special desk and special staff were reserved for elite guests checking in and out. Guests on these top four floors of the sixteen-floor hotel had access only by special keys, and guests received VIP attention in their mini penthouses. However, the remaining twelve floors were also extraordinarily luxurious.

Madame Sofia led them into the private area of the VIP receiving suite, muttering to Paul in French. As the tour continued, Lance agreed with a nod at everything he saw but never gave Paul an answer. At the end of the tour and back on the first floor of the hotel, Lance learned the hotel would open in the spring.

"What's your opinion of the hotel?"

"I do not doubt that you've built a wonderful oasis for those who are looking for an escape."

One of Paul's brows flew upward. "Are you ready to commit?"

Lance pondered his answer. "This is a mammoth decision; I can't make without any forethought."

The older gentleman eyed him disdainfully. It appears Lance wasn't going to be an easy target.

"Well, enough talk about the job. We must head back to the house. I'm having a small dinner party this evening, but before we leave, I have a phone call to make."

Lance was so surprised that something else was planned, so for a moment, he didn't know what to say. In truth, something was nagging him about Rachel's nonchalant demeanor the night before.

"Paul, I was hoping to leave late this evening."

While studying Lance, Paul perceived something almost heavenly about him. Much as Paul needed Lance to remain, he was somewhat hesitant to continue with his plan.

"Please stay and allow me at least two more days to convince you. I want you to meet some affluent people from different countries starting tonight at my party."

CHAPTER 19

The Appearance of Deceit

L ance opened his bedroom door and leaned against it. He wasn't happy with the delivery of a tuxedo and put it on the bed. He shook his head in disgust at Paul's deliberate manipulation. Lance thought mockingly of his days dealing with some of his mother's manipulation. With much deliberation, Lance had reached a decision: he was leaving before any guests arrived. But in the hallway, Paul's personal man's servant interrupted him.

"Good evening, sir," he said civilly. "Mr. Van Fitzgerald wanted me to inform you he's waiting for you."

"I'm sorry, but I must leave," Lance's voice was calm, trying not to overreact.

The faithful servant politely said. "Sir, I believe Mr. Van Fitzgerald would be highly disappointed if you did."

Lance's upbringing shaped him never to disrespect his

elders and bombarded his mind. Therefore, he swallowed his pride. "Very well, tell Mr. Van Fitzgerald I'll make my entrance in ten minutes."

"Thank you, sir," the servant replied, desperately relieved.

Lance's display of testiness wasn't lost on the manservant. Dutifully, Lance went back into his room and put on the tuxedo; he decided to be on his guard.

Upon Lance's entry into the living area, he was greeted by sounds of chatter vibrating around the room.

"Lance!" Rachel crooned like a cat on the prowl, "Come, I want you to meet some of Father's friends," she reached out for his hand.

The guests within her circle turned toward the incoming hunk. The next several hours were the worst nightmare for Lance. At times, Lance was an exhibit of what some might interpret as the lover of the spoiled Van Fitzgerald heiress. Lance had to constrain himself not to think about Grace. He would concentrate on finishing the evening with a speck of decency.

◦◦◦◦

Lance had never known two days and nights to crawl so slowly. He attended meetings, parties, and small dinners, meeting the hotel's staff including concierges to bellhops, and in between.

Ready to return home, Lance was packing his bag to depart in the morning when Paul's manservant notified

Lance, that he was needed in the study. A few minutes later, Lance stood in Paul's study. It took about one hour to talk it out, but Lance agreed to meet a business person from Dubai for breakfast before leaving for New York that evening. Upset by the outcome, Lance was grateful to find a cup of cappuccino on his nightstand. Sipping the drink, he became mellow, and within minutes, Lance was in a deep sleep.

In the early morning hours, Rachel shook Lance. "Good morning, darling," her voice resonated in sweetness.

"What's going on here?" Lance was awake but confused and disoriented. His usually mesmerizing shade of blue-green eyes shifted to a hostile, icy blue while a callous determination took hold.

"Lance," she reached for him, but he vaulted from the bed.

With growing resentment, he wanted to shake her violently, but he calmly asked between clenched teeth. "Rachel! Tell me, what are you doing in my bed?"

Rachel flirtatiously raised her arms above her head. "Sweetheart, we made lovely music last night," she hummed.

Taking a few seconds to think this through, he asked, "What game are you playing?"

"No game, Lance, you were very passionate."

"I didn't touch you last night!" he thundered. "You will leave my room instantly before the household awakes.

"Don't be such a prude. You enjoyed yourself last night."

"Get out! You have one minute before I…"

"No need," her tone was hard. "I pity you, Lance. Understand this, you'll be mine, completely!" With that, Rachel scrambled off the bed and out of the room, grinning like an enchanted tigress.

Gradually, Lance's equilibrium returned. Distracted, he pondered, was the cappuccino drugged? Dressing quickly and holding his breath, Lance demanded to see Paul immediately before the hotel manager from Dubai arrived.

"What's the matter?" Paul suddenly asked.

"Let's get right down to business," Lance spoke with authority. "I regret that I can't accept your offer."

"With the added incentives, I think you will reconsider."

"I've concluded my answer is no," Lance stated emphatically.

"Worthington Steel may not reinstate you?"

"That's a chance I'm willing to take."

Paul stared at the young man before him, and when he spoke, his voice held all the command he expected. "I freely admit that I'm a man who likes to get his way," Paul said, laying the contract face down on the desk. "Nevertheless," Paul leaned closer across his desk. "Give me one more day to prove to you Paris is good for you."

"I'm sorry, the answer is no," Lance said without preamble. "My rescheduled flight to New York is this evening."

Paul was unsatisfied at Lance's assertiveness but also amused.

"Lance, I am not trying to influence you," Paul stated. "But I am suggesting you seize this unique opportunity."

Lance stood erect, his garment bag in his hand, arms hanging stiffly at these sides. "My family comes first. I'm leaving now for the airport."

Paul discounted his angry tone and began to speak. "I do believe you know our ideas about family are similar," Paul said, regarding Lance's piercing gaze.

"Goodbye, sir," Lance said, expressing his appreciation for Paul's hospitality and offer. He departed to a waiting cab he had called earlier.

South Hampton

"Pardon me, madam."

"Yes, Janet?" Grace looked up from her bible as Janet entered the library.

"You received a letter by messenger.," Janet stated. "Mrs. Worthington asked me to bring it immediately. It's from Paris."

"Thank you. If Mrs. Worthington isn't busy, I would like to speak with her."

"Very good, madam."

Grace closed her bible and laid it aside, waiting for Ava, the envelope in her hands. Minutes later, Ava waltzed in and sat in an identical powder blue chair opposite Grace. Ava couldn't understand how Grace appeared to be a picture of tranquility when her husband hadn't called in five days.

Smiling, Grace sighed and spoke.

"I suppose you're wondering why I didn't want to open this envelope apparently from Lance, privately."

"Well, I must admit, I'm curious."

"I wanted you here because we are family."

Ava savored the word *family*. Her relationship with Grace started with hatred and fear. She recognized that Grace had given her a second chance.

"Open it, and let's see what Paris has to say," Ava gushed.

Grace laughed a little and ripped the seal off the large envelope. Blinking rapidly, Grace pulled out pictures upon pictures of Lance and Rachel in many intimate situations.

"No...it... it... can't...," Grace cried in a high-pitched voice, "be...be...true!" Paralyzed in her chair, a ship sinking without a lifeboat, Grace seized her chest.

Ava gazed at Grace's troubled look, her forehead was wet with perspiration, her fingers antsy and trembling.

"Rachel, what have you done?" Ava muttered under her breath.

Tears welling up, Grace pulled out the last item inside. Through blurred vision, Grace choked on the newspaper clipping. *The Worthington Steel's dethroned heir has deserted the company and his pregnant wife for fetching Rachel Van Fitgerald and her family's millions.*

Fighting back tears and failing, Grace recoils and places her hands on her extended abdomen, knocking all the contents from her lap onto the floor.

Ava rushed to Grace's side, dodging images of Rachel's arms wrapped around Lance's neck, kissing him, with Paris as the backdrop.

"Grace!" Ava called her name gently as she touched Grace's shoulders and knelt beside her. Grace flinched from her touch.

"Don't fight me, Grace," Ava grew intently worried and walked to the intercom. Ava couldn't repress her shivering as she summoned Janet to call the doctor.

Grace hadn't spoken since she opened the envelope. Feeling totally helpless, Ava knew Lance wouldn't maliciously hurt anyone, even if the pictures told another story. Janet quickly retrieved the contents and gave it to Ava.

Several hours later, there was no change in Grace's condition. Ava summoned Janet to start getting Grace ready for travel. Her stomach was churning with fear for Grace and the babies. Ava made a phone call.

"Come, Grace, we're leaving for Penville," Ava said to Grace, who was unresponsive.

Ava had no idea how she and Janet managed to prepare Grace for the journey; however, working in tandem, the lady of the manor was ready within an hour. Like a ghost, Grace wobbled and swayed several times. Janet and the staff were truly afraid for their mistress of the manor.

Having settled Grace into a comfortable position on the Worthington's private jet, Ava reminisced about her conversation with Caroline.

What I've shared with you breaks my heart. I know Lance has been trying to be the man Grace needs, but evil forces are fighting him. I'm so fearful this may cause Grace to go into early labor. When Lance returns, please, Caroline, have him come quickly to Penville.

Late that Tuesday night, Ava and Grace appeared on Stone and Labella's doorsteps without any pleasantries or questions. Stone grabbed their suitcases while Labella positioned herself on the other side of Grace, and everyone went upstairs.

"Ava," Stone whispered. "Labella will settle Grace; your room will be across the hall. We will talk in the morning."

"Thank you," she said with a dry throat, trying not to fall on her face from sheer exhaustion.

Returning from Paris on the Concord, Lance landed in New York at ten in the morning fighting jet lag. Lance was happy to see Jeffrey, however., Lance felt Jeffrey's piercing eyes on him, and wondered if everything at home was well. With a glance at Jeffrey's tense posture, and receiving only a nod of acknowledgment, Lance knew something was amiss.

"Jeffrey, anything wrong?" Lance questioned him the moment the car started.

"No, sir."

"My wife?"

"Fine."

Lance thought it rather strange that Jeffrey sidestepped all his questions. He wondered what his driver was not telling him. Resolved not to be alarmed, Lance decided to wait until he arrived home. However, he was met with a quiet and mournful household. Taking two steps at a time, Lance kept reassuring himself until he found Grace's bedroom empty. Where was Grace?

Caroline had been weeping uncontrollably for hours at the stench of images Ava had dropped off. Seeing Lance sprinting into the solarium, Caroline quickly composed herself and told him the whole story.

Lance, remembers Paul Van Fitzgerald, to be a good businessman, wonders, *could Paul have done this sadistic act?*

"Those pictures were altered," Lance yelled.

Caroline's face gave nothing away; it never did.

"I will have my investigator look into this."

Lance spent the next hour detailing his trip. However, there was no denying the fact that, at one time, Lance had been romantically involved with Rachel. He needed to go to Grace immediately.

Penville, North Carolina

To put her mind at ease, Ava went to check on Grace the next day, finding her sound asleep. Ava did nothing to disguise the tears in her eyes as she relayed to Labella and Stone what pushed Grace over the edge.

Ava beseeched Stone not to hate her son, indicating that Caroline believed that the photos had been altered. To Ava's amazement, their treatment toward her was gentle and kind while they listened to her reasons. They continued to talk as Ava answered all their questions.

~

Fueled and cruising at 39,000 feet, Lance and Caroline settled comfortably in Worthington's corporate jet for its six-hour flight to Penville—the second such trip in two days. Considering that they left late in the afternoon, their arrival was going to be after 9:00 that evening.

Lance looked out of the large panoramic window, seeing stunning views and mountains. He was horrified at Paul's attack on his family, and he was sure Rachel was at the center of this destruction. A glance at his grandmother told him she wanted to talk with him. Caroline paused for a moment.

"I warned you!" Her voice was a bit testy.

"True, Grandmother," Lance said humbly. "I regret not heeding everyone's advice."

With a heavy heart, Caroline weighed her next words carefully.

"Lance, you fit so well in your new position within the family and company that I forgot you didn't grow up in this world."

Lance studied his grandmother for a moment. "I believe you've given me a compliment; however, I feel a "but" coming."

"You're right," Caroline was glad he sensed it. "Lance, you should've trusted me and waited before talking with Paul Van Fitzgerald."

The temptation to defend his decision was strong, so he reminded his grandmother he had no job, and his wife was expecting.

"You're not an ordinary working man, Lance," she said firmly. "Your pride got in the way."

Some of Lance's exasperation disappeared when Caroline explained he had no idea how to live the life he was born into since he was deprived of it. She then turned his attention to his responsibilities as the heir of the Worthington legacy.

"What if Paul's goal was to take over the Worthington Company, using your unfortunate situation as leverage? I'm sure you realized that since the death of your grandfather, the corporate business crocodiles are lurking for any opportunity to snatch up Worthington Steel."

His sigh was audible, and his eyebrows rose. Caroline orders him not to forget the legacy he carries and that his unborn babies were in line to inherit it. She clarified the idea that he had the right to forfeit his inheritance but cautioned him not to do it out of desperation.

"Grandmother, I'm truly sorry," Lance whispered, sitting back in his seat, utterly drained.

"I don't want you to punish yourself over this. I want you to succeed."

At that moment, Lance's heart was tattered and threadbare. Grace absolutely deserved an apology for his careless actions. He silently asked his Heavenly Father for assistance. Midway into the six-hour flight, the pilot anxiously announced a thunderstorm was heading their way and said they must land at the nearest airport.

It was almost nightfall when Caroline and Lance arrived at a small town a few hours away from Penville. Acquiring rooms at the only bed and breakfast, they walked a couple of blocks to a small quaint restaurant. Lance questioned his grandmother.

"Did you have the opportunity to see Grace before she left?"

"No, it seemed the right decision at the time."

"I hope she will listen to me," Lance looked unsure.

"I can't promise she will, but maybe with the two of us, you'll be successful," Caroline said.

Before retiring for the night, the pilot informed them that the weather was clearing and that they would be able to leave in the morning. It was a relief to be in their rooms, to reflect on their tumultuous thoughts. Caroline was well acquainted with Paul Van Fitzgerald's history of preying on his competitors' weaknesses. Lance was brooding over his failure as her protector, which assisted Grace in fleeing their home. Both, unable to reconcile this reality, wept silently in their rooms.

CHAPTER 20
A Shattered World

Labella and Ava checked on Grace during the day, encouraging her and making sure her needs were met. Grace was given broth before she rested for the evening. In expectation of Lance and Caroline's pending arrival that evening, a melancholy cloud dangled over the entire Forrester family.

Halfway through dinner, the ringing of the doorbell disrupted everyone's thoughts. Wyatt, closest to the entryway, departed to receive the expected guests. The weight of inquisitiveness drove everyone to leave the table. They were shaken to see a strange man standing in the entryway.

"Good evening," the stranger said, greatly encouraged by gaining entrance. He wasted no time introducing himself. "My name is Mr. Carl Jasper," his eyes looked at the group with disdain.

"Can you tell us what your visit is about?" Stone questioned politely, stepping in front of Wyatt, barely holding his temper for being treated rudely.

Jasper tried to dismiss the scorn on everyone's faces. "I'm sorry," he began, not sounding sorry, judging the burly man in front of him, wearing a red massive bushy beard.

"State your business, sir, and do it quickly," Stone's voice roared.

"I need to speak with Mrs. Worthington," Jasper's eyes narrowed.

"I'm Mrs. Worthington," Ava spoke up.

Confused, Jasper looked at the older lady. He was given the impression that Mrs. Worthington was younger. Leering at Ava, Jasper rationalized that he had the right people. Their questionable stares didn't deter him from his job. Therefore, he spoke deliberately to the group.

"I represent Mr. Paul Van Fitzgerald," he spoke cautiously.

"Why are you here?" Stone yelled.

"I wish to speak with Mrs. Grace Worthington about the defamation lawsuit against her husband."

Grace woke at the sound of her father's resounding voice vibrating her room. Silently, she lay looking around her room, wondering what instigated her father's anger. She carefully crawled from her bed and shuffled to the staircase. She whispered.... *It's concerning Lance and Rachel.*

"You need to leave now," Stone demanded as Wyatt opened the door, and Edmond moved to stand alongside Stone, both son replicas of their father.

"I had expected you to be angry," Jasper smiled with a bitter twist to his mouth, his focus never leaving the three men.

"I can see you believe your son-in-law isn't guilty."

Throughout Stone's heated wrath, Labella monitored his fortitude while his steely blue eyes scanned the stranger. Using a carefully controlled tone, Labella spoke hastily.

"I'm not saying your claim is true," Labella said. "Explain the reasons for the suit."

Amused by their misery, his voice became animated. "Months before marrying your daughter, Lance Worthington made love to Rachel Van Fitzgerald, promising to marry her," Jasper stated, exhibiting a gleeful smirk. "Recently, while in Paris, they renewed their relationship, but Mr. Worthington expeditiously left Paris when Ms. Van Fitzgerald showed proof, she's carrying his child."

Upstairs, Grace heard the words, *carrying his child*; she was saturated with rage and shame, her life shattered into debris. She tried to move from her spot but couldn't.

"Get out!" Stone exploded, snatching Jasper's left arm high in the air. With Edmond's help, they literally lifted Jasper's feet off the ground, tossing him out the door. "Tell your client he's suing the wrong person," his voice thunderous.

"Mr. Van Fitzgerald always gets what he wants," Jasper screeched, his words lost in the wind of the slamming door.

Beset by scandalous accusation, the group limped into the living room. Ava collapsed on the sofa; her sobs muffled as she leaned forward against her arms. Some minutes passed before Edmond saw Grace bent over, holding onto the banister, moaning. Everyone rushed to Grace's aid.

Grace was lifted and carefully put back into bed when a

sharp, indrawn breath filled the room. Stone ran to call the ambulance.

Suddenly, a contraction hit. "Mami'," Grace yelled, gripping Labella's hands.

As the contraction subsided, Grace spoke. "That hurts," she gasped.

"Yes, it does, but you're going to be fine."

"It's so painful," Grace grasped. "I didn't realize."

"You can do this. You're going to be a mother. Ava and I are here with you."

"Oh… I wish… Lance was here."

"He's on his way," Ava said.

"Will he come?" Grace moaned as another contraction hit.

Labella sat on the edge of the bed, holding her daughter against her chest, rocking her back and forth. A short time later, another contraction was soon on her. Grace felt warm liquid running down her legs. Grace lifted the sheet and saw red fluid.

Frightened, Grace screamed as another contraction hit her hard.

"Something is wrong. I'm wet, and my sheets are red."

Within minutes, an ambulance arrives at the Forrester's home, ready to transport Grace to the hospital. Grace squeezes Labella's hand, as another hard contraction almost render her unconscious. Grace floated on the brink of losing consciousness before another contraction startled her alert. Stone and Ava follow behind the ambulance, leaving Wyatt and Edmond to wait for the arrival of Lance and Caroline.

Penville Memorial Hospital

The doctor on call, decided to try and slow or stop Grace's contractions. Combating the smell of antiseptic, she was hit with a wave of nausea.

"Lance, Lance," she moaned. "I need you now."

"Please, Mrs. Worthington, it's important you stay quiet."

The nurse had given Grace something to relax her. Too weak to fight the effect of the medicine, sleep rushed in, and Grace gladly welcomed it. In the waiting area, Stone paced while Labella and Ava sat side by side on a sofa, their eyes on the automatic doors that had whisked Grace away. Almost two hours had passed before they were told the contractions had stopped, and she was sleeping. She would be admitted for a few days for observation.

For a moment, all three were silent.

"Stone?" Labella said softly, her eyes suspiciously moist. "Call the boys, and if Lance and Caroline haven't arrived, tell them to make haste."

Stone shook his head yes. Tears had come to his eyes. He bent down, kissing her cheek. "I will be back soon."

"Oh, Labella," Ava whispered, "I'm sorry. So very, very sorry."

"No, Ava, don't torture yourself…"

Wringing her hands, Ava wouldn't let Labella continue.

"My interfering has caused this travesty."

Labella quietly said. "Ava, in the book of Psalm 139:2, it reads," *thou knowest my down sitting and mine uprising, thou understand my thoughts afar off.*"

Labella calmly enlightened Ava that the verse means that God is aware of every detail of their lives, even the innermost thoughts, even before they are expressed.

Ava nodded, and thought in the future, she would ask Labella to expound further. This God thing was becoming real to her.

Subsequently, mid-morning, Edmond and Wyatt found everyone gathered in the family waiting room. Labella's heart lightened a bit, seeing her sons. However, she wondered where was Lance. In subdued voices, everyone contemplated what the outcome would be.

"Does anyone desire something from the cafeteria?" Edmond asked.

Even after surviving on black coffee all night, no one had an appetite. Sitting quietly and waiting for an update, the family bolted upright when the doctor entered. Fretful for Grace, one after the other, struggled to focus on the update.

"Mrs. Worthington is going to be all right," the doctor said. "No contraction in the last seven hours; things are looking promising."

A huge sigh was audible.

"Can we see her?" Labella questioned.

"She's being monitored right now, but she's fine. We'll bring more updates soon."

"What about the babies?" Ava interjected while her sorrow of losing a baby at birth unfolded in flashbacks.

"At the moment, mother and babies are doing fine."

The doctor finished his report and left. Stone's eyes rose to the ceiling, and his heart cried out thanks to God as he reached for Labella. The brothers bruised themselves, hugging each other, as Ava sat sobbing.

"It's going to be all right, Bella," Stone said, hugging her tightly.

It was such a relief to hear that Grace and the babies were fine; the emotional exhaustion was lifted, and hunger quickly took residence. The men left in search of food.

Several hours had passed when the doctor emerged again to give another update on Grace's condition. Suddenly, Code OB was paged over the intercom, and a whoosh of nurses and machines rushed past the waiting area to Grace's room. A nurse hurried inside the waiting area and whispered in the doctor's ear; his face became dark with panic and fear.

It was clear something wasn't right. In a daze, the family of five followed behind the doctor, but a frightful woman in scrubs halted them. Quietly, they watched in horror as the door closed in their faces. As they leaned against the cold grey wall, their eyes were glued to the door. It seemed like forever when the doctor finally opened the door and motioned them to the waiting area.

"I'm sorry, but Grace's contractions have started again, and we can't delay them any longer."

Labella took a deep breath. "The babies…"

"Their hearts are dropping slightly, so we must do an emergency C-section. She's being prepared for surgery," the doctor said softly.

Ava found solace in the presence of Edmond and Wyatt while Labella clutched Stone's arm, murmuring. "The babies…"

Stone, unable to process what was happening to his only daughter, crudely detached Labella's grip, turned and left as the family peers at his retrieving back.

Lance and Caroline arrived at the Forrester's home, where the housekeeper informed them that Grace had been taken to the hospital the previous evening. Staring blindly at the housekeeper who was closing the front door, Lance stood stationary, holding his stomach.

"I've caused this, Grandmother. If Grace and the babies die, I'm to blame."

Caroline firmly guided Lance's body so they were looking directly at each other.

"Nothing could be further from the truth," she said softly.

Lance's entire body convulsed in agony as they silently rode to the hospital. He felt nauseous from the pain in the pit of his stomach. As spots danced before his eyes, he knew Grace deserved a better man than he.

"My heavenly father has given me a second chance. Grandmother, I don't want to fumble," he whispered. His last thought before they reached the hospital was that Grace needed him.

Lance was appreciative to find Stone standing outside the entrance of the hospital. However, being a few feet away, Lance saw something that stopped him in his tracks.

"Stone?" Lance questioned.

Stone stood rigidly near the front desk, watching nothing specifically. He carefully turns around at the sound of his name. In spite of Lance's contrite expression, Stone remembers the doctor's words and lashed out. "You're not wanted here," Stone hissed; specks of water covered his eyes.

Lance comprehended his father-in-law was angry.

"It's your fault," Stone yelled. "My daughter is getting ready for surgery at this very moment because of you."

"Please, sir, don't shut me out," Lance spoke softly, but Stone didn't look at him.

Caroline covered her mouth with quivering hands while onlookers passed through the automatic doors.

"Sir, I beg you, please, let me see Grace," Lance's voice quivered.

"No!" Stone finally looked at him, his voice detached.

"I'm not leaving until I see my wife," Lance angrily replied.

"That's a laugh, your wife?" Stone snickered. "You're not wanted here. Leave now."

Lance hadn't expected this greeting, and he felt as if he'd been slapped. "Where shall I go?"

"I don't care where you go; just leave from my sight."

Lance couldn't believe his ears. He knew Stone was upset,

but he wasn't prepared for this. Lance turned to his grandmother.

"Go, Lance," Caroline breathed. "It's best you check into the hotel downtown. I will send for you later."

Like a disobedient child, he finally nodded. He squeezed her hands and walked away, looking over his shoulder. Lance had no idea when he would see his wife again, if ever. He couldn't bear leaving, so he wandered around the grounds of the hospital.

Caroline had gone deathly pale, hoping Stone would come to his senses. Fixated by a large potted plant, Caroline continued to watch Stone wrestle with his anger, never mumbling a word. Completely unconscious of their surroundings, Wyatt's approach went unnoticed.

"Dad, you look miles away," Wyatt commented as he stood next to his father, studying his expression. "Mom sent me to find you."

"I don't wish to return yet," Stone told Wyatt with a voice of finality.

Wyatt had no trouble understanding his father's wishes, but he also knew the wrath he would receive from his mother. Believing that the old man would do anything he wished, he pressed on.

"Are you ready to go?" Wyatt asked, tucking his arm in his father's, gently leading him to the elevator. Stone nearly protested, but he followed his son, Caroline followed close behind.

Ten minutes later, Labella abruptly stopped in mid-sentence, struck by the sudden appearance of Caroline without Lance. One question swirled in her mind.

"Stone, where is Lance?"

Too stubborn to admit he was wrong in his actions, Stone refused to answer. Speechless, Labella and Ava looked at Caroline for an answer.

"As a matter of fact, Lance was here," Caroline stated.

For the first time, Labella was disenchanted with Stone. Lost for words, she sighed quietly, searching her husband's face.

"All right, Stonewall Forrester, what have you done?"

"I don't think I need to answer."

"That's absolute nonsense." Labella's voice was very earnest but not accusing or angry. "I love you, Stone, but I think the very reason for your willfulness is that you're afraid. You have allowed the devil to take your peace away."

Stone wanted to cry out but now wasn't the time. He had been disrespectful to Lance and Caroline, and he knew it. A heavy silence fell within the room, and Labella prayed, asking God to guard his heart and mind. She loved Stone so much; it was at times like this that Labella had to remind herself that God loved him more. It was hard to admit that the man you have always loved and respected was wrong.

"Sons, please," Labella's voice was low. "Go find Lance."

Stone moved to one of the end chairs and stared at the floor.

Grace's family huddled in the waiting area, praying for her safety and her unborn babies. It has been over an hour since she went into surgery to deliver her babies by C-section. Edmond, Wyatt and Lance, looking disheveled, arrived at the precise moment the doctor made his appearance.

Stone and Labella lurched to their feet, searching the doctor's expression. For twenty-eight years, Grace had done nothing but give them joy. Now, they were on the verge of finding out if their sweet angel was alive or dead. Holding each other close, they held their breath.

"Is Mr. Worthington present?" the doctor whispered.

Lance swiftly backed up against the wall. He was rendered speechless, displaying a vacant, glassy glare.

"Speak, man!" Stone boomed at Lance, throwing his hands up.

Confused by the commotion, the doctor cleared his throat and spoke directly to Stone in a detached tone. "Mrs. Worthington has lost a lot of blood," he confided. "At one point, I thought we were going to lose her."

Labella swallows hard. "The babies?"

"I'm sorry we couldn't save the twin boys," the doctor explained. "Due to her severe loss of blood, she's currently in an induced coma."

Lance exhaled loudly, doubling over in pain. Time seemed to slow down as the truth materialized in a chilling mist.

"I suggest everyone go home and return in the morning. If you're a praying family, continue to pray for her recovery."

Feeling as though he was in a dream, Lance watched Labella bury her face in Stone's chest. His eyes moved across the room, beholding sneers of disgusted pinched lips, and shaking heads. In that instant, torment entered his heart.

Adverting everyone's gazes, Lance moved away from the wall, speaking to no one; he left. He absently thought as he left the hospital in the dusk of the night that he really ought to have spoken to his mother and grandmother.

Stone saw that Labella, Ava, Caroline, and the boys were settled in the family room. No one spoke, but Stone sat close to Labella, and others joined them at a slow pace. Forrester's live-in housekeeper entered with coffee and sandwiches. Seeing Labella shiver, Agatha returned, covering her with a blanket.

"I can't stop crying," Labella said as Ava nodded in agreement.

"It's alright, Mother," Wyatt chimed in. "We're all mourning."

This unexpected tragedy had left the family feeling numb. Unable to process the reality of the situation, Stone spoke. "Ava, you may not agree with my decision, but Lance isn't in a position right now to make a sound decision."

"It's fine; if he returns, his hurt won't allow him to have a clear perspective," Ava whispered.

"We must first establish a plan and schedule, so that Grace won't be alone in ICU," Labella stated.

"Yes, that's a great idea," Stone answered quietly, wondering about the funeral arrangements.

"Stone," Caroline said, distressed but not crying, "Let me help you with the funeral."

"Thank you, Caroline," Stone replied, wanting to make his wife's life less painful.

Stone stared at his somber family, still amazed that this had happened to them. But he also knew that grief or not, they must continue living. Stone and Labella said goodnight while the rest went their separate ways. Wyatt and Edmond promised to return early in the morning, and Ava and Labella proceeded to their rooms.

"My heart's broken in two," Labella admitted while she and Stone held one another desperately in the privacy of their room. "It's beyond my wildest dreams; God would allow our child to experience a loss, just as I did."

"We must comfort one another to survive," Stone whispered.

"Stone!" Labella suddenly said, seizing his shirt with urgency. "What about Lance? We must find him and tell him about the burial."

"Bella, listen carefully," he explained. "Our daughter needs us more than ever. Ava and Caroline can deal with Lance."

"But he's Grace's husband, and she needs him."

"True, but we need to allow God to work on Lance."

Not until morning did Labella find out how swiftly word traveled. They received phone calls from the church family, townspeople, and family and friends of both families.

CHAPTER 21
The Nightmarish Misery

Aday later, mourners gathered around two small graves. André, Stella, Perry, Lance's father and stepmother, and a few board members from Worthington Steel had traveled from New York. However, Lance seemed to have vanished like smoke. Deeply drawn in their grief, the families didn't hear the pastor's final words or scripture: *The Lord giveth and the Lord taketh away; blessed be the name of the Lord.* Their eyes were filled with sorrow, compassion, and love. They found it difficult to say goodbye to little Parker and Shaun, who they never had a chance to meet.

Everyone gathered back at the home of Stone and Labella Forrester afterward for a meal prepared for the family and other mourners. Caroline, acting as hostess, saw to it that all were comfortable. At one point, when there was a lull in the activities, Labella and Caroline found themselves alone.

They embraced warmly.

"Why don't you slip out to visit Grace," Caroline stated. "Ava and I will help Stone until the guests leave."

"Oh, Caroline, thank you." Labella's voice was awed, her eyes wide with contentment.

"Grace is going to be all right," Caroline's voice was soothing. "It's inconceivable. I would believe in God, but I'm starting to." Caroline had to stop. Sometimes, additional words weren't necessary.

"I've already talked to Stone about you going to the hospital. He's charged Edmond to escort you."

Labella nodded and departed.

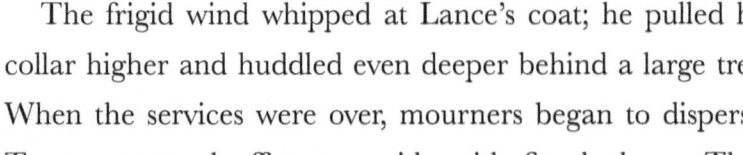

The frigid wind whipped at Lance's coat; he pulled his collar higher and huddled even deeper behind a large tree. When the services were over, mourners began to disperse. Two men stood off to one side with fitted gloves. They gripped the handles of the small caskets and lowered them into open ground.

Once all the mourners had left the cemetery and the grave diggers departed, Lance made straightway to his sons' everlasting cradles. He stood looking at the freshly covered graves; cries of woe echoed throughout his words. *Father, why did you allow this to happen? How could you take our sons? Grace isn't at fault. I'm the one to blame, not Grace. If someone needed to be punished, it should've been me, not my wife and babies. In addition,*

I wasn't even allowed to see or grieve with my wife. I wish I were dead. Lance's throat clogged as he spat those words at God in anger and bitterness.

The storm of anger raged within him, leaving him completely adrift on the churning waves of sorrow, tossed about with no control. Lance took one last look at the two graves and stiffly walked away. He climbed into his car, closed his eyes, and tried to erase the newspaper's announcement. *It's with deep sorrow that we announce the passing of two precious angels, Parker and Shuan Worthington, newborn twins of Lance Worthington and Grace Worthington-Forrester. A memorial service will be held tomorrow, 10:30 a.m., at Penville Cemetery.*

Across the street from the Forrester's home, a grieving Lance sat quietly inside the car. He looked out the window at the mass of people dressed in black from head to toe. He caught sight of his father-in-law at the door, his face a mask of gloom and disappointment.

Lance hesitantly paused at the hospital information desk. With his hands tightly gripped inside his pants pocket, he cleared his throat. The volunteer behind the desk looked up. Lance detected a look of pity and instantly knew he looked as sad as he felt.

"Excuse me, madam. Can you tell me the room number of Mrs. Grace Worthington?"

"Are you a family member?"

"Yes, I'm her husband, Mr. Lance Worthington."

A smile stretched across the volunteer's face. Next, she checked the visitor's list and, with a quick hand to her mouth, told Lance something was amiss.

Blinking, "I'm sorry, sir, but your name isn't on the visitor's list."

Lance didn't bank on being left off the visitor's list. His normally fearless personality was crumbling at his feet. All of Lance's suppressed hopefulness drained away, and he left without speaking. The words, *not on the visitor's list,* seemed to stretch from the desk to the automatic doors.

Feeling discouraged, Lance saw no reason to hang around Penville. He hadn't spoken with his mother or grandmother, and a future with Grace was gone; he caught the next flight to New York.

On the fourth day of Grace's ordeal, Stone and Labella's hearts were near to bursting as they watched Grace's lids flicker from the induced coma. The doctor and nurse stood close to their patient.

"Mrs. Worthington, can you open your eyes," the doctor beseeched her. Grace made inconsistent moans. "Mrs. Worthington, please open your eyes; your parents are waiting for you."

Once her eyes were open and her vital signs checked, the doctor departed, leaving the family with a promise to return after lunch.

"Mami, Papi," Grace spoke softly,

"We're here," they said, gripping each other's hands.

"Where's Lance?"

"He isn't here, my wee one," Stone whispered.

Grace fixated her eyes on her father with bated breath.

"Where is he?"

"We don't know," Stone answered. "We believe he went back to New York."

Grace's eyes flew to her mother. "The babies…"

Labella quickly shook her head no, and then watched Grace whimper like a broken melody. Neither parent knew how to tell her the past events; however, they shared it and allowed Grace's quietness to continue.

Grace didn't have the slightest inkling as to why her father sat with a granite face until Labella left the room for some ice chips.

"Grace, every father, wants the best for his daughter, but Lance ran the first moment of hardship. You should divorce him."

What he said struck Grace as heart-wrenching, as she married Lance for better or worse. For the first time, it was important for her father to see her as an adult and not his little girl.

"Father, thank you for caring and loving me my entire life, but now, with God's help, I must work on my marriage."

Grace has always been special in his heart, a gift from God. A side glance at Grace told him the conversation was finished. Upon the uplifting news, Grace was awake and on the road to recovery; Caroline and Ava left for New York to find Lance and squash the Van Fitzgerald plans.

Days went by, turning into two weeks. Lance was doing well in regaining the board members, and stockholders' trust once again. Lance wasn't to know the day of reckoning was near. However, the surprise arrival was in the form of Mr. Jasper, a brazen lawyer representing Paul Van Fitzgerald.

"What's your reason for this visit?"

"Mr. Worthington," Jasper laughed. "You're familiar with my reasons."

"Am I?" was all Lance said. He didn't want Mr. Jasper feeling too overconfident.

"Did you receive my correspondence?"

"Well, a certified envelope did arrive a while back, but it's still unopened."

Jasper gestured with his hands, looking somewhat flustered. "Interestingly, you're taking this so calmly," he said in a hostile voice.

Lance kept silent, curious about what Mr. Jasper's next step would be. Mr. Jasper altered his stance, resting his briefcase on his lap and taking out an envelope.

"What this?" Lance stared at the envelope.

Mr. Jasper jerked his head violently, "Rachel Van Fitzgerald is suing you for defamation."

"Why!"

"Ms. Van Fitzgerald is carrying your child?" Mr. Jasper laid the summons on Lance's desk. …. your job is at stake. Here's my card. I expect to hear from you in three days," He turns and walks out.

Never would Lance have dreamt his life would be in such pandemonium. He spent the next three hours talking with Caroline. It took everything Lance had inside not to disagree with his grandmother's instructions.

In view of Lance's long absence having a cruel effect on Grace, Stone felt she should remain in Penville. To salvage her marriage, Grace left Penville the first week in November.

The first day back at the manor, Grace found it difficult to relax. Not knowing Lance's whereabouts, she went to the library in search of a book to read. Noticing a large stack of condolences on the desk, she began to open them one by one. Reading the encouragements and prayers from people she didn't know brought tears to her eyes.

Pulling out thank you cards, Grace wrote from her heart. Janet stood quietly, attempting to get her attention.

"My lady, Mrs. Caroline Worthington, is here to see you."

"Thank you," Grace answered. "Make her comfortable in the great room."

Grace lowered her pen and dutifully walked into open arms.

"It's good to see you. Your mother called to say you were back."

Grace smiled.

"Lance is back with the company," Caroline stated as she watched Grace stiffen.

Grace didn't comment.

"There's something you need to know." Caroline regretfully informed Grace of Mr. Jasper's visit and the summons. Grace listened with only half an ear to the conversation as she recalled the night her father's voice woke her. Instantly, she remembered the words, *Rachel's having Lance's baby.*

Grace made her apologies and left. Caroline, dumbstruck by the action, didn't wait for Janet or anyone to see her at the door. Grace took herself off to bed to fall into a dreamless sleep.

Even though she was hurting, Grace ached to see Lance. Each day, her mind pondered why he hadn't returned. Anxiously, she looked for him to walk through the doors. As a drunken woman full of wine, Grace earnestly pleaded with God for answers, receiving nothing.

On the anniversary of one month of the twins, Shawn and Parker, entry into heaven, Grace was drowning in stormy seas. She ordered the nursery with all its furniture, clothes, and toys to be locked. Yet, for endless days and nights, Grace lingered near the locked room, longing to hold her babies. Many nights, she would sneak inside the nursery, cradling two teddy bears, bearing their names, and screaming, *it wasn't supposed to be this way.*

Feeling numb, Grace brushed her hands over the cribs and the hanging sports theme mobiles from her father. While fixating on the football field mural, an overall sorrowful feeling had taken root in her soul.

CHAPTER 22

Death

The week prior, Lance sat in stunned silence after Caroline said he must accept Paul Van Fitzgerald's demand to move in with Rachel, or he would go public about the lawsuit. Caroline didn't believe Rachel was pregnant, no matter if she had a sonogram as proof. In addition, Caroline knew it wouldn't do any good to take the Van Fitzgeralds to court. People would always have doubts, even if Lance won the lawsuit.

Her office clock read 1:00 p.m., and momentarily forgetting her lunch, she sat down and made her usual daily call to Lance. However, this call was met with a cry of outrage. He was losing his patience.

"Lance, you can't give up," Caroline whispered into the phone. "It's only been one week."

"I'm so tired of this farce." The words came on bated breath. "I can't stand it any longer, Grandmother."

"It won't be much longer, Lance."

Moments later, hearing his loneliness and desperation, Caroline hesitantly placed the phone on the receiver. Lance looking at the dead phone, honestly believe he would never see Grace again.

Rachel stepped out of the elevator as Lance made his way to the kitchen, carrying an empty plate. Rachel had imagined that when Lance arrived, they would act like husband and wife. But Lance made it clear he wanted no part of the charade.

"Let's just imagine that we are married and excited about the baby," Rachel said reasonably.

"No! And you should stop this madness immediately." Lance roared.

"Not on your life. Your precious wife lost your sons, but now you can love our son."

"I don't love you, never did, never will, Rachel. Let me go."

"I suggest you concentrate on how to be a good father."

To Rachel's amazement, Lance shook his head and smiled.

"Lance Worthington, you're crazy."

"Crazy in love with God and Grace."

Rachel watched him walk down the hall toward his room, catching his shoulders shaking in glee. Enraged, she re-entered the elevators, swearing out loud, *Lance, you will regret the day you ever met me.*

Rachel interrupted her father's nightly solitude and night-cap. Her goal was to humiliate Grace, which meant that she had one additional favor to ask of her father.

For many years, it's been just the two of them since his beloved wife died when Rachel was a young teen. Paul's past tendencies were to indulge his daughter's every whim. Now, she believed that the universe revolved around her. She uses people and then discards them when she has no more need for them.

"Father, I want you to give the biggest party New York society has ever had, announcing the birth of my child with Lance."

Paul was shocked by her request.

"That's not possible," Paul said; for the first time in his life, he denied his daughter.

"I'm not asking you, father. I'm telling you. I want this!"

"I'm not sure this is the best time," Paul told his daughter kindly.

"Why not?"

Paul shook his head. His voice was gentle, but he held his jaw at a stubborn angle. "Lance is still legally married, and that being said, we must wait."

"Father," Rachel reaches out for him, panic on her face. "I'm sure Lance will get used to the idea. Anyway, it doesn't matter; I'm having his baby."

Paul opened his mouth to say more, but as he turned, he spotted the gilded frame on the bar. His loving wife's smiling eyes arrested him to face the truth about how he raised their only daughter.

"I must think of our stockholders and board directors. Besides, you've waited for him a long time; a little longer would be worth it."

"Father, please don't deny this request," she said, water building up in her eyes. "You must do this for me. I'm carrying Lance's baby!"

Paul went to his daughter, putting his arms around her. Her statement was a hard blow to him. He had never seen Rachel so helpless and weak. It had never occurred to Paul that Rachel would want something so badly; she would change her whole outlook on life.

"I've dreamed for so long," Rachel cried, "and now it's so close."

Paul smoothed her long hair off her face.

"It's not forever," Paul soothed. "Just a little while longer."

Rachel disregarded her father's calm voice. *You need to have patience; with time, Lance will gladly marry you, and happily, you will raise a child.*

The father and daughter exchanged a long look.

Paul nodded. His heart beat fast while he comprehended the irrationality of their conversation. He recognizes his company couldn't bear an unsightly scandal, but on re-examination, the possibilities were present.

Returning to her penthouse, Rachel pushed her father's words far from her mind. Her chest heaved from the exertion of his disapproval. She reasoned this was her last chance to win Lance's love. How in the world did a man such as Lance love such a socially inept woman? The very thought of Grace being Mrs. Lance Worthington made Rachel madly insane.

Moving very slowly, she took out her address book and diligently added names to her party list. Barely holding her elation, Rachel was certain her plan of revenge would surely drive Grace to start the divorce proceeding.

∽

The last couple of days, Lance heard furniture crashing against the tile floors outside his room. On the third day, Rachel told Lance she was giving a soiree within an hour. She briefly explained he was expected to attend. In truth, Lance stood in the middle of his room with an expression of puzzlement on his face. He wasn't interested in playing the fictional role of the *man of the hour.*

"What I need to say won't take long," Rachel said, wearing a long, flowing evening gown that accentuated a teeny bump in the front. "You'll be charming, adoring and most of all gracious to my guests."

Lance stared at her. He questioned within, *why must I play this charade?*

Side-stepping his weird look, Rachel continued. "And don't keep me waiting."

Lance shrugged and waited for her to leave. Instantaneously, Lance knelt by his bed to pray.

Father, I am tempted to beg you to let this suffering pass, yet I mustn't. Thank you for these dark hours of my life. I have no doubts about you, and I'm immensely contrite and sorry for the injury I have caused. I've learned a valuable lesson in humility. Please help me to trust you for Grace and my future continually.

Lance continued talking from his heart to God until he heard music and much laughter. Putting on his attire and the finishing touches of his appearance, he departed his sanctuary of privacy to stand strong in the battle.

The penthouse was marked by grandeur, elegance, and extravagance, highlighting luxurious fabrics, rich colors, and ornate details. The room buzzed with a lively atmosphere, with music, food and drinks. Energy flowed as Rachel's globetrotting friends, dressed to impress and notable reporters, danced and chatted. Everyone had gathered to celebrate Rachel's fresh start.

"Hello," Tim Archibald, III greeted Rachel as soon as he entered into a glorious golden age of Hollywood glam. "It's hard to believe you're pregnant," Tim said, remembering their many exotic and mischievous vacations together.

"Well, now," Rachel smiled at him. He was so handsome in his tux; she wondered why she hadn't fallen for him. "You're certainly looking attractive this evening."

Tim smiled in return and did some admiring of his own, causing Rachel's face to flush.

CHAPTER 22

"We are so glad you came," Rachel began, not able to keep the enthusiasm from her voice.

"Where's the man of the hour?"

"He will be here shortly," Rachel gushed.

"How did you meet this glorious creature?"

"We met at one of the country club events."

Whispers resonated strongly the moment Lance made his appearance. The party had been in full swing for more than thirty minutes. Rachel would have blatantly screamed if he hadn't looked so debonair. She suddenly appeared at Lance's side, slipping an arm through his.

"Everyone!" she said, speaking over the noise, "I'm proud to introduce my fiancé Lance Worthington of the Worthington Steel Company." It took all Lance's etiquette skills to smile while Rachel introduced him.

Shaking hands and smiling at the right moments, with proper courtesy, Lance listened, bending his head to all the congratulatory words.

"Good evening, Mr. Worthington," Tim began. "I'm sorry we didn't have a chance to meet sooner; Rachel is a wonderful person."

"It's a pleasure to meet a friend of Rachel's, and please call me Lance."

Tim was so eager to meet this young man who had risen from anonymity to notoriety in such a short time and who had stolen his prize. He knew she was spoiled and judgmental, but he fell in love the moment his eyes rested upon her. He thought getting to know this man might allow him to forget her.

335

"If I recall, you're the grandson of Sterling Worthington, Sr."

Lance nodded.

"I understand you have inherited Worthington's fortune and are now the new CEO."

"Yes, that's correct."

"May I interrupt?" a female voice broke in at Tim's side."

Lance stayed quiet, listening to the two of them talk about how delighted they were for Rachel and her luck meeting such a wonderful man. However, another group of guests caught the female's attention, and she was off.

At that point, Lance had had enough of Rachel's friends, and he knew he wouldn't be able to keep up this pretense any longer. He was still musing over it when Tim smiled at him.

"I want to extend an invitation to you and your lovely fiancé," Tim continued, trying the word fiancé for the first time. "You're welcome to sail with me on my yacht before Rachel's unable to.

For a moment, Lance was speechless. Had Tim truly been fooled by the charade? Finally, Lance mustered out a *Thank you.* He glanced over to see Rachel enjoying a group of men and women. Observing the scene, Lance still believed that God had a hand in his problem. How long would it be before things would change? He didn't know; only God did.

Lance told himself not to be angry when Rachel beckoned him onto the dance floor. Not taking any chances of overreacting, he worked to close the distance between them.

Rachel allowed Lance to lead her onto the dance floor. The ballad was half over when Tim cut in so smoothly that Lance bowed away graciously.

"You've your whole life to dance with your future husband," Tim stated, his voice soft.

"I suppose that's true," she admitted.

"I find it hard to pretend, but I hate you're engaged."

His statement brought Rachel's eyes to him for a moment, so Tim felt the need to continue. "I'm not sure how to tell you, but I have always loved you, and how deeply I regret not telling you sooner."

This time, Rachel looked up longer.

"I suppose you think I've lost my respectability for you and Lance," Tim suggested. "I'm not ashamed, only stating my case."

The dance ended, but Tim still wasn't certain where he stood. For the moment, he proceeded as if nothing had happened. "We're still friends?" Tim asked.

"Yes"

They parted, leaving Rachel trying to dismiss her strange feelings. Tim's pronouncement had scared her substantially. She knew his proclamation couldn't be acknowledged. Rachel was still thinking about it when the evening soiree began to dwindle. Lance and Rachel bid everyone a good night.

The party was hailed as a success, and the fake couple could finally seek their rest. Walking to their respective rooms, Rachel hesitated.

"My friends adore you," she stated. "Thank you, Lance."

"You're welcome," he whispered. "But I won't do it again, Rachel. Good night."

Rachel nodded silently, turned, and walked in the opposite direction.

It was a good night for both of them but for very different reasons. Rachel repeatedly relived the dance with Tim and his statement. Despite facing numerous obstacles, Lance's unwavering spirit and determination were the characteristics of a man who loved God. He fell sound asleep, thanking his Heavenly Father that he had passed the test.

The morning sailed into the afternoon, and Lance was still asleep when Caroline made her usual phone call.

"Lance, I have some interesting news," Caroline stated.

His heart throbbed with anxiety, his exhaustion fleeing.

"Grandmother, will you please tell me what you heard."

"I have uncovered a doctor in the Bronx who received over twenty-five thousand dollars from Mr. Van Fitzgerald. Around the same time, Mr. Jasper produced Rachel's sonogram."

Lance jerked upward from the bed, and joy rushed through him.

"Then, we have proof: Rachel isn't pregnant!" Lance blurted.

Thinking back to a fight with Rachel, Lance remembered she let it slip about the baby's gender, which was impossible to know, considering she was only a month pregnant.

"Yes, but we must handle this with caution."

Lance sighed. "Why, I don't understand; I'm finally free from this bondage!"

"You don't have to agree, but remember, your previous impulsive behavior led to a regrettable outcome."

Lance decided not to fret and wait on God's perfect timing. He couldn't do anything, but his eyes lit with excitement. It took Lance several moments to realize he should try to get out of bed. Selecting a pair of dark jeans and a sweater, he ventured to the kitchen to have a snack. Relieved Rachel was nowhere to be found, and she had given the staff a day off, he sat back in his chair, his legs stretched out, thinking *soon he would be released from his prison.*

Heading back to his room, Lance mindlessly picked up the morning newspaper off the side table in the living room. Facing the view outside his window and newspaper in hand, he gave a surreptitious glance at the society page. His eyes locked onto an article that caught his attention. Speechless, he slowly read: *A wealthy socialite is expecting, and the father-to-be is the newly re-installed married CEO. Lance's brows rose. Well, he thought uncharitably, at last, they have no hold over me.*

Hitting his hand with the rumpled newspaper, Lance had no idea if Rachel was awake, but he was going to speak to her at any cost. Cutting across the living room to get to the opposite side, Lance found his target sitting on the sofa, looking indifferent.

"Rachel, put the magazine aside; we need to talk," he announced.

"Fancy seeing you out of your cocoon," Rachel gaily spoke as Lance walked toward her.

"What brings you out of your cocoon?" she stood up slowly. "Have you resolved we are a couple?

"No," Lance growled.

"Wrong!" she replied, annoyed. "Admit it, I'm in your blood."

"I don't love you," Lance's eyes were smoking hot. "I'll always love Grace."

"The days will come when you'll love me," she playfully ran her slender red fingernails up and down his chest. "No matter how long it takes. I will wait."

Lance jerked away, his eyes burning a hole in Rachel. "Do you ever hear the truth?"

"Stop it, stop." Her once immaculate features now seemed to ripple with the intensity of her fury.

"You and I will never be," his shirt strained against his taut muscles.

"Lance, I know you love me," Rachel said as she breathed heavily.

"You've believed in your lies for so long that you can't distinguish the truth from a lie. I'm leaving Rachel," he turned to walk toward the elevator.

"Don't you walk away from me," she sizzled following him.

"You're a fool," he said with venom in his voice as she grabbed his wrist.

"How dare you call me a fool," she screamed, hitting Lance's chest using her free hand. Her eyes flashed dangerously as they struggled back and forth. I'm more valuable than your precious Grace."

"Rachel, you don't know the meaning of valuable!"

The belligerent atmosphere in the penthouse was quickly escalating; embarrassed Lance released her.

"Get it through your entitled head; there will never be anything between us."

"You…you can't see that you married beneath your social standing."

"Now, we are coming to your expertise," he laughed mirthlessly.

"I don't know what you mean."

"You see yourself a privilege soul, someone who feels that they deserve whatever they desire."

"So, what," she snarled, spreading her arms wide. "I can't help it if I was born in wealth, just like you."

"But my wealth doesn't define me. That's the difference between us. On the other hand, you're a pompous, pampered heiress."

A low rumble came from deep in Rachel's chest. Slowly, she picked up a crystal vase.

"It's immoral for you to marry so far beneath you," Rachel yelled, seizing a vase full of white roses and water in her hand.

"Rachel," Lance's brows knit. "Please put the vase down."

"This little thing," she purred.

"Please, Rachel," his heart was throbbing while he snatched his luggage and slowly moved backward.

With sheer force of rage, Rachel reared back and threw the vase.

"You're nuts!" Lance said through gritted teeth, escaping the vase by mere inches.

"Get out!" Rachel exploded with rage. Grabbing a pair of stone lioness bookends, she simultaneously threw them while yelling, "Get out, get out."

Eluding each thrown item, Lance rushed to the elevator, frantically pushing the button while weaving and dodging shattered items hitting the walls and floor. Lance literally fell into the elevator as Rachel screamed, "I never want to see you again."

CHAPTER 23
Intense Heat

C lose to six weeks since Lance left for Paris, the day broke into a clear, sunny day. Yet, teasing snow wasn't far away, and Grace woke once again without a husband. Time seemed to be whisking by without her experiencing the joys of living. Can her devastation be restored into something positive? Every bit of her life was flying around her in shattered debris.

Grace knew that she was going to have to make some changes if she was going to survive the loneliness. So, she went to the study to work on her correspondence. At first, it looked as if her day would be fruitful. However, she couldn't concentrate, so she picked up the morning paper to read.

The tranquility swiftly turned into an absolute frenzy. Grace screamed as her heart skipped a beat, and her jaw dropped in total disbelief, her knuckles turning white as she gripped the paper.

"Rachel...I've had enough!" she howled. "You can have him. I'm done!"

Hearing their mistress' outburst, Janet dashed into the study.

"That woman!" Grace stomped her foot, not talking to anyone in particular.

"What woman?" Janet curiously asked.

Grace was mesmerized. The article held a hypnotic spell on her, drawing her into the abyss of desolation. The night of her own engagement party swept across her mind, glazed with a vivid remembrance of Rachel's declaration *Lance would always belong to her.*

"Rachel did this to humiliate me," Grace shook the news-paper vehemently in the air. Her face was distorted as she continued. "Rachel has gone too far, and Lance has no recourse but to choose between us."

"My lady, what can I do?" Janet pleaded again.

"Nothing," Grace snapped. "How could Lance broadcast his indiscretion to the public? For weeks, I've been waiting for him to return home. He isn't coming back!" she cried out.

Janet had never seen her mistress in such a state. She scurried over to Grace. Everything around Grace started to fade, and the air in the room was surrounded by a voice beckoning *Grace, Grace.*

"My love, please, open your eyes," Lance whispered.

Grace had been unconscious for more than a couple of minutes when Lance swooped down at the critical moment.

"Grace, I'm here; open your eyes."

Lance encouraged Janet to get a warm cloth for Grace's forehead, and when she did, Grace's eyes drifted open at a turtle's pace. It took Grace several moments to focus, but it was obvious Lance was leaning over her, his face close.

"Lance!" Grace gulped. "You're here! 'How…how…am I dreaming?"

"No, Grace, I'm here," his voice soothed. "We can talk in the morning."

"No! Lance, no," her voice turning frantic. "I can't believe you're finally here."

"Grace, please," Lance's voice saddened. "You're frazzled. Try to calm yourself and close your eyes."

"I can't," she declared. "Weeks, with no communications; where were you?"

"Please, my love, soon you'll know everything."

Refusing to listen to his petition, Grace started to bawl. Lance, lost for words, gathered her wiggling body tightly against his chest. Upstairs in their bedroom, his mind very much on his task, he carefully undressed his wife and laid her between the sheets. Worn out by the aftermath, Grace surrendered to the warmth of the bed.

Grace's outpouring of hurt was too much for him. Using a free hand, Lance gently placed the comforter over her.

Unexpectedly, Grace gripped his jacket with a strength he didn't know she had.

"Don't leave me, please, I beg of you, don't leave."

Lance's spirit sagged under the weight of guilt.

"I must let the servants know you're alright."

"Lance…" she whimpered.

"I promise I'll return soon."

After exchanging words with Janet, Janet took Lance's position, sitting in the chair near the bed. It was a quiet husband who said *I would be back*, his eyes still watchful, kissing Grace's forehead. He exited, and Grace thought it was too wonderful to be true.

Grace woke the next morning to find Lance asleep on the other side of the bed. She tip-toed her way to the bathroom to be presentable when he awoke. *Should I forgive him and take him back?* Her mind asked. Without warning, Ephesians 4:32 came to mind. *Be kind and compassionate to one another, forgiving each other, just as Christ forgave you.*

The shattering discovery of her husband's affair clearly defined her life. Could she possibly move on from something like this? Is it possible to create a life that's beautiful again? Grace had shuffled through hellish heartbreak and humiliation. Could she truly forgive?

An hour later, the awkward couple settled in the study far from prying eyes and ears. Lance looked into Grace's vacant face and took her hand.

"I'm so remorseful, and it isn't easy to explain."

Grace inched forward. "Please try. I've been waiting a long time."

"My foolishness considering Paul's offer has caused unnecessary pain for all. I want you to know I never stopped loving you."

"What I know is that your actions spoke volumes. I saw pictures of you and Rachel, and then I read the announcement of your pending marriage and baby with Rachel!" Grace screamed. "And to add salt to my wound, you weren't at the memorial."

"That isn't true, I was there."

"My father told me…" Lance interrupted her, "Your father forbade me to see you before you went into labor. I tried to see you on the day of the memorial, but your father erased my name off the visitor's list!" Lance roared.

Despite Lance's explanation, Grace felt the hardness of an iron railing pressing against her heart. "On the contrary, you could have stood up to my father for us, but again, you cowered."

Lance winced at Grace's hardness. "My heart longed for you every day. Believe me, I never stopped loving you," Lance explained, drawing in a long breath.

"Lance, my heart was forever yours. God knows I cried and cried for you, afraid of losing you. I can't wipe away the history of the pain because my heart is in a cloud of sorrow. I can't see us back together. I have put us in God's hands."

Grace rose from the table, leaving Lance slumped back in his chair, his head buried in his hands, allowing all his suppressed tears to erupt.

CHAPTER 24
Bee Sting Heart

With a change in his schedule, Paul decided to visit his daughter on the way to work. Standing just five feet inside the entryway of the penthouse, Paul let his eyes roam the living room. Rachel stood gazing out the large picture window at the picturesque Central Park.

"Rachel?"

Paul's voice startled Rachel from her musing, and she stammered through her greetings.

"I'm sorry," she said softly.

"Daughter, you seem so far away," Paul murmured, finding her behavior and response odd.

"I've lost Lance for good," Rachel covered her mouth to muffle the sob, threatening to be released. At a loss for words, she moved away from the window to meet him. They stood still for several moments in the middle of the living room.

"Father, I wasn't expecting you this morning."

"Chalk it up to a father's need to see his daughter," he said, giving her a hug and a kiss.

"What were you pondering so deeply?"

"Lance Worthington," she whispered. "I can't fathom why he prefers his wife over me."

Paul wasn't going to argue over that statement. He was eager to tell her his news. Rachel stood in stunned silence upon hearing his plans for them to move to Paris permanently. She was incapable of speaking or moving.

"I've shocked you," Paul asked.

"Yes."

"Is this your way of putting distance between Lance and me?"

"I'm afraid so," Paul said. "What would your answer be?

Rachel thought about this, but honestly, she didn't have an answer. Hot tears filled her eyes.

"I truly love Lance," she whispered, while Paul noticed her stricken face.

"But my daughter, he doesn't love you."

"I can't imagine my life without him," she said, her voice unnaturally pitched.

Paul wrapped his arms around her and led her to the small settee, both in a tempest of difficulty.

"Ever since your kindhearted mother died, I have given in to all your aspirations. But until now, I realize my actions have been detrimental to you. I'm determined to be a better role model for you."

Working hard not to overreact. Rachel wished she could stop shaking. Hearing her father's voice, she tried to comprehend his meaning. Rachel was about to comment when her father spoke again. "Please, my sweet daughter, try to understand my reasoning."

"Father, it isn't fair for such an inferior woman to have the name of Worthington. Grace Forrester dares to believe she's in my league," Rachel gave a sinister laugh.

"I love you very much, but I have one question. "What woman doesn't wish to marry for love?"

In the beginning her father agreed with her wish to marry Lance, even though it was one-sided. However, she's baffled why the change of heart. Now she has a question for him.

"Father, why the sudden reversal?" Rachel inquired.

"I had a conversation last evening with Caroline Worthington. There's a strong probability that charges could be brought against us. We're in a precarious situation."

Rachel gawked at Paul. "They wouldn't dare!"

"Given the damaging report they have and your antic of the news article, it has nailed our coffin shut."

Father and daughter stared at each other. Rachel appeared helpless in her frustration.

"If I agree to move to Paris with you, will we be able to return at a later date?"

Silently, Paul cupped his daughter's chin with his manicured, chubby hands.

"I have been shortsighted about you marrying Lance, and

our deeds have harmed many. I really don't know if that will be possible."

Rachel blinked, and her head dropped.

"I must leave for work. We will discuss further, I promise."

They both stood.

"Father, I love you," she surprised him with a smile.

"And I you."

At the end of the two hours of much-needed discussion, father and daughter embraced one another for strength and support.

Penville, North Carolina

Hearing the news that Lance was back home, but Grace was staying with Caroline. Stone purposely left the week before Thanksgiving for New York. He hadn't visited South Hampton since both families visited for Labor Day weekend. During his flight and his drive to Long Island, Stone berated himself for treating Lance so insensitively. In truth, his marriage to Labella has been tense ever since he'd dealt Lance such a painful blow. She had disagreed with his handling of the crisis.

The taxi pulled into the driveway of his daughter's lovely home, and he felt as though he hadn't visited in years. Soon, he would know if Lance would accept him with open arms. Lance had taken a few minutes of quiet time to fully think and pray what his next step was going to be, but Bently interrupted him, knocking softly on the door and entering.

"What is it, Bently?" Lance asked, his voice sounded tired.

"Mr. Forrester is here, sir."

"Bring him right in," Lance shouted.

Lance was on his feet when Stone entered the study but had no energy to move around his desk. Stone pressed forward and shook his hand.

"How are things?" Stone asked of the younger man.

"In my soul…things are getting much better…but my heart's torn to tatters," he said.

Stone began to speak. "My folly in blocking your rights as a husband has caused deep pain. Not just for you and Grace but for both of our families. I'm here to ask for your forgiveness."

Lance swallowed and admitted. "My actions were utmost careless. It bothers me I've persistently failed as a husband."

"Son, I'm glad you recognize and confess it."

Lance softened on these words, and his face revealed it.

"What did I just say?"

"You called me son," Lance said with triumph in his voice. He went on quietly. "So that you know, I love your daughter very much."

"Thank you for that. However, I didn't doubt it. Both you and Grace are undergoing a great deal of grief and sadness. With God's help and the family's support, there's hope."

Lance only nodded. He hadn't expected Stone's mercy. Some of his fatigue drained away, and the two men managed to talk for several hours until Stone left to fly back to North

Carolina later that evening. Lance appreciated the heart-to-heart chat with his father-in-law. It wasn't easy at times, but both were glad they had it. Lance gained a new lease on life and was on the road to recovery.

After Stone visits with Lance, both families tried to persuade Grace to return to her husband, but she rejected their interference. Terrified that he has lost Grace for good, Lance fretted days and nights worrying.

Grace's refusal to return to Lance was a severe blow to everyone. Family and friends were praying Grace would find a way to reconcile with Lance.

Two days before Thanksgiving, Grace felt like her pain would never end. She maddeningly didn't believe she could forgive Lance and even God. *Why should I go through the hardship to ask or give forgiveness? It won't make any difference.*

Hiding in her bedroom, trying to block out God's nagging prompting, Caroline attempted to comfort her granddaughter.

"May I come in? I will only take a few moments of your time," Caroline said.

"Alright," Grace answered gently.

"I've missed seeing you."

Grace didn't answer, so Caroline plunged forward. "Grace, I lost my mother to cancer at the age of twelve. Her illness had been a long and frightening time for me. My father, lost in his grief, left me to care for myself. Losing my mother at a time when a young lady needs her mother, I thought I had no one to lean on."

For a moment, Grace only stared at her.

"How did you get over the loss?" Grace asked quietly.

"It wasn't easy. For a long time, I was angry because someone whom I loved dearly was gone. When you're suffering so much, and each breath you take seems excruciating, it will take over your life."

Suddenly flustered, Grace looked down at the floor.

"My heartbreaks are massive," Grace said angrily. "Healing feels impossible."

"But all isn't lost. You can have more babies, and your husband still loves you, Grace. I recently learned forgiveness is a choice."

Grace fell quiet, still breathing heavily with frustrations, when Caroline bid her goodbye. Deep down in her soul, Grace blamed Lance and God for everything. She had asked Lance why he didn't fight for her, but when the tide was turned, Grace didn't fight for them; she gave up. She knew God was waiting on her to acknowledge her pain and hurt, and that she needed to show mercy and forgiveness.

"Oh, Father," Grace cried. Y*our daughter comes humbly weighted down by past sins. I acknowledge my shortcomings with a remorseful heart. I have been prideful, headstrong, and self-righteous. Help me to forgive those who have caused me harm, as carrying the* *weight of resentment harms me more than it affects them. She paused to catch her breath. Let your love wash over me and cleanse my heart from all that taints it. Amen.*

CHAPTER 25
The House of Sadness

L ance was alone in the big room reading his bible when Grace arrived the day before Thanksgiving. Because he was concentrating on a particular scripture, he didn't hear Bently going to the door. The sound of her voice caused him to jump.

"Hello."

"Grace! It's you," he gasped. "You look so beautiful to me."

"I," she faltered, her hand fluttering.

"You talked with our Heavenly Father?"

"Yes," she moved from the entryway and sat close to Lance on the sofa, his eyes never leaving hers.

Swallowing past the lump in her throat, she said: "I'm terrified of disappointing you."

"Oh, Grace," Lance said as the months of loneliness came rushing back. "I feel the same way; however, I have so many things to ask for your forgiveness," he sighed. "I've made some horrid mistakes against you. I need you!"

"Everything is behind us, Lance."

"Grace, we have much to be grateful for; this is a new beginning for us."

Janet came into the room and told them breakfast was on the table, but they refused. Grace and Lance's conversation never stopped. They talked to each other like they never had before, each having dozens of questions for each other.

Lance hugged Grace for a long time before they fell quiet, as though God had renewed their vows. They moved gently with a deliberateness. Each was sharing a breath, their lips connected, feeling warm, tender, and safe. As the kiss ended, they shared a smile with a renewed sense of closeness. Lance said to her, "You're my beautiful butterfly, whom I almost lost."

Reunited with Lance from a long and difficult journey, Grace listened with genuine interest to André describing her new assignment. She believed this unplanned opportunity arrived for a specific reason.

"Are you sure?" Grace questioned André.

"You've no reason to question my judgment," André suddenly laughed. "The assignment is only for three months in Greece, leaving the first of the year."

"Lance left this morning for a business trip to Chicago with Caroline; I'm not sure how he's going to take the news."

"After having your unwavering devotion, I've taken for granted you would jump at this opportunity. I can see this bit of news has arrived at an inopportune time."

Grace knew her mentor spoke the truth. It made perfect sense. However, the task of informing Lance wasn't going to be easy. She was torn between overjoy and alarm.

"Well," André said thoughtfully, "I don't need an answer now. You must discuss this with your husband and family."

Grace bit her lower lip. Was she ready to be thousands of miles away from Lance so soon after their reconciliation?

"Are you positive you can wait?" Grace asked, feeling she had forced him into a difficult situation.

André couldn't stop smiling. "Actually, the director of the Museum of Archaeology has given me two weeks for an answer."

Grace sighed with relief. Anticipating a nod of agreement from both Lance and her family, she would spend the next few hours in a relaxed discussion about a possible departure date for Greece. Settling in for the evening, Grace was eager to tell Lance the extraordinary news.

EPILOGUE

Three Weeks Later
Mykonos, Greece

Lance and Grace stood on the edge of one of Mykonos, Greece's northern beaches. Remote and quiet each day, they have enjoyed the crystal-clear azure waters and golden sandy beaches.

Their Christmas vow renewal ceremony was a joyous occasion. It offered a chance for Lance's mother, father and stepmother to attend. It helped each family reflect on the journey and challenges the couple has overcome.

"I've never seen anything so perfect," Grace said to Lance. They had been honeymooning in Greece for a few days, and she couldn't get over the wonder of their new life together.

Tears came to her eyes, thinking how the renewal ceremony was larger and more pretentious than the first. It seemed every high society family relinquished their own

Christmas traditions to attend the wedding of the century, Mr. and Mrs. Lance Worthington. Grace loved every minute of it, especially the vows they spoke to one another and how the ceremony healed many wounds of both families.

"What time is it?" Lance asked softly.

"Time for dinner," Grace whispered. "But can we enjoy the peace and tranquility a little while longer?"

Lance gathers Grace in his arms. "Yes, lets relax in the stillness of this night filled with millions of stars."

Grace smiled. "We have three months to enjoy this."

Grace reflected on the difficult pain and loss she once carried, and the resilience that had resided within her. After profound pain, she found the inner strength to rebuild and found the true meaning for living. New possibilities may have been obscured by agony, but with God's mercy and help, Grace emerged as a new creation. She realizes having a flicker of hope, she could and did survive.

"Grace, where did you go?" Lance asked.

"Not far, my love."

"Oh, by the way, we received a letter from Caroline," Lance said as he led Grace to sun chairs on the balcony.

"Please read it," Grace begged as they nestled in their sun chairs.

Dearest Lance and Grace,

Your families are thankful you've arrived safely and enjoying the beautiful Mediterranean weather. I'm ecstatic to give you some highlights since you left. First, Ava, Betty, your father, and I attended our first church services with Grace's parents. I never in my life thought I would enjoy the praise and worship services. When the pastor made an altar call, all four of us literally ran to the front. I'm shaking with joy at the peace I have.

Lance had to stop. Grace was gasping and crying with such joy that he stopped to join in. Both thanked God for his glorious work in their families.

"Shall I continue?"

"Please."

I thought you would like to know Rachel married Tim Archibald, III, and they are now on a six-month trip around the world on his yacht. Paul Van Fitzgerald has moved permanently to France to be close to Rachel and Tim when they return to live in Rome. Everyone sends their greetings, love, and support, including your families and friends from Worthington Steel and Dupré Museum.

God bless you both. Take care of yourselves and take lots of pictures.
Love,
Grandmother Caroline

"How fantastic," Grace said, her voice dreamy.

Lance laid the letter aside and moved his hand up to frame Grace's face. "I honestly can't remember a time I didn't want you in my life," he said, his eyes searching hers for a moment. "I must tell you, there was a time I thought I had lost you for good," he whispered.

"Oh, Lance," Grace reached for him, kissing him as if her life depended on it.

Not in a hurry to go inside their bungalow, Lance returned the kiss with his entire being, thinking no one could argue he wasn't a bless man.

ACKNOWLEDGEMENTS

The title of this book, *Seduction of a Butterfly: The Art of Forgiveness*, describes much more than the story within the cover. It speaks of certain seductions in my own life. Below are the ones I need to thank for throwing me a lifeline.

I accepted Jesus Christ into my life at nine years old. Living next door to a bar, at a young age, I saw and heard things that, during my time, were unheard of. I want to give him praise and honor, had he not interrupted me on many detours in my life, I have no idea how my life would have turned out.

The late Reverend and Missionary Ben Matthews obeyed God's command, leading him to drive thousands of miles from Grand Rapid, Michigan, to Oakland, California, searching for relatives to tell them about the gift of God's son and eternal life. Through their obedience, three generations came to know God and his son and are still seizing our family's next generation from the borders of sin.

My mother, Ruby Wiley, I thank you for your diligence in steering me on the right path when I strayed. I thank you for all you have instilled in me and the benefits of having a life of prayer. A day doesn't go by that I don't miss you. But I am comforted in knowing that you're in the presence of God. You were my traveling buddy and best friend. I love you.

My spiritual father, Pastor Charles H. Webb. I didn't always agree with your chastisement, like the time I was silenced for almost two years for dating a man not in the faith. But I am so grateful that it taught me the true meaning of Hebrews 12:6 – *For whom the Lord loveth he chastens.* Thank you for caring for my soul.

About The Author

Patricia Monserrate lives in Texas with her husband and two daughters. She is a licensed evangelist with a passion for writing captivating stories of triumph over adversity. Her debut novel, *Blueprints of Shades*, received rave reviews for its charismatic characters and exhilarating plot, which leaves readers asking, *what's next?* In her second novel, *Seduction of a Butterfly: The Art of Forgiveness,* Patricia delves into a woman's journey from joy to brokenness, finally to forgiveness. She explores God's grace in the presence of pain and the hope that refuses to die.

Connect with Patrica:

Patricia@patriciamonserrate.com

Facebook.com/blueprintsofshades

patriciamonserrate.com